SACRED DOG

THOMAS W. SAVAGE

Tommy Savage 2018

EDITED BY MARJORIE KRAMER

Disclaimer and Copyright

Sacred Dog ©2017 by Thomas W Savage.

Acknowledgements

I would like to thank my daughter Kelly, a rangeland specialist for the Bureau of Land Management, for the inspiration to write this story.

I would like to thank my youngest daughter Katrina for her encouragement to write this story in the context in which it is written.

I would like to thank my wife Pat for her help in the creation of this book. Her unending patience and support enable me to pursue endeavors such as this one.

Thomas W Savage can be reached at tommys@3rivers.net.

Table of Contents

From the Author

My best friend, Tae, has shared my journey for nearly three years. He has walked beside me every step of the way and listened carefully as I shared with him the words that would eventually become "Sacred Dog."

Each significant character that appears in my stories has played an important role in my personal life. In this book, Alan Williams is one such character. His name was inspired by the combined names of two wonderful friends who shared my journey in life for many years. Sadly, the lives of Alan Schwendiman and Danny Williams have ended. It was my intention that they share my journey again for a short while in the pages of this story.

Chapter One

The once moonlit sky had quickly grown black and ominous. The moon was now hidden by sinister, boiling clouds whose ragged edges shone silver as they raced through the sky above us. I stood braced against a howling wind that had sprung suddenly from the west. Lightning hissed through the sky, and as thunder reverberated from the peaks around us, rain began to fall. I stood with my head lowered, beneath a weathered and twisted old tree as driving sheets of rain drenched both Yellow Tail and me. Lightning flashed again and again through the sky, illuminating distant peaks as it held fast for a moment to their towering cliffs. The terrifying lines of light exploded in deafening blasts as it danced on outcroppings of rock around us.

Yellow Tail, a young member of our tribe, stood unflinching on a rocky precipice near me, his arms outstretched. Reaching fearlessly toward the fiery sky, the young brave performed one of the most sacred ceremonies of our people, the *Vision Quest.* Undaunted by the rapidly growing storm, he stood as unmoving as the rocks around him in the lashing wind and driving rain. Wailing urgently into the gale, he pleaded for the gift of knowingness from the spirits he knew surrounded him in the angry skies above. A strange illness had overtaken him, and his time for passage into the spirit land, he knew, was near. In defiance of his fading strength, with the might and determination of a true warrior, he had ridden me to the top of the ominous cliff upon which we now stood. Yellow Tail was the son of the great Ogallala war chief, Talking Bear. Yellow Tail knew he had failed his father. He had become sick and weak. The sickness within him had ravaged his body and rendered him unable to be the son he knew his father wanted him to be.

Our village lay in a sprawling valley hidden far below us in the darkness. The churning, black clouds had approached us from the west. In the west, Yellow Tail had told me, lived the mighty spirits, the *Thunder Beings,* known by our people as the, *Wakia.* He told me that the Wakia stalked the raging skies hidden in the threatening clouds that came from the west. Hurling terrifying bolts of light to the earth as they came, they were feared by all but the bravest warriors. Any who lived after having been touched by the terrifying light of the Wakia were given their great power. With this grand power he knew he would soon receive, Yellow Tail would surely find his strength.

The thunder beings rampaged through the sky with fiery rage, each streaking pulse of light followed immediately by a horrific crash of thunder that shook the very ground upon which I stood. Recoiling with fright at each terrible explosion, I stood beside Yellow Tail where he had tethered me to the reaching, old tree. A tether though, would not have been necessary, for I would never leave my friend and master.

Four-legged ones such as myself are called *horse* by my kind, but being highly revered possessions by Yellow Tail and his people, we were known by them as, *Sunka Wakan*, or *Sacred Dog*.

Our journeys had become one, when three years earlier, Yellow Tail had heard my cries from deep in a swamp where I lay exhausted and starving. I was helplessly trapped, held fast in the sticky mire. A group of enemy warriors had doggedly pursued my herd for days, trying in the most brutal of ways to ensnare our stronger members. The greatest prize of all, the dream of all Indian warriors in our land, was to somehow capture and have for his own, the grand, white stallion that led our herd. His feats of eluding capture were legendary. The white stallion had come to be known by all in our land as *Nya,* "the ghost one."

9

Beneath a full moon, our two-legged foe had burst upon the place where our herd lay sleeping. The hunters had blocked all ways of escape. Nya, realizing this, stomped and snorted angrily as he paced menacingly between the hunters and our herd. In a chaotic rush, the screaming warriors charged suddenly forward. Ropes flew from all directions at our great leader, and finally, the white stallion was ensnared. Upon his capture, our panicked herd bolted blindly into the night. As I ran frantically behind the lunging form of my mother, I turned to see our magnificent leader fall to the earth, unmoving, in a hopeless tangle of ropes.

Far from the hunters, my mother and I took refuge in a swamp. The two-legged ones were stealthy trackers though, and upon finding our hiding spot, had charged suddenly upon us from the brush. Into my memory was etched forever, the wild eyes and bleeding face of a warrior that only a short while before, I had seen knocked to the ground beneath the flailing hooves of Nya. I watched helplessly as the crazed one, whooping and hollering, threw a rope around my mother's neck. With the help of others, he dragged her from my side. I listened in horror as her cries of angst became distant, and then ceased. They had left me alone in the swamp to die. At my age and size, I was worthless to them.

The storm intensified, and the rain turned to hail. The white crystals of ice pelted us mercilessly, as they were driven now by a stiffening wind as the storm brutalized all in its path. Unyielding, seemingly oblivious to the chill, Yellow Tail stood bravely at the cliff's edge braced against the lashing gale. His face turned upward toward the pulsing sky, he cried unceasingly for a vision of guidance and knowing. He had surrendered his life completely to the one that he called *Great Spirit*, the mysterious entity to which he now offered, without condition, all that was his to give.

The jagged boulders that lay around us in the darkness, seemed to dance and move in the lightning's throbbing glow. In the terrifying light, I could see the brooding silhouette of towering mountains on the far side of the valley, their tops dotted by battered old giants like the tree beneath which I stood.

Lightning sizzled and crashed through the sky nonstop. The boiling clouds above us pulsed with energy, illuminated in colors I had never before seen.

Suddenly, in a terrible explosion of blinding light, the specter of an enormous white horse burst from the mountain of churning clouds above us. The mighty beast, kicking and rearing wildly, bound across the storming sky. Its flowing white mane and tail shimmered in the pulsing light, and lightning shot from its flared nostrils at each mighty leap. On its back desperately clung a strange, light skinned rider. The two-legged one's face was gaunt, and its eyes were shadowed. It was clad in bizarre clothing I had never seen worn by my people.

In the clouds surrounding the apparition, appeared a chaotic throng of many two-legged ones. Like the ghostly rider, their skin was the color of snow. They were like no men I had ever seen. Their thunderous chorus of howling voices brimmed with excitement as the magnificent horse twisted and leapt, bucking wildly through the ragged sea of clouds before them.   Unable to pull my eyes from the fiery display, I watched as the frightful vision streaked and loomed in the turbulence above.

The brutal ride of the two-legged-one ended abruptly as he spun helplessly from the great horse's back. The incredible spectacle disappeared in yet another dreadful blast of light.

The night was alive with the strange power of the mighty storm. My skin now tingled, and the hair at the ends of my ears twitched. Yellow Tail's hair was suspended from his head, drawn mysteriously into the night by the crackling energy that filled the darkness around us.

Our world was engulfed in a blinding roar of simultaneous light and thunder, as a twisting streak of light danced suddenly at the top of the tree to which I was tied. I was knocked instantly to the ground, writhing in pain, lost in the horrific blast of thunder that immediately followed.

Dazzling bands of light throbbed behind my eyes as I struggled to my feet. I saw that Yellow Tail had somehow held his footing on the rocky ledge. His gaze fixed upward yet, he knelt painfully on one knee. With one hand lowered to the rocky surface to steady himself, his other was outstretched still, toward the storming sky.

Through the rampaging sea above us, there now charged an army of angry warriors locked in violent battle. A great war chief, wearing a magnificent bonnet of eagle feathers, fought bravely in the midst of the battle. His retreat was not possible. One end of a red sash wrapped around the chief's waist had been staked to the ground by his war lance. His knife in one hand, his war club in the other, the looming warrior fought tirelessly. Enemy warriors lay dead and bleeding at all sides of the embattled chief. His horse, rearing and kicking, fought loyally beside him as enemy warriors, screaming hideously, at last overcame the great chief. In a mighty explosion of light, the apparition vanished.

An enormous white-headed winged one appeared suddenly in the churning sky. At each thrust of its mighty wings, deafening peals of thunder crashed through the mountains around us. In each of its mighty talons, the eagle clutched a twisting bolt of white light. The gigantic bird hurled its sizzling light earthward as it drew overhead. Instantly, from both Yellow Tail's outstretched arms, and the tree to which I was tied, shot a blinding bolt of light.

There was no thunder. No sound. Nothing. I fell helplessly through a sea of blackness.

Suddenly before me in the darkness appeared Yellow Tail. His body was no longer ravaged by sickness. Muscles rippled in his shoulders and arms as he held a feather-bedecked war lance above his head in a sign of victory. He sat astride a great white stallion that I was certain was my father, Nya. Yellow Tail smiled at me from the darkness. In his gaze was a look of knowing. His glowing image began slowly to fade, and I somehow knew that the mortal journey we had known, had ended.

My dream world vanished as I awakened suddenly from my sleep. I raised my head and with pounding heart fought to wrest myself from the grip of my frightful dream. Anxiously, I scanned the area around me. As my world slowly focused, I realized finally, that I lay near my mother beneath a small bunch of scrub oak where we had taken refuge the night before. My mother, apparently oblivious to my terrible night's journey, lay with her head down, sleeping peacefully still.

'*Sunka Waken? Sacred Dog?*' I wondered breathlessly, as I remembered the strange dream from which I had just awakened. An involuntary shudder coursed through my body and my eyes shot skyward as the visions in my dream played again in my mind. Stars twinkled silently, though, where only a short while before, terrifying images had thundered through my dreams.

I lay trembling for a long while, staring into the darkness, as my nightmare faded slowly in my memory. My pounding heart quieted finally, and my ragged breathing soon matched that of my sleeping mother.

Bazaar night journeys would become my constant companion in my years to come. My dream world, I would soon learn, would afford my nightly passage to another life.

Chapter Two

A smattering of rain fell softly as my world became light the next morning. The tiny drops of rain caressed me gently where I lay trembling on the ground in meager, yellow grass. The astounding events that had consumed my dream world only a short while ago, were soon forgotten in the growing light of day. Fully awake now, I lay quietly watching as the world around me appeared from the darkness. The smell of moist earth, and the pungent scent of creosote awakened by the sudden rain, hung heavily in the air of my desert home. I became slowly aware of a towering black and white horse that stood looking downward at me in the early morning grayness. This beautiful horse, I knew, was my mother. I had been born into this remote desert land only days before.

Lowering her nose to me, she lightly nuzzled my neck and ears, then said softly, "Come little stallion, follow me." She gently nudged me upward, until with her help, I gained my feet. A brilliant bolt of light shot suddenly across the sky above us, followed by a terrifying boom. The memory of the terrible shooting light in my dream danced instantly across my mind. Terrified, I stood unmoving, struggling to make sense of this flashing specter that had somehow followed me from my dream world.

My mother, lowering her head once more, said, "Don't be afraid little one, it is only lightning. The spirit of the Wakia honor you with their presence. The Thunder Beings are the most powerful of all forces in our world, little one. From them, I give you your name. From this time, until your journey ends, little stallion, you will be known by our kind as, *Wakia*. The Thunder Beings will walk with you always."

I gazed in awe at the sky, wondering about the origin of the terrible crashing light as I stood safely beneath the protection of my mother. My mother turned at last and led me from the grassy opening. I followed behind her on quaking legs as she walked slowly into trees on the backside of a gentle hill where we were protected from the stiffening breeze. I had come into the world in a remote, mountainous desert land known as, Nevada. Towering mountains loomed skyward in all directions around us. Craggy, broken ridgelines of brown and black rock tumbled downward from the gigantic spires to form finally, the rugged hills in which we now took refuge.

There was little in the way of growth clinging to the upper reaches of these rocky giants. Only where the twisted and scarred ravines of the upper mountains gave way to our foothill home did an abundance of greenness suddenly exist. Even in in these smaller hills, the landscape was a jumble of huge rocks and was scarred by jagged, twisting ravines. Mountainous piles of rock lay strewn in disarray everywhere, as if hastily stacked then abandoned by some ominous force. The hills in all directions were covered by a tangle of gnarly, twisted brush that was to my head in height. Growing on the ground around us were small cactus of all shapes and colors. Some grew in clusters of small, round plants bristling with sharp needles. Others grew in a chaotic jumble to heights nearly as tall as I, covered with glistening spines nearly as fine as hair. Tall, green cactus dotted the landscape for as far as I could see. Like brooding sentinels, they stood on even the highest and most jagged ridges and peaks. Their bent and crooked arms reached silently from their slender bodies as if to catch the elusive raindrops that now fell on this dry land. Beneath these great cactus grew an unruly tangle of smaller bushes and trees. Like their larger relatives, each one regardless of size, possessed either needles or thorns that at the slightest touch brought stinging pain. Passage through the brush, I would soon discover, was difficult at best.

"It is early in the season called spring," said my mother, as she slowly lowered herself to the ground beside me. Nestling now in front of her, my curiosity growing, I continued my visual adventure through the strange new land that surrounded us. Around us, beneath the protection of the trees, lay other four-legged ones of our kind. I carefully studied each of them.

Seeing my curious gaze, my mother said from behind me, "We are called *horse* by our kind, Wakia. Together, all the horses that you see around us, form a *herd*."

There were many large horses like my mother. There were all shades of brown ones, black ones, and ones who were dappled both black and white. In front of only a few of them though, lay smaller ones like myself. They, like their mothers, were a hodgepodge of soft colors. Only I, was the brilliant white color of the horse that stood nervously alone at the edge of our herd. Like him, I too, had a mask of black hair that covered the area from below my eyes, to the base of my ears.

The dazzling white horse was much larger than any of the others in our herd. Muscles rippled beneath the shining white hide of his shoulders and rump as he moved boldly through the brush around our herd. His flowing mane and long white tail shimmered in the sunlight as he tossed his head from side to side. With nose held high, the great horse continually tested the wind.

My mother, following my gaze, stared quietly for a long moment at the magnificent horse. Lowering her head to me finally, she said, "That stallion, Wakia, is the leader of our herd. Without end, he guards us. He watches now for any danger that might be present. He watches especially for our greatest enemy, the two-legged ones known as, *man*. Man has pursued our herd for years and has taken many of our kind. The captured ones, ensnared by strong ropes thrown by the men, are dragged from our herd never to be seen again. Our leader is known by these hunting ones, as *Banshee,* for he eludes them, and leads our herd through this land as if he were a ghost. It is known by all of our kind that within him flows the blood of great leaders. Stallions like him, it is said, once carried ancient two-legged-ones known as *Indians,* into battle. All who know Banshee, know that the pale skinned ones will never possess him. He will never be taken alive."

"Nya," I breathed aloud, as my mother's words evoked the bewildering memory of the white stallion in my dream.

Each of my days was similar, it seemed, to the day preceding it. We would rise early in the morning from our resting place carefully chosen for protection the night before. Our herd would begin grazing, moving slowly along, to ensure finding enough browse to fill our stomachs.

"The constant moving," said my mother, "Also made it difficult for our natural predators and the two-legged-ones to stalk us."

When the sun was high overhead each day, the white stallion would lead us to one of several waterholes that lay hidden in secluded pockets between the hills. Here, we would quench our thirst and sometimes frolic in the water near the pond's edge to cool ourselves. Our visits to the waterhole were always pleasant and the highlight of my day. After drinking our fill, we young ones would often crash through the water running with all our might in exuberant forays of pure bliss.

It was at one of these places, though, that I first experienced the harsh reality of death. Our herd had approached a small waterhole surrounded on three sides by rocky ledges. After drinking our fill from its cool water, several in our herd waded into the pond to their bellies. Suddenly, amid a clatter of hooves at the edge of the pond, I heard the painful squeal of a young colt. Turning quickly toward the frightening sound, I saw the young one rear onto its rear legs, its front feet pawing frantically in the air. From the colt's nose hung a twisting snake. The frantic shaking of the young one's head finally dislodged the serpent, sending it flying through the air to land in nearby rocks. Upon its landing, the snake immediately coiled into a tight ball, and from its shaking tail came an ominous buzzing sound.

The young horse, bucking and rearing, ran quickly to the protection of its mother's side. But for the colt, it was too late, a deadly mistake had been made. I watched in horror as the young one staggered and fell onto its side kicking helplessly beneath its shaken mother. Tearing my eyes from the gruesome scene, I looked questioningly into the eyes of my mother.

"It is a snake, Wakia," she said. "Never forget the buzzing sound that you now hear from it. Should you ever hear that sound again, quickly move away from it. And as this young horse did today, never make the mistake of lowering your head in curiosity to sniff at one."

Banshee quickly gathered our unsettled herd, pushing us onward through the narrow gully that led away from the waterhole. As I entered the gully, I looked back to see the young horse kick feebly one last time, then lay quietly at the feet of its distraught mother.

I grew stronger with each passing day. I could now run effortlessly beside my mother for long distances through the desert. Each day was a learning experience. The brutal environment that was our home held many difficult lessons to learn. The huge white horse, Banshee, guarded carefully over us, and only once far in the distance, did we see the dreaded one known as man.

One afternoon as we grazed quietly across a rocky ridge, we saw a small group of men moving methodically toward us in the thick brush on the side of a faraway hill. A chill coursed through me when I realized these men sat astride four-legged ones such as ourselves. As they rode from view into a small wash, our leader guided us quietly into a canyon where he led us skillfully away from the sinister ones.

At night, my dreams were filled with journeys through a beautiful land where I lived among two-legged ones called, Indians. These mysterious dreams occupied my slumber with greater frequency as time passed. Always it seemed, in these strange night visions, a great war chief named Talking Bear sat proudly astride my back. Curiously, I did not object to this two-legged burden. Together, we traveled across grassy plains and climbed towering mountains. We often sat quietly watching from high alpine meadows as herds of bison grazed far beneath us. Beside meandering ribbons of sparkling blue water, the great beasts moved slowly across the plains in an immense wave of brown. Often, I woke exhausted from these strange travels walked in the darkness of night.

It had slowly become the season my mother called, summer, and the days in our desert land had become long and hot. We now grazed in the coolness of the early morning, then, as the sun climbed higher in the sky, sought shade in cliff-lined canyons beneath clumps of mesquite and manzanita trees. As our herd rested quietly in the shade through the heat of the day, we often heard the screeching call of huge birds circling far above.

"These" my mother said, "Are vultures."

They were large birds with featherless, red-colored heads. Their bodies were dark in color, with large, reaching wings that slanted forward. They soared endlessly through the sky without movement of wing, their ominous screeching calls echoing from the canyon walls where we lay resting.

'They seem very unlike the beautiful white-headed birds that fill the skies on my nightly journeys,' I mused.

Often, as our herd grazed slowly through the brush and rocks of our desert home, small four-legged ones darted beneath our feet as they skittered away in fright.

"These small ones," explained my mother, "Are called lizards. They present no danger to us, Wakia."

But there were lizards, I had learned, that could bring death. Larger, four-legged ones whose skin was covered with stripes and splotches of orange and black, often sat quietly on rocks bathing in the sun. These four-legged ones, when startled by our passing, quickly raised themselves on all four legs and hissed menacingly.

"Like snakes," said my mother, "These four-legged-ones should be avoided at all cost."

We saw the ones known as man more often as summer passed. They had seen our herd and the great white stallion that led us had become their quarry. At times we saw them pointing excitedly in our direction from some distant ridge. Sometimes, they snuck so closely to us that we could hear the heavy footsteps of their horses, and their strange, droning voices. Always though, Banshee led us safely away from our would-be captors.

25

Everywhere, it seemed, could be seen the evidence of man. Sometimes, far below us on the flat plains of the desert, we heard the muffled rumbling of shiny beasts that crashed in a frenzy across the desert floor. They threw great plumes of dust into the air as they went. And in the skies far above even the highest of the circling vultures, we often saw the birds of man. They were fearful craft with shimmering bodies, and voices of thunder. They roared through the sky leaving long, white scratches that stretched from horizon to horizon.

"All are devices used by the two-legged ones," said my mother.

When the long, hot day had ended finally, I lay beside my mother in growing darkness. As I drifted slowly to sleep, haunting thoughts of the one called man, filled my mind. My dreams were tormented and filled with images of the two-legged ones as they stalked toward us through the brush. Into my dream world on this night, though, suddenly came yet another puzzling image.

As was often the case, my dreams on this night were again filled with an Indian I knew as, Yellow Tail. The young warrior sat triumphantly astride a great, white stallion as he appeared suddenly before me in the darkness. Without speaking, Yellow Tail held my gaze for a long while. From in the darkness around him came the sound of sorrowful chanting. In my dreams each night, the strange chanting song grew louder.

One day as we lay in the shade beneath the manzanita, the two-legged ones swooped suddenly upon us from the brush growing at the canyon's side. Hollering and screaming, with ropes twirling above their heads, they charged at us from all sides. Banshee sprang to his feet from the side of our herd, and pushed us frantically upward in the canyon. But suddenly from above us in the canyon came more riders. Brandishing their lariats, they yelled and screamed excitedly as they sought to surround us. Banshee, realizing we were trapped, charged bravely forward toward the chaotic group of hunters. Their horses, overwhelmed by the specter of our storming leader, reared, and sprang to the side as Banshee thundered through their midst. Riders screamed in pain as the panicked retreat of their horses sent them careening into the prickly trunks of gigantic saguaro cactus. Men were thrown to the ground writhing in pain, their horses bucking wildly away as our herd thundered past them behind our charging leader.

Banshee crashed relentlessly upward in the canyon, leading us through a maze of creosote and desert willow.

Reaching the canyon's head finally, we followed him across a broad plateau. Deep in a canyon that fell from the plateau's far side, we stopped in a large stand of palo verde trees. With fearful eyes, we stood with our nostrils flared and ears erect, as all in our herd watched and listened for any hint of the two-legged ones. There was no sound or scent that told of man's continuing pursuit. The hunters had given up. I shuddered as I remembered the fading calls of anguish from members of my herd as we charged upward and away in the canyon. Looking at the shaken horses that stood around us, I realized that our herd was smaller in number now.

That night we rested beneath the protection of manzanita trees at the crest of a small hill as darkness gripped the land. I lay for a long while staring into the darkness, reliving the events of the day. I trembled with fear as the image of riders crashing toward us from the brush loomed again in my mind. One man had thrown a rope around the neck of our charging leader, but Banshee had pulled both him and his horse to the ground and broken the rope in his headlong rush toward freedom. I wondered what the two-legged-ones would do with those unfortunate members of our herd that they had captured.

Trembling still, I lowered my head to sleep.

From the shadows of my dream world again came the soft haunting chant that filled my nightly journeys. Louder and louder it grew. To my nose suddenly came the smoky scent of sweet grass and sage.

I recoiled suddenly in fright from an unexpected touch to my neck. But the soothing stroke drew me deeper into my dream world. Slowly, I became aware of a two-legged-one who knelt near me. His form was shadowed by the brilliant sun that shone in the sky beyond him, and I was unable to see his face.

As my world focused, I realized I lay painfully on my side. Chanting softly, while gently stroking my neck and shoulder was Yellow Tail's father, Talking Bear. The great chief, seeing the fluttering of my eyelids, leaned forward and whispered softly in my ear.

"You live, *Sacred Dog*," he said quietly. "The Great Spirit has given you another day! Stand now, White One."

Pain shot through me as I raised my head from the ground. Lunging upward with all my might, I rose painfully to my feet. Near me, at the cliff's edge, Talking Bear had erected a burial platform beneath a huge, old tree. It was the tree under which I had stood as Yellow Tail and I watched the fiery visions dance in the sky above us. In the fork of the

29

twisted old tree, Talking Bear had tied a large bison skull, and below that, he had fastened the lance of Yellow Tail. Beneath the tree, he had driven four posts into the ground and at a height equal to mine, he had draped and tied a large buffalo hide. In the hide, lay the mortal body of Yellow Tail.

His father had dressed him in his finest ceremonial clothes. Yellow Tail lay as if sleeping. He wore a buckskin shirt, and pants. Long, leather fringe ran the length of his sleeves and pant legs. Colorful beadwork covered both the breast of his shirt and the knee-high moccasins that he now wore. A necklace of bear claws hung from his neck. On Yellow Tail's cheeks, Talking Bear, in paint the color of night, had drawn the crooked, lightning shaped sign of the mighty Thunder Beings. Beneath my friend, on the ground, lay his bow and war club. Beside them was his quiver filled with arrows, and all his worldly possessions.

Though in my strange dream world I had been shown that Yellow Tail's mortal journey had ended, I was overcome with sorrow as I saw the reality of my young friend lying before me. For a long while Talking Bear and I stood silently facing the lifeless form of Yellow Tail.

Talking Bear turned finally, to me.

"Sacred Dog" he said, looking into my eyes, "It is the custom of my people that when we pass to the spirit world, beneath our death scaffold is placed the greatest of our worldly possessions. In this way, the one whose journey has ended, will have all they need as they travel through the spirit world. To our people, the most important and prized possession is that of their sacred dog, their horse. You were my son's most trusted friend, White One. You were certainly the most prized possession in his life."

With his voice cracking with sorrow, he continued, "It is my duty as his father, that I now take your life, White One. I must place you beside the burial platform of my son. For all of time, you and he will ride together in the land of spirits."

The chief moved me slowly to the side of the burial scaffold where he knelt and pulled a bundle of smoldering sage from a small fire that burned at its side. He bathed himself in its curling white smoke, then passed the sage under, and around me. Chanting, and praying softly, he enveloped me in a cloud of sweet-smelling smoke. Talking Bear knelt then, and drew his war lance from his bundle.

Turning slowly to me, he said quietly, "Oh, Sacred Dog, you are a fine animal, you were my son's closest friend. His, and your journey in this great land were *one*. You stood bravely at his side here at this sacred place when the Thunder Beings came for him. Only you, White One, know the bravery with which my son faced the mighty Wakia." Looking down then, at the lance he held in his hands, the chief studied the weapon for a long while.

Softly, he said finally, "Long ago, my father gave me this war lance. The translucent seam of yellow that divides its black tip, gives it great power. With it, my father said, I would defend my people and my family. Now, White One, with this most prized possession, I must find the strength to take the life of one I love."

The chief's face was drawn, and his eyes were filled with remorse. He hung his head and wept.

From the sky there suddenly came a thunderous explosion. A strange fog moved quickly across the sky and covered the sun. Lightning shot to the earth from the dark, threatening clouds. Again, and again, came a shuddering explosion of light and sound. In the clouds above us, suddenly appeared Yellow Tail. He sat proudly astride the white stallion that all in our land knew as, Nya. As in my dream, he held his war lance above his head, and in his unblinking gaze was a look of knowing. With unspoken word, his voice thundered through the hills around us.

"Father," he said, "You must keep for your own, this sacred dog that stands beside you. He is the son of the great stallion I now ride. He is the son of Nya. Keep him always by your side, Father. Within him now lives the strength and courage of the Wakia. With him beneath you, you will lead our people with great courage and knowing, and you will return always from battle."

A bolt of light shot from the heavens striking the earth near us in a blinding torrent of light and sound. Throbbing bursts of light pounded behind my eyes. When at last I could see again, Yellow Tail and his grand white mount were gone. The sun sparkled brilliantly in the sky above us.

I limped painfully behind Talking Bear as he led me slowly from the steep ridge. In a small opening on the lower part of the mountain, we came upon a small group of warriors that had journeyed with Talking Bear in his search of Yellow Tail. The men stared in disbelief as Talking Bear told them of his son's fateful encounter with the mighty Thunder Beings. He told them to go to the village and prepare a spot in its center where upon his arrival he could address the people and share with them the story of his brave son's vision quest.

As the riders rode from view, Talking Bear mounted his spotted horse and turned one last time toward the crest of the steep ridge. The platform upon which Yellow Tail lay, could be seen clearly outlined in the blue sky at its top. The eagle feathers Talking Bear had fastened to the top of each corner post danced slowly on the breeze, and the bison skull he had lashed securely in the crotch of the old tree watched silently from far above.

The journey from the mountain to the broad valley at its bottom, was agonizing as I hobbled slowly along behind Talking Bear. The huge encampment of our people lay near the center of the valley, on the banks of a broad river. For as far as one could see, rolling hills climbed upward to the base of towering mountains at both sides of the valley. On the hills, tall grass shone softly in the midday sun, caressed by a gentle breeze. As we slowly descended, white plumes of smoke rose suddenly from an outcropping of rock near the valley floor. Almost immediately came a billowing answer from sentinels at the edge of our encampment.

In the deep grass at the outskirts of our village stood small groups of tepees, erected there by visitors from friendly tribes. Beyond them, were tepees that sat alone where some members of our tribe sought to live in solitude, apart from all others. In all directions around our camp, grazed countless horses, their heads down, feeding in the deep grass on the valley floor. Around them sat young boys barely visible in the deep grass, carefully guarding the feeding animals.

People lined the entrance of the village as Talking Bear and I approached. Dogs yipped and whined nervously, and small children clung bashfully at the side of their mothers as we walked slowly through the remorseful throng. With a nod of his head, the great chief acknowledged the sorrowful gaze of each man and woman as we slowly passed. Talking Bear stopped and dismounted at last, in a large circle that had been prepared in the center of the tepees.

Talking Bear drew me near and rubbed my neck as the villagers gathered around us.

After a long silence, Talking Bear took a deep breath, and exhaled slowly. Drawing himself to his full height, he said finally, "Brothers and sisters, today, my heart is very heavy and I am filled with sadness. My young son has followed his mother, Standing Deer, on *Wanagi Tankancu, the trail of stars.* He watches now from the spirit land. Three days past, Yellow Tail climbed to the highest of peaks," he said, turning slowly to point at the towering mountain at the far side of the valley.

"There, on a ledge of rocks, he cried for a vision. *Wakan Tanka,* the Great Spirit, heard his prayers and carefully watched him as he prayed. Seeing the strength that filled Yellow Tail's heart, and the fearlessness in my son's gaze, the Great Mystery summoned the Wakia, from the West. Brothers and sisters, the Wakia, the mighty Thunder Beings, have taken my son. Forevermore he will live with them, in the crashing light of the storming skies."

"This sacred dog that stands beside me now," he continued, "Was Yellow Tail's mount. It stood bravely beside him as he cried for a vision. This great animal truly knows the strength that filled Yellow Tail's heart when the Thunder Beings came. As is known by all, it is our custom that all worldly possessions are placed beneath the burial platform upon which rests our departed relative. Beside the platform, the life of their favorite stallion is taken, so that together, they will ride in the spirit land forever. This, I was prepared to do, but as I raised my war lance to take the life of this horse, a terrible blast of light filled the skies. Above me in the clouds, sat Yellow Tail astride a gleaming white stallion. It was the stallion known by all in our land as, Nya. Thunder rolled through the skies as he told me in unspoken word, to spare the life of this grand, sacred dog that stands beside me now. Yellow Tail told me that with it beneath me, I would lead my people with wisdom, and I would return always from battle."

"Brothers and sisters", continued Talking Bear, "Know that like my son, this fine animal too, has been touched by the fearful light of the Thunder Beings. His heart is now filled with their courage."

Talking Bear had covered my shoulders with his ceremonial robe as we entered the village, and now slowly pulled the robe from my back. A mighty gasp came from the huge gathering as with disbelief, they studied the singed hair and winding burn that ran jaggedly across my neck at the base of my mane.

"The Thunder Beings have taken my son, but have chosen to leave this sacred dog to walk among us as proof of their mighty power. In their honor, I now name this horse, Wakia," said Talking Bear.

The sun had risen well above the horizon, when in a dazed stupor, I suddenly awoke. The smell of cactus and creosote bushes hung heavily in the desert air around me. The heat from the sun's intense glare was already uncomfortable. I became aware of my mother standing near me as my world began to focus. Remembering suddenly, the screaming hunters that had nearly captured us the day before, I jumped excitedly to my feet. Horses grazed quietly around me in the manzanita where we had taken refuge the night before.

"My herd," I whispered with relief, as the strange visions of crashing light, and dark-skinned two-legged ones that had filled my dreams, began slowly to fade.

I felt as though I had slept for days. I took a tentative step toward my mother, bracing for the shooting pain that I knew would come. Strangely though, the terrible pain that I had known in my past night's journey was no longer present. Standing safely at my mother's side, I thought quietly about my strange dream. From the hair of my shoulders and neck came the baffling sent of sweet grass and sage.

Chapter Three

Banshee led our herd carefully across the desert as the sweltering days of summer drew slowly by. Through an endless sea of creosote and cactus, our herd followed the great stallion. Behind him, we walked through narrow, twisting canyons and climbed through seemingly impenetrable mountains of rock as he led us skillfully from waterhole to waterhole. We had traveled far from that place where the two-legged ones had nearly captured us, and the members of our herd had grown relaxed and confident once more. Banshee though, had not forgotten. He circled our herd constantly, testing the wind and listening carefully as he went.

This day had been blistering hot. As the sun drew lower in the sky, we rose from the shade of the palo verde, and began to graze along the banks of a small arroyo. The little canyon was flat and sandy. In places, saguaro cactus towered above desert willow that grew at the top edges of the arroyo. Our herd moved slowly into the bottom of the ravine, toward green clumps of grass that grew beneath mesquite at its far side.

Suddenly, from the rear of the herd, Banshee threw his head into the air, and charged forward, blocking our path. Angrily, he forced us backward on the trail upon which we had just come. Standing again on the bank of the arroyo, all in the herd curiously scanned its sandy bottom below us. Beside the clumps of grass at the ravine's far side were bleached bones nearly covered by sand.

"Quicksand, said my mother breathlessly. "Had we crossed to eat the grass on the arroyo's far side, many in our herd would have died in the sandy quagmire that lay hidden beneath the surface there. The bones you see, tell of the animals whose eyes were not nearly as keen as are Banshee's. Banshee led us upward along the arroyo's bank, then, in a short way, led us confidently across the small canyon.

After all in our herd had eaten their fill beneath the mesquite at the canyon's far side, we lay in failing light beneath palo verde in the arroyo's bottom. My mother stood patiently while I fed beneath her, then together, we joined the others beneath the trees. The pungent smell of palo verde and mesquite filled the warm summer night, as a soft wind murmured through their twisted branches above our heads. From in the darkness around us, came the soft, grinding steps of Banshee's feet in the sand as he moved endlessly around our sleeping herd. I was grateful to be led by such an amazing horse as was Banshee.

'Would I ever be as powerful and wise as Banshee,' I wondered, as I drifted into slumber?

My sleep was shattered by the chaotic thunder of pounding hooves around me. The predawn grayness of morning was filled with panicked cries and wrenching groans, as my herd sprang frantically from their beds. From around us in the brush came the terrible, excited calls of man. The hunters had found us.

Dust filled the air as the panicked members of my herd spun and reared in confusion. Appearing suddenly beside me in the shadowy turmoil of bodies, was my mother.

"Come, Wakia," she said anxiously, as she whirled and thundered upward in the canyon toward the screaming cries of Banshee. In the ever-narrowing draw ahead, was the great white stallion, rearing and snorting as he called anxiously to our terrified herd.

As we reached Banshee, he turned and thundered up the draw. With our herd rumbling upward behind us now, we knew that we would again escape the hunters as we crashed onward behind our charging leader. Suddenly a hidden rope fence sprang from the brush in front of Banshee, pulled upward and held tightly by men concealed on the rock walls that lined the narrow canyon. Banshee reared and pawed the air with anger at this attempt of capture. With a mighty snort, he spun and charged downward in the canyon. Again, from the brush jumped a hidden rope fence, held by yelling and screaming men that now appeared in the rocks at our sides. Dust boiled upward from beneath pounding hooves as our panicked herd reared and milled in confusion. From within the rising cloud of dust came the angry, screaming cry of Banshee.

With neck bowed, shaking his head in anger, Banshee charged with all his strength at the rope fence. The great horse hit the fence with a mighty groan, but the fence did not fail. Rather than breaking through it, Banshee became hopelessly entangled, and was pulled to the ground by the excited throng of men. Kicking and pawing, snorting with rage, Banshee sprang to his feet, but was held fast in the entanglement of ropes. The swarming mob of hunters soon had many ropes around his neck, and these were held fast in all directions by mounted horsemen that had appeared at the canyon's edges.

Banshee's anger quickly grew, and with it grew his mighty strength. For the first time in his life, the great stallion was held helplessly fast by the two-legged-ones that he so loathed. Rage boiled within him. Grunting and groaning, twisting wildly in uncontrollable fury, he pulled two of the horses and their shaken riders to the ground. The other horsemen, frightened by Banshee's stunning prowess, moved their horses steadily backward, pulling the ropes around Banshee's neck ever tighter.

With a mighty heave, Banshee sprang once more toward his captors. A resounding snap echoed through the little canyon, and the mighty stallion slumped to the ground. The boisterous pack of hunters fell suddenly silent. The riders quickly loosened their ropes that had been drawn so tightly that they were nearly hidden in the hair of Banshee's neck. But it was too late for the great stallion, his neck had been broken. By his own strength, Banshee had fulfilled the promise all horses in our land had long known. Indeed, Banshee would not be taken alive by the two-legged ones. Our great leader was dead.

The hunters, yelling and screaming excitedly once more, turned their attention to the bewildered herd that milled nervously around me. Soon the men had their terrible ropes around the necks of all the members of my herd, including me and my mother, and we were tied securely to trees. Then, held fast from each side by a mounted rider, each horse was pulled kicking, and bucking, down the draw.

43

As the men approached me finally, my mother's ears pressed immediately back against her head in anger and she raised onto her hind legs pawing furiously at them.

"Well!" exclaimed one man, "Feisty huh? Looks like she's up fer a fight!"

"Might make quite a bucking horse," said another.

"The horse ain't yet been born, that I couldn't ride!" barked the apparent leader of the hunters. "Get my saddle," he said to one of the others, as he tightened the ropes that held my mother.

As the leader approached my mother, now carrying his saddle, she fought wildly against the ropes that bound her. When he threw his saddle across her back, she lunged toward him with all the strength she had. With a loud snap, one of the ropes that bound her broke. Twisting now against the other rope, she flailed wildly with her front feet at the startled man, striking him in the head. The hunter tumbled to the ground with blood gushing from the side of his face. Screaming with rage, the bleeding man jumped to his feet, drawing a pistol from his side. A terrifying thunder filled the canyon, and my mother fell quivering, to the earth.

Horrified, I fought in vain against the cutting ropes that bound me firmly to a weathered old manzanita tree.

"Damn!" said one of the hunters. "You killed her! We've killed them both! The stallion, and now you shot this one!"

"Well," groaned the leader as he staggered to his feet, "Look at my face! She deserved it! Most of these horses won't barely make good cannery meat anyhow. The only one that was worth a damn was that white stallion. This little white one though," he said, pointing his pistol at me now, "Just might be worth keeping."

I bucked and kicked with all my might as the men approached me.

"And spirited too," said the hunter, his pistol still in his hand as they drew near. "I wouldn't be surprised if this'n weren't the son of that big white leader horse we just killed," said the bloodied leader looking me over carefully. Turning from me finally, he said to the other, "Now help me get my saddle off that dead mare."

Having re-saddled and mounted his horse, the leader fastened the rope that bound me, securely to his saddle. With him on one side, and another hunter holding me firmly from the other, I was pulled roughly down the draw. Straining to look back, I could see the lifeless form of my mother lying motionless beneath the creosote bushes. Beyond her, lay our leader, Banshee.

The journey down the canyon was terrifying. The hunters, holding us firmly from each side, dragged us brutally through ravines and onward through the desert on our tortuous trek.

When the sun was high overhead, the hunters dragged us toward four shiny beasts. Until now, I had only seen creatures such as these from afar, rumbling across the desert in rising plumes of dust. Behind these strange beasts that our captors called *trucks*, were fastened small enclosures called *trailers*. The men quickly passed a rope through the front of the trailer and out its rear. With these ropes, they dragged each member of my herd, kicking and fighting, into the frightful enclosures.

The trucks to which our dark prisons were affixed, began to rumble, and with a jolt, we began to move. In a choking cloud of dust, we bounced across the desert. When the sun hung barely above the horizon, we came at last to a group of large structures where we slowed, then, stopped. Through small gaps in the walls of my prison, I watched in horror as two-legged-ones poured excitedly from openings that appeared suddenly, in the structures.

Light flooded my dreadful prison as with a resounding screech, the rusty door at the rear of my trailer was drawn suddenly open. We were dragged from the trailers, and the members of my herd were placed in a large, round enclosure that the men called a *corral*. Held at each side by one of the hunters, I was led away from the corral and pulled into a huge structure that the men called a *barn*. The air in the darkened barn was rich with the musky smell of manure and grass. A rope holding device called a *halter*, was put over my face, and buckled securely behind my ears. To this was fastened two ropes, and they in turn were fastened to the sides of a tiny enclosure in which I was put. A creaking wooden door was swung across the opening of my stall, blocking any escape. Trembling, I listened carefully to the fading footsteps of my captors. Through narrow openings in my enclosure, I could see my shaken herd as they milled nervously in the corral outside.

Soon, I heard the grinding crunch of approaching footsteps in the gravel of the barn. Suddenly appearing at the opening of my stall was the leader of the hunters that had captured me and my herd. Held fast by the ropes, I was unable to turn from him, and stared fearfully into his cold eyes. Dried blood clung still, to a wound that ran crookedly down the side of his face. The wound, I knew, he had suffered beneath the flailing hooves of my mother.

Drawing close, his foul breath floated over me as he breathed raggedly, "Little man, I figured on keeping you for my own. Breakin' you to ride. But I need money, so I sold ya. By this time tomorrow, you'll be on the way to the cannery with the rest of your herd. From your hooves they'll make the glue I'll use to fix my saddle that your mother ripped when she fell. I'll be feedin' you to my dog soon," he growled.

Turning finally to leave, he stopped and glared unblinkingly back at me. "Bet you'da been a real spitfire to break. But like I said, little stallion, there ain't never been a horse born I couldn't ride."

A shiver coursed the length of my body as the sinister two-legged-one turned at last, and trudged from view. I stood quietly peering from my shadowy enclosure as the day ended. My throat was parched and dry, and I stood shaking fearfully long after darkness had fallen. I could hear the once proud, wild horses of my herd, as they paced unceasingly in the corral outside the barn. I thought of the lonely canyon where the bodies of my mother and the mighty stallion lay in the night. I wondered what would become of us.

Overcome finally by exhaustion, I lowered my head toward the ground. Slumber settled slowly over me and mercifully, I soon slept. Freed once more by the darkness, I lay suddenly in the beautiful mountains that I had come to know in my mysterious night time dreams.

It was not yet fully light, and in the air around me, hung the heavy mix of smoke and mist in the chilly, predawn gloom. It was now the time known by my people as the season of ripening berries. My life through the previous season of growing grass had been largely one of rest as I grew strong and healed once again after my terrifying encounter with the Thunder Beings. I lay in the grass at the edge of our village amidst the herd of horses that was Talking Bear's. Being the great chief's favorite horse, I was usually tied on a long tether near his tepee, but this past night, Talking Bear had walked me into the deep grass near his other horses and set me free among them for the night.

"Eat well, Wakia," he had said, "Tomorrow, sacred dog, we will ride."

It was often the custom among the people of the Sioux nation that after the death of a family member, the soul of the departed one was kept in a sacred way for a time of one year. A lock of hair was taken from the head of the deceased one and with a piece of their clothing, was rolled up and bound firmly in buckskin. This *sacred bundle* was then carried at all times by the keeper of that soul. This sacred right was known by our people to bring them closer to the Great Spirit, and it helped to ready the soul of their loved one for their journey along the trail of stars. Talking Bear had chosen to keep the soul of his son, Yellow Tail, in this way.

Talking Bear approached me from the circle of tepees as the sun was climbing above the far horizon. With him, he carried the sacred bundle that I knew to contain the soul of Yellow Tail. He carried the buckskin bundle secured by a leather thong over his left shoulder with the bundle held securely over his heart.

"May our journey begin, White One," he said, as he gently patted my neck. He placed a leather bridle on my head, and swinging powerfully onto my back, we walked quickly away from our encampment.

We walked through a large stand of cottonwood trees that stood at the edge of the village, then moved upstream along the river until the huge encampment of our people was miles behind. The deep grass beneath me rustled noisily as it parted before my driving legs. Talking Bear guided me across the river finally, and with the warming sun at our backs, we started upward on the mountains at its west side.

We camped that night in a saddle overlooking a huge valley that lay beyond. It was the place our people called the Valley of Shiny Stones. We had descended from our camping spot and started across the broad valley's floor when the sun at last brought light to the new day.   At the valley's far side, we came to the mouth of a small canyon, and without stopping, began the gentle climb upward in its bottom.

Talking Bear whispered softly as we walked. His words, I knew, were directed to the buckskin bundle he clutched to his heart. As we approached a rocky knob that lay at the canyon's side, Talking Bear pulled me to a stop. He dismounted and for a long while stood looking at the rocky hill that lay before us.

"Yellow Tail," he said quietly, as if the boy stood beside him, "Upon your death, this knob of rocks above me grew to bear the silhouette of your face looking down. Walk with me now, son, here in this sacred place, where so often we walked when you were a boy."

With that, Talking Bear led me slowly from the trail where we crossed the small creek that meandered down the

51

canyon's bottom. We walked a short way upward along the bank of the creek and soon entered a forest of gigantic sagebrush. The sagebrush was taller than me, and their trunks were as large as trees. Beneath the sage were impressions in the dirt where herds of bison had pawed and lay as they sought shelter from winter storms. Piles of dung were scattered everywhere throughout the sage. We moved quietly on a well-beaten path that in places wound through giant sage so closely growing that I could barely fit.

"Yellow Tail," said Talking Bear, as if he were beside him now, "Do you remember when we walked here together when you were but a boy?" he asked. "This was not our longest hike, Yellowtail, but this hike that we made along this little creek beneath these huge sagebrush, was one of our best."

Coming to a place where the gnarly, reaching limbs of the sagebrush blocked the trail, Talking Bear stopped and stood quietly looking. He said aloud finally, "Do you remember Yellow Tail, when you were able to easily walk beneath these brushy limbs? Due to my size, I struggled to find paths around them." Then, chuckling to himself, Talking Bear said quietly, "Yes, Yellow Tail, I remember the laughter that danced in your eyes as you watched my toil."

In a short while, we came to a place where a small pond had been formed by the tireless work of beavers. Here, we stopped, and the chief dropped my reins to the ground. He slowly knelt in the grass and stared downward into the water, his eyes brimming with emotion, as he quietly remembered.

"Yellow Tail," he said, "I remember still, the wonder that filled your eyes as I shared with you the story of the *Wiwhila*, the tiny water spirits that inhabit places like these. Looking everywhere, you were frustrated when you were unable to find them. I explained to you finally, that the Wiwhila could only be seen with the eyes of one's heart."

Talking Bear slowly closed his eyes, and tears streaked down his face.

"Yellow Tail," he said softly, "My heart feels as though it has been ripped from my chest. You came to believe, I know, that in your diminished state of being, you could no longer be what I needed. Son," he sobbed in barely a whisper, "I needed you so badly then, and now, I am but half a man without you. Had the spirits allowed you to stay, I would have gladly carried you on my back until the end of my time."

A weak smile pulled finally at the corners of the chief's mouth, as wonderful memories, I was certain, danced again in his mind.

Behind us rose the rocky slope of the mountain that formed the likeness of Yellow Tail. Talking Bear slowly rose from the grass and turned to face the rock ledge that climbed abruptly from the sage. In the rough, weathered rock, twisting veins of gold glistened in the sunlight.

"Yes, Wakia," he said to me, "Our land is truly blessed." He reached out and ran his fingers slowly along the gleaming seams in the rocky cliff.

"Yes," he whispered quietly, "The hand of the Great Spirit has truly touched our land."

Talking Bear turned then, and we retraced our steps along the secluded trail. Soon we emerged from the sagebrush to stand once again on the trail in the bottom of the small canyon.

Turning back, we stood quietly looking at the tiny mountain of rock.

Talking Bear said softly, "Yellow Tail, as your sickness grew, I stood in this place where I stand now. With all my being, I prayed to the Great Mystery that you be healed. But son, it was not to be so. I stood here again, with aching heart, what seems only days ago. I told Him that your steps had become weak, Yellow Tail, and were small in number. I prayed, Son, that you walk with strong steps to your last day, and that the Great Spirit not let you suffer. My prayer was answered, Yellow Tail," whispered Talking Bear. "You climbed the mountain and sought vision beneath the raging skies with the strength of a great warrior. I will return often to this sacred place where together, we walked when our journeys were one. This place, Yellow Tail, where I made powerful prayers for you to the Great Spirit. With trembling heart, I now make you this final promise."

"When I think of you, my Son, and remember your passing, I will not be overcome with sadness and grief. I will instead, remember the many steps we shared when our journey was one. My heart will then be filled with happiness. I will live this promise, Yellow Tail, but I am filled with wonder that the place in my heart in which you dwell, is at the same time filled with such sorrow, and joy."

Talking Bear stood for a long while staring at the rocky knob in silence. Turning finally, he gathered my reins and with a smile on his face, swung onto my back.

"Thank you, Great Spirit," he muttered skyward, as he nudged me forward.

We climbed steadily upward in the canyon on a deeply rutted trail, and soon we walked beneath giant fir and large juniper trees. We crossed the little creek often as we weaved between huge boulders in the canyon's bottom. As we walked steadily upward, the canyon became increasingly steep, and a band of cliffs loomed above us at the canyon's sides. The gigantic rock walls formed an impassable barrier where they joined at last, at the canyon's head. In a narrow gap between two soaring pinnacles of rock, a tiny creek plunged misting downward, and disappeared amidst gigantic fir trees at the cliff's base. The canyon steepened and became ever narrower as we moved upward. The gentle creek along which we walked became increasingly angry and loud. Its surface was now covered with foam from its turbulent journey.

As the sun drew near to the horizon, we stood at the bottom of one final pitch where the trail wound precariously upward through loose shale rock. With heart pounding and sides heaving, I carried Talking Bear finally, onto a hidden shelf of land that lay at the foot of the daunting wall of rock.

Huge trees grew sparsely on the narrow plain, and nearly encircled a sparkling pond that lay at the foot of the towering waterfall. In many places on the small flat stood tiny structures in various stages of ruin. Shelters I was certain, that had been used by other two-legged-ones long ago. In small openings between the trees, large circles of rock nearly hidden in the grass, told of places where tepees had long ago stood. The setting sun cast a scarlet glow on gigantic scars etched in the rock at the cliff's top. Here, huge slabs of rock had been sheared away by some strange force of nature. Left behind was the looming image of an enormous eagle's head staring unblinkingly downward. With its beak parted menacingly, it warned any who would approach the sacred wall in other than a humble and sacred way.

Dismounting from my back, Talking Bear led me to the pond where I sucked greedily at its surface while Talking Bear knelt beside me cupping handfuls of water to his mouth. We then walked quietly forward and stood directly beneath the towering wall of rock.

"The sacred wall of words, Yellow Tail," the chief muttered quietly, as he held his sacred bundle to its weathered surface. "Our leaders have journeyed to this place for generations, Yellow Tail," he continued, as if his

57

son were beside him. "They have stood beneath this great eagle, and with all their hearts they have prayed. Here in this sacred place, we have heard the voice of the *rock spirits,* and on this towering wall, have been shown images of the future. With this wisdom we have led our people wisely for all of time."

Turning from the cliff, Talking Bear led me to a small opening where he dropped my reins to the ground, freeing me to feed in the tall grass beneath the trees. From the darkening forest around us reverberated the call of *Hinhan,* the great night-bird, owl.

"The winged ones call to one another, Wakia," he said as he turned to listen. "They talk of the vision that the great eagle will soon bring."

When darkness gripped the land finally, Talking Bear made a small fire and spread his bedroll out in the grass near me. The chief sat hunched over his fire as the night drew on, his silhouette boldly drawn before its dancing red flames. With his sacred bundle clutched to his heart, he chanted quietly to the echoing calls of owl.

Talking Bear stood straight and tall, facing the rock wall long before the first rays of light shone on our camp.

With his eyes closed and arms outstretched, he prayed quietly to the huge mountain.

We camped beneath the great ledge for four days. Long before daylight, until long after darkness fell, Talking Bear stood before the craggy wall, arms reaching relentlessly forward as he prayed and chanted to the towering cliff.

The great wall was bathed in a fiery glow as the sun dipped below the horizon at the end of the fourth day. From somewhere above, at the cliff's top, came the haunting cry of a wolf. As the echo of the ominous cry died in the distance, a quiet rumble began to grow within the rock. From the fissures and ledges of the weathered cliff, slowly grew the image of a large village. From all directions in the sky, menacing black clouds crept toward the encampment. Soon, the village was consumed. Billowing clouds of snow swirled through the tepees, driven by a blistering wind. When the clouds at last lifted, huge drifts of snow loomed everywhere throughout the village. Smoke from warming fires rose from the top of only a few tepees. Burial scaffolds stood in many places beyond the village. Countless numbers of black winged scavengers sat in trees at the encampment's edge, patiently waiting their turn to feed at the burial racks, and on the carcasses of dead horses.

59

The piercing call rang once more from the cliff's top, and the image vanished.

Talking Bear stood unmoving through the night. No longer chanting, he stood quietly in the moonlight facing the sacred wall.

The chief walked slowly toward me the next morning as the skies first began to lighten.

"We must go," he said, "We must share this vision with our people."

Talking Bear swung onto my back as the sun climbed above the jagged ridgeline behind us. Beams of light shone between its reaching spires, striking the sacred wall before us with rays of shimmering light. Curiously, though fully light now, the call of owl came from the forest behind us and echoed ominously from the huge rock wall. From far above grew the thunderous whistling of great wings. In a great rush of wind, an enormous white-headed eagle swooped from the sky and landed in a weathered old tree that grew at the foot of the sacred wall. With wonder, we watched as the white head of the eagle turned slowly to red. Soon, where the mighty eagle had sat, lurched the hulking form of a great vulture. Talking Bear slid quietly from my back and stood facing the sinister bird.

On the weathered rock surface behind the lurking winged one, appeared the image of riders. Four warriors on horses painted with images of darkness, galloped down a gentle hill toward our village. Behind each of the riders rode a ghostly, light-skinned companion. The faces of the strange passengers were chalky white and blurred, and they were dressed in black, flowing robes that danced in the wind behind the charging horses. Strangely, the people of the village were unaware of the approaching riders, and did not see the horsemen when they entered. The warriors circled through the huge ring of teepees one time before leaving the encampment, then disappeared over the rise from which they had come. As the horsemen rode from sight, their ominous companions were no longer with them.

In a torrent of wings, the vulture leapt suddenly from the snag before us, and with a terrible volley of screeching cries, disappeared from view. The image on the cliffs' weathered surface was gone.

Stunned, Talking Bear stood for a short while quietly facing the cliff. Then, visibly shaken, he turned from the rock wall, gathered my reins and swung once again onto my back.

"We must go, White One," said the chief, as he turned me from the rock wall and nudged me downward in the canyon.

Slipping and sliding in the loose shale, we retraced our steps down the steep canyon's side, and soon walked along the small creek that gurgled down the canyon's bottom. Talking Bear sat quietly astride my back as we moved steadily along the trail. He was lost, I knew, in thoughts of the visions we had seen, and puzzling, I was certain, over the ominous image of the four horsemen and their ghostly companions.

When at last we came to the small canyon where the rocky image of Yellow Tail stood, Talking Bear turned me from the trail. We crossed the creek and circled the small butte, then from the mountain's rear, followed a narrow ridgeline carefully upward between large rock and juniper trees. Soon we stood atop the natural likeness of Yellow Tail. Talking Bear slid from my back, and while clutching his sacred bundle to his heart, silently studied the rugged mountains that surrounded us.

Softly he said finally, "It is easy, Yellow Tail, to find comfort in the old ways. But if we use wisely, the knowledge the Great Spirit has given us, we can bring much good change to our world. It is hard for me to understand much of what has passed in my life. I find myself ill at ease with much of what has now come to be. Like the waters of a great river, time is rapidly passing. At times I feel I am lost, and I struggle to find the soul that is mine. When at last I do, I realize that the spirit I have found, stands already in the past, and the one I seek, has moved onward. I am growing old, Yellow Tail," said Talking Bear to his son. "Though I am leader of all Ogallala, I am tired, and my eyes are growing dim. For a warrior, I am old, but within my chest still beats the heart of the great bear. The air that I breathe, I draw within my chest with the strength of the bull elk. Though the sun is setting on the long journey that has been mine, I am not yet ready to slow."

Done voicing his thoughts, Talking Bear drew a mighty breath, and exhaling with an air of finality, turned to me,

"We will stay the night on this sacred mountain, Wakia," he said.

Deep in thought still, the chief quietly spread his bedroll in the grass, and with a quiet sigh he lay down. The night was warm, and a gentle breeze moved slowly around us. The sky was luminous with the glow of countless stars. I lowered myself to the grass near the chief, and was soon lost in the soft sounds of the night.

Chapter Four

An ominous rumbling sound wrenched me from my sleep. I raised my head anxiously, and struggled into consciousness. I no longer rested near Talking Bear on the tiny mountain. The chief was nowhere to be seen.

As I drew fully awake, I became aware that I was securely fastened still, to the sides of a small, dark stall. Exploding suddenly in my mind were images of my herd's brutal capture. Nausea settled sickeningly upon me as the memories of the past day returned. Hoping to disprove this terrible reality, I peered frantically between the slats of my enclosure. Outside the barn where I was held prisoner, stood my herd gathered fearfully together in the center of a large corral.

The rumbling sound grew steadily louder, and soon, a huge truck came into view. In a cloud of dust, the great beast ground to a halt near the front of the barn. The truck was very large, and the trailer fastened to its rear was much larger than the ones in which we had been held captive on our long ride across the desert. Men appeared from the structures beyond the corral and the morning calm was soon filled with their excited voices. Dogs barked eagerly as they swarmed nervously at their feet. My herd stood tightly grouped in the center of the corral watching the growing commotion fearfully. The huge truck backed up to a narrow wooden chute on the far end of the corral, and soon the men and dogs entered the enclosure. In a rumble of clattering hooves, the anxious horses were prodded snorting and grunting into the wooden chute, and upward into the huge trailer.

I heard footsteps approaching my stall, and its wooden door was pulled suddenly open. Two men, one on each side of me as before, pulled me from the stall. Behind me, walked a third man who prodded me painfully along with a strange stick that sent agonizing shocks rocketing through me at its slightest touch. The men pulled me into the corral and to the chute at its far end. The halter, that for the past day had so tightly bound my head, was removed, and the terrible sting of the prod sent me bounding up the chute and into the trailer. With a groan, the trailer's door was drawn shut behind me, and soon the huge truck began to rumble once more. On the ground outside our darkened enclosure, I suddenly heard the menacing voice of the scar faced one.

"You nags ready fer yer last journey?" he asked menacingly, as he sauntered toward the huge truck. He pulled himself upward onto the side of the truck, and with a thud, closed the opening into which he had disappeared. Amidst the pounding clatter of hooves, we sought to balance ourselves against sudden movement as our journey began.

We rocked and swayed in our moving prison as we bounced along a rough, dusty trail. After what seemed a long time, the huge truck swerved onto a trail that was much smoother. The wind whistled ever louder through the narrow openings in our trailer as we quickly gained speed. Peering fearfully out, I was shocked to see the hills at our sides passing at a rate that I could never have imagined.

Flashes of light from a gathering storm shot through the sky as darkness began to settle. Soon, we could hear booming peals of thunder above the endless wind that lashed at our trailer. Rain began to drum on our enclosure's top, and quickly became a deafening roar as the storm worsened. Water found its way through the trailers top, and soon showered steadily down on us as we rumbled onward through the growing darkness.

The lightning became nearly nonstop. Its flashing bursts lit the passing hills with a flickering blue light. At each crashing bolt of lightning, sparks shot across the ceiling of our trailer in terrifying lines of sizzling light. Beneath the pulsing light of the storm, I could see water cascading down the hillsides at the edges of the road. Great saguaro cactus stood flickering in the night, bracing against the frothy torrent as the water drew upward on their trunks before parting, and rushing past. In a terrible crash of hooves, we struggled to hold our balance as time and again, our trailer thundered through floods of water that raged across our trail in the night.

As our prison sped downward into yet another canyon, we were suddenly sent toppling over one another in the darkness. Our trailer and the huge truck to which it was fastened, came to a halt in a thundering wall of water that filled the canyon's bottom. Water gushed through the openings in the walls of our trailer, and we felt our terrible prison shudder as the boiling surge drove it sideways.

Our enclosure leaned sharply as the roaring flood pushed it from the road, and with a mighty groan, both truck and trailer rolled onto their sides in the raging torrent. Our darkened prison was filled immediately with water. The terrified members of my herd kicked and fought with all the strength they had against the terrible rush. Panic stricken, I stood on my hind legs fighting for each breath of air, my nose held into a small pocket of air trapped in the upper corner of the trailer. With a groan, our enclosure shifted again in the boiling surge, and with a soft gurgle, my pocket of air was gone. Completely submerged, I could see the flickering silhouettes of the horses around me in the terrible flashing light of the storm. Muffled thumps and groans rang eerily through the water as my herd desperately kicked and twisted, fighting their watery graves. I could hear the terrible ripping and tearing of the walls of our trailer as we rolled again and again in the terrible flood. In a mighty rush, I was pulled suddenly through the opening where the trailer's gate had been. Choking and gasping, I bobbed to the surface of the raging water. The terrible screams of my herd faded quickly behind me as the thundering surge pulled me relentlessly along. I struck rocks and collided painfully with cactus as I was swept downward in the darkness. A large blockage of logs and brush stood suddenly before me, and I was drawn helplessly beneath it by the driving water. Kicking and flailing with all my might, I fought to reach the surface, but my long struggle had taken its toll. Exhausted at last, I could fight no more. A weary calmness settled slowly over me as I swirled helplessly beneath the surface. I could see the hills far above my watery grave as they shone beneath the flickering light of the storm. Suddenly, near me in the water, I saw the form of the scar faced hunter. His arms were outstretched and his unseeing eyes stared blankly upward as he floated slowly by me in the pulsing light.

As consciousness drained from my body and I succumbed to darkness, I thought with curious satisfaction, 'the scar faced one who brought this terrible plight to me and my herd, will die with us tonight.'

My head shot from the earth. I lay atop the rocky butte where Talking Bear had made camp the night before. With my heart pounding in my chest, I peered anxiously into the night, to determine what had awakened me, but no imminent danger was near. Stars shone silently in the sky above, and I could hear Talking Bear's slow, even breathing where he lay sleeping in his bed roll at my side. The ridge top around us was quiet, and there was not the slightest hint of a breeze. I lay quietly studying the brooding silhouettes of the rugged mountains that towered around us as the sky began to lighten, signaling the beginning of a new day. I thought again, about the great vision that Talking Bear and I had witnessed one day ago, and remembered the chief's anxiousness to share it with our people. We were now one day's ride from our village.

Beside me, Talking Bear stirred from his bed roll, and stood quietly facing the spot where the sun would soon rise. He raised his arms skyward and prayed softly as the fiery orb climbed into view. When the sun was well above the horizon, Talking Bear mounted me once more, and we retraced our steps downward from the top of the sacred mountain.

Billows of white smoke boiled skyward signaling our approach, when at last we dropped from the mountains and entered the broad valley where the encampment of our people lay. We soon waded the huge river and passed through the forest of cottonwood that stood at the village's edge. Many people called happily to Talking Bear as we entered the encampment, and the excited throng grew steadily as they followed us to the chief's tepee at its center.

Sliding from my back, Talking Bear turned to his people. "Brothers and sisters," he said, "I have journeyed to the sacred cliff of talking rock. Upon the face of the mighty wall, I was shown a vision. Tell all in our village to gather here tonight. We will feast, and I will tell you of the vision that the rock spirits have given me." The crowd of people quickly dispersed, chattering excitedly to one another as they went.

After darkness had fallen, a huge fire was made beside Talking Bear's tepee. I stood tethered in the darkness at its side. Dressed in their finest ceremonial garb, the members of our tribe danced and sang before the great fire. The celebration slowed only occasionally, when the people stopped to gorge themselves on fresh bison and elk

71

meat, and savor tantalizing, fresh picked berries. Young ones ran gleefully through the crowd laughing and screaming, pursued by their barking companions. Talking Bear sat at the edge of the fire surrounded by other leaders of our tribe. When he stood at last, and walked before the fire, the people immediately saw him, and fell respectfully silent. A sea of faces shone in the fire's light, as the people anxiously faced Talking Bear, waiting for his words.

"Brothers and sisters," he said, "As I have told you, I traveled to the sacred wall of talking rock. Beneath the great cliff, I stood for four days. From daylight to darkness, I prayed for a vision of guidance with which to lead you. As the sun began to fade on the fourth day of my quest, I heard the call of the mighty wolf spirit. From within the great mountain then came its quiet growl. On the towering wall before me, slowly appeared the image of our village. From all directions above our encampment, loomed black, menacing clouds. When the ominous storm was above our village, the clouds settled from the sky. A terrible wind ripped at our tepees, and clouds of snow billowed through our village. When at last the clouds rose, our village was buried. I saw no one walking, and smoke rose from only a few of our tepees. Black winged ones sat in trees everywhere beyond our village. Beneath them, lay the carcasses of many dead horses. Again, came the haunting call of the wolf spirit and the vision was gone. I stood before the wall through the night, but the rock spirits spoke no more.

"The rock people have shown me, brothers and sisters, that the season of renewal will come to our land before it is time. Though it is still the season of ripening berries, we must begin our preparation for winter. We will soon leave this Valley of Shining Mountains and begin our journey southward across the great divide. When the sun rises tomorrow, prepare for the first of our great bison hunts. We will fill our drying racks with much meat. Our baskets will be filled with the berries and fruits of our Mother Earth long before the season of renewal grips our land. Our trail southward across the great divide will long be cold before the deep snows come."

The people danced jubilantly through the night. Chanting and singing to the sound of drums, their excited, happy voices could be heard ringing everywhere through the darkness of our village. Only when the skies began to lighten, did the people disperse to begin preparations for the coming hunt.

During the year in which one keeps the soul of a loved one, it is not permitted that the keeper should kill, or touch blood. The keeper of the soul must instead seek solitude, and pray for guidance.

Talking Bear watched stoically from his tepee the next day as the huge hunting party mounted their horses and left the village. Laughing and talking cheerfully, many women and older children followed behind the hunters on foot. Their help would be needed after the kill, to cut and prepare the meat for drying.

It was now seven days since the hunting party had left the village. Talking bear mounted me as the sun rose. We crossed the river and climbed to a place high in the mountains at the edge of the valley. We spent the day scanning the horizon, watching for the rising cloud of dust that would tell of the returning hunters. Suddenly a series of smoke signals rose from the edge of the valley floor telling of the approach of strangers. In a short while, four riders appeared on a small rise to the south of our village. Onward they came, and without stopping, entered our encampment. Talking Bear mounted me, and urged me quickly down the mountain toward our camp. Upon entering our village, the chief was told of the arrival of four messengers that carried important news for our people. Word of the riders passed quickly through our encampment.

As darkness fell, the people gathered beside Talking Bear's tepee where the four messengers sat before a large fire. The warriors were from a tribe far away and spoke in tongue we did not understand. Sitting cross-legged on the ground opposite Talking Bear, their hands and fingers danced in the flickering light of the fire as they excitedly shared their story in *sign language*. With the surrounding group of people pressing ever forward to watch, the messengers told the chief of white-skinned men who had appeared on the shores of our great land.

The white ones, they told the chief, had come from a faraway place. A land in which countless others like them lived. They had arrived in a huge, wooden craft that was driven across the water by the wind. The white men, they said, had come in peace.

From a large leather pouch, the four warriors then produced a colorful blanket.

"A gift to your people from the strange, white-skinned ones," they told Talking Bear.

The blanket was thick, woven from very soft material. It was dyed in colors our people had never seen. With much excitement, each muttering sounds of approval, the people passed the blanket from person to person through the gathered crowd. Reaching Talking Bear finally, the chief carefully inspected the gift, then quietly placed the blanket back in the pouch from which it had come. Talking Bear had not told his people of the apparition that he had seen appear beneath the great vulture on the wall of talking rock. He did not yet understand its meaning, and therefore had not shared his vision. A strange uneasiness settled over Talking Bear at this news of odd, white-faced ones appearing on the faraway shores of our land. After a long silence, the chief stood and faced the messengers. Scrambling to their feet, the four warriors stood quietly before the chief. With clenched fist, Talking Bear pounded his heart four times, then, pointed skyward in a show of love, and thanks to the Great Spirit for this important news that had come to his people. Then, in a sign of respect and thanks to the messengers, Talking Bear raised his arm skyward, his palm forward toward the four men.

Talking Bear sat quietly awake in his tepee through the night. The pouch containing the gift from the white-faced ones lay before him on the ground. The chief pondered the troubling vision he had received at the wall of talking rock. Again, and again, in his mind, he saw the image of riders and their ghostly companions as they entered our village.

Early the next morning, the chief approached me long before the skies had begun to lighten. He quickly slipped the leather bridle over my head, and with reins in hand, swung onto my back. The sacred bundle of Yellow Tail was secured tightly to his chest. The pouch that contained the gift from the white-ones was tied to his back with a leather thong. Beneath the starry night, we crossed the great river that ran beside our village. For a day, we walked southward down the valley before entering a small canyon that climbed upward from its side. Beneath a tall spire of rock that stood at the canyon's head, Talking Bear pulled me to a stop, and slid from my back. As darkness fell, the chief built a small fire beneath a tree, then sat quietly beside it. Opposite him on the ground at the far side of the fire, sat the pouch that contained the white man's blanket. Through the night, Talking Bear sat chanting softly, rising only to place small branches on the fire. I stood in the grass near him and listened. From in the darkness around us came the soft, resonant call of owl.

When morning at last came, Talking Bear rose from the fire and carried the pouch to the foot of the cliff. He dug a hole, and placed the pouch in its bottom. Chanting softly still, Talking Bear buried the pouch, then rolled a heavy rock over the place where the fresh dirt lay. He stood for a short time, staring at the rock under which lay the strange gift. His eyes were troubled when he turned finally, and mounted me. Quietly, we retraced our steps downward in the canyon.

Early the next day, messengers ran through the camp excitedly announcing the arrival of the hunting party. Far off to the south of our village, a cloud of dust rose from the flats, signaling their approach. Soon, the jubilant band of hunters rode into camp. Behind them, the women and children led horses pulling travois piled high with fresh bison meat. The people of the village quickly fell to work cutting and preparing the meat. In two days, drying racks filled with thin strips of fresh meat stood at the front of each tepee in our village. That night, a huge fire was built in the center of our encampment, and a huge feast of celebration was held before Talking Bear's tepee. While the hunting party was in search of bison, the remaining members of our tribe had worked diligently to collect berries and roots of all kinds for our journey to the south. With the drying racks now full, and baskets brimming with berries and roots, we were ready to begin our long journey to the land of the Red Rocks. Talking Bear announced to the people that at sunrise the following day, we would break our camp and our journey southward would begin.

As the sun rose the next morning though, many of our people lay sick in their bed rolls. A strange illness had overcome many in our tribe who had stayed behind when the hunters went in search of bison. They burned with fever, and their faces were covered with red spots.

Talking Bear sent word through the village that we would not depart on our long southward trek. We would wait while our people healed. More and more people felt sick as the days passed. Many people remembered the ominous vision of winter that Talking Bear had seen at the wall of talking rock. Many in the tribe were now growing restless.

A meeting was called by sub-leaders in our tribe, and all those people well enough to attend stood anxiously around a counsel fire burning before the tepee of Talking Bear.

Talking Bear appeared from his tepee, and without speaking, looked from face to face of those who had gathered.

Finally, he said in a loud voice, "Brothers and sisters, many in our tribe have fallen sick to a strange disease. With so much sickness, it is not possible that we travel southward. We must wait until all in our tribe are strong enough to go."

One of Talking Bears leaders, a burly man named, Spotted Fox, stepped forward.

"Talking Bear," he said, "We cannot wait, we must go now. We must leave those behind that are too sick to travel. To do otherwise would be to deny the vision that you received at the wall of talking rock. We will be caught by the coming of winter, here, in the Valley of Shining Mountains. We will perish. Each day, more of our people succumb to this red spotted sickness. Should we stay, we will soon all be sick. If you will not lead us, I will lead the people southward."

Talking Bear stared into the eyes of Spotted Fox for a long while before finally, he spoke. "Spotted Fox," he said, in a voice void of emotion, "I will not leave the sick ones behind. We will go as one, or we will stay here and die as one, but I will not abandon my people."

Looking beyond Spotted Fox now, Talking Bear said, "Brothers and sisters, those of you who wish to journey southward, I grant you my permission to travel with Spotted Fox to the land of the Red Rock. I will stay behind. I will stay here with the sick and dying ones that cannot travel. We will either live together here, in the Valley of Shining Mountains, or we will die, but it will be together that we do this." Talking Bear turned then and disappeared into his tepee.

The next morning as the sun climbed into the sky, an enormous throng of people moved slowly across the plains away from our encampment. On travois pulled behind horses were the tepees and belongings of those who had chosen to follow Spotted Fox southward. Talking Bear stood quietly watching as the departing members of his tribe crossed the river and dropped from view over the rise below the village. When the cloud of dust that marked their progress had disappeared, he turned and entered his tepee. Sitting on the ground in the darkness, he understood finally, the ominous vision he had seen at the talking wall of rock. The ghostly white companions in flowing, black robes, that had been left behind by the unseen riders, was this strange sickness that had befallen his people. The red spotted disease had been carried to them in the blanket that had come as a gift from white ones.

Each day, more of our people succumbed to the grip of the red spotted sickness. Many of our elders died from the mysterious plague. Soon, burial scaffolds of both young and old stood beyond the village at the edge of the forest. Feathers and prayer ties fastened to their corners, danced in the wind. Talking Bear had come to know that his people would not migrate before the season of renewal gripped the land. It was here, that together, they would live or they would die.

Men, women, and children, who had not yet fallen sick, worked diligently each day, carrying firewood from the surrounding forest. Soon, all available space within the tepees was stacked high with wood, and tall woodpiles surrounded each. The bark was stripped from the wood and stored. It would be fed to the horses of the tribe when they could no longer fight the deep snows to forage for themselves.

Each day, Talking Bear swung onto my back, and we climbed to a place in the mountains where the chief sat quietly staring at our village far below us on the valley floor.

"If on my journey I should ever cross the path of the strange white men," Talking Bear muttered angrily one day, "With my lance and war club, I will kill the white plague. I will push them across this land until they drown in the sea upon which they came."

One day as we sat watching from high above the village, we suddenly heard the call of geese. Soon, the sky above our encampment was filled with the great water birds, calling excitedly to one another as they flew steadily southward. Talking Bear, deep in thought, sat watching the majestic birds until the great flock had disappeared from view. In his mind he clearly saw again, the vision of the village that was buried beneath deep, driving snow. He knew the season of renewal was near.

One afternoon as the sun dropped toward the horizon, towering clouds began to build above the mountains to the west. Brilliant beams of light shone between the ominous, dark clouds as the sun dropped slowly from sight. Late that night, as the people in my village slept, a light breeze sprang suddenly from the north. In the darkness, I felt a gentle touch on my nose and ears, as the first flakes of snow began to fall. What had been a gentle breeze, soon became a driving, blistering wind. When the skies became light the next day, the sun was hidden above boiling, gray clouds. The tepees around me were lost in a torrent of falling whiteness, hidden from view behind swirling billows of snow.

Talking Bear appeared suddenly in the blizzard, and stood at my side. Gently caressing my neck, he said finally, "The season of renewal has arrived, Wakia. When the season of ducks returning, comes again to our land, I hope that we will live still, and will ride again, together. Let the snow build deeply on your back, White One, for it will help shield you from the cold. I must go now. I must check the tepees of my people." Talking Bear turned then and disappeared in the swirling whiteness.

The blizzard pounded our village for days, and the biting cold steadily worsened. Endlessly it seemed, I stood in the deepening snow beside Talking Bear's tepee, bracing against the driving blizzard. Late one night, I heard trudging footsteps in the snow, and suddenly Talking Bear appeared beside me in the blinding storm. He brushed the snow from my back, then said, "Come, White One."

The chief led me into his tepee where he stood beside me in the near darkness, rubbing my neck and ears. "White One," he said, "If you are to carry me as I know you will, there will be times when I must carry you."

Long after Talking Bear lay sleeping in his bedroll, I stood gratefully basking in the heat of the flickering fire, beside him. I listened as the storm beat mercilessly against the walls of our enclosure.

Chapter Five

Torturous, stinging pain wrested me suddenly from my dream world. Gone was the soft warmth of our tepee where I stood huddled in the darkness beside Talking Bear.

As my eyes fluttered open, they focused on a darting, yellow beak that tore at my face. Adrenaline pounding through every fiber of my being, my head shot from the ground dislodging the shaken vulture. In a clatter of wings, the greedy scavenger and his flock leapt into the air screeching their disapproval, then brazenly settled in trees near me at the edge of the wash. My world spun sickeningly around me as I struggled to make sense of their odd presence. As I came to full consciousness, my surroundings came slowly into focus. I realized I lay in the sand in the bottom of a small ravine. Around me was stacked a jumble of debris, and the sun beat mercilessly down with ferocious heat.

The horrifying memory of rampaging water, and my improbable battle for survival slowly returned. Remembering the wreck of the truck and trailer, I struggled dizzily to my feet, my sudden movement sending the flock of winged predators squawking noisily away. I remembered the terrible death cries of my drowning herd as the trailer in which we were imprisoned was driven helplessly down the draw by the raging floodwater. Somehow, I had survived the torrent. My eyes shot furtively up and down the ravine. No hunters were present, but my herd was nowhere to be seen.

Slowly, I became aware of a growing sound far above me in the ravine. The sound grew steadily louder until with a great roar, a strange craft appeared suddenly in the sky at the canyon's edge. Moving very slowly in the air above the ravine, the great bird sent clouds of dust boiling from the ground as it moved toward me. It was the most fearsome creature I had ever seen. The beast carefully hunted for something in the draw as it hovered slowly along. Fear pounding in my chest, I toiled upward through the brush on the side of the wash, hiding finally, beneath a gnarled clump of manzanita. I stood breathlessly trembling as the huge bird slowly passed, its thundering wing churning blistering clouds of sand and debris stinging against me. Far below me in the draw, the craft sank from the sky and landed. It had found the quarry for which it hunted. Satisfied apparently with its find, the sky above the ravine remained quiet, and I dragged myself from the brush in which I hid and crept into the desert.

The thundering beast had long ago retraced its path and disappeared in the sky above the draw when darkness began to fall. As the land around me grew dark, I realized that for the first time in my life I was truly alone. I had no way of knowing how long I had lain unconscious among the debris in the bottom of the wash. I became aware of wounds on my shoulders and back as I quietly remembered the nightmarish flood. All had scabbed over except those that had been torn open by the sharp beaks of the vultures. My mouth and throat were painfully dry, and my lips and tongue were swollen from dehydration. There was no sign now, of the boiling water that had ripped through the ravine. Only twisted stacks of brush and cactus laying between boulders in the bottom of the wash told of the horrible torrent.

I listened fearfully through the night, hiding in a small hollow in the protection of mesquite trees that grew at the canyon's side. I was certain, that at any moment the two-legged hunters would crash through the brush, and again I would be captured. The night was deathly still though. The inky sky above me shone with stars, and there was no noise telling of the approach of the dreadful hunters. The silence was broken only by the occasional call of night birds.

When the sun had at last risen the next morning, my burning thirst drove me back to the wash in search of water.

When I remembered the raging flood that had so recently filled the ravine, it seemed impossible that now only sculpted ridges of sand and piles of twisted brush remained. As I walked upward in the narrow canyon, I looked carefully for any sign of my herd. There was none.

I came finally, to a small pool of water that lay shimmering in a flat, bowl shaped rock. The rock lay nearly hidden in the shade beneath overhanging brush. The churning water had unearthed the huge rock as it tore at the bank in the arroyo's bottom. Trotting quickly to the tiny pond, I lowered my head, and with eyes squeezed tightly shut, savored each gulp of coolness that I drew greedily down my throat.

I stayed near the unlikely pool of water for several days. I satisfied my hunger feeding on desert willow that grew on the banks of the wash. In both the morning and evening, I drank from the ever-shrinking puddle. At night, I lay beneath the manzanita at the edge of the ravine. In my dreams, I walked a beautiful land, filled with rivers and creeks, but as the sun rose each morning, I awoke alone again, in the desert. I wondered often about the strange craft that had floated slowly over me in the sky above the wash. I was certain that it had seen me, for it hovered above me for a bit before it moved on. I wondered why the great bird had not crashed down upon me and fed.

It apparently sought a different quarry,' I reasoned, 'one it had found a bit farther down the wash where it had finally landed.'

As the days passed, I worked slowly upward in the draw searching for new pools of water from which to drink. One morning while rounding a tight bend in the wash, I was suddenly startled by the rush of thundering wings. A flock of vultures screeching noisily, sprang skyward from the carcass of a dead horse. As I approached the pitiful animal, I realized that it was one of the members of my herd. Fear gripped my heart as I quietly studied the dead mare. The terrible memory of my herd's capture played instantly in my mind. Again, I saw myself choking and gasping for air as I was pulled helplessly along in a torrent of water.

Gathering myself finally, I turned from the dead horse, and continued carefully up the draw. As I moved slowly along, I found the remains of others. They had been precariously buried in mounds of debris by the raging water. Nearly overcome with sorrow, I walked quietly upward in the arroyo.

Rounding yet another bend in the wash, I came suddenly upon the twisted wreckage in which I had been held prisoner. Shaking with fright, I studied the mangled remains of the ominous structure before me. The huge truck that had pulled the trailer was gone, but the ominous enclosure in which my herd and I had been held, lay twisted and mangled on its side. The dreadful torrent had rolled it downward in the wash, and it lay wedged between huge rocks in the arroyo's bottom. The rear of the trailer lay agape, torn open by the raging floodwater, but between the slats in the trailer's side, there protruded the legs of still others of my herd who had been unable to escape. Sadly, I was certain finally, that all had died in the terrible flood. I was alone. Shaken by my grisly discovery, I turned and thundered down the draw.

The pool of water from which I drank became smaller by the day. One morning, when I lowered my head to drink, the water was gone. I licked longingly at the moisture that remained in the cradle of the rock, then turned, and climbed quietly from the arroyo.

I crossed many draws as I move steadily across the desert, but I found no evidence of water in any of them. I spent my days lying in the shade beneath joshua and manzanita trees. The coolness of night found me lying atop

90

small hills. From the terrible capture of my herd, I had learned to never rest in a place where your escape was easily blocked by the two-legged ones.

It had been five days since I had last drunk water. My mouth and throat had become so dry that I could no longer eat and swallow, and the dryness in my nose had ravaged my sense of smell.   My eyes were sunken and burned from thirst, and my strength was beginning to wane. I knew that if I did not soon find water, my fate would be the same as that of my herd.

No longer able to rest at night, I now wandered aimlessly in both darkness and the heat of the day, moving desperately from canyon to canyon, in search of water. One afternoon, I was startled by the sudden rush of beating wings. A covey of desert quail flew closely overhead and disappeared over a rise beyond me. Filled with new hope, I followed the path of their flight. As I crested the rise I saw an area of green, flowing grass in the bottom of a sandy basin that lay beyond. Excitement burned within me, as I crashed downward into the basin. My anticipation growing, I galloped across a small rise, the other side of which I was certain, lay a hidden pond.

Skidding to a halt, I stared in disbelief at a small, round depression in the grass that lay dry. There was no water. At the edge of the sunken place where water had once stood, lay the scattered bones of others of my kind. They, like me, had come in search of water.

"How could so many plants grow green and tall in such a hostile place where there was no water to be found," I mumbled?

Turning from the dried waterhole, I stumbled aimlessly into the desert. As the sun climbed higher in the midday sky, I was overcome finally by dehydration. My legs buckled, and I fell helplessly to the ground. Through partially opened eyes I could see vultures circling above me in the sky. I heard the flutter of wings as they landed near me on the ground. As my eyes slowly closed I thought to myself in resignation, I hope the winged ones feast quickly so my suffering will finally end.

Suddenly, I heard the thunder of beating wings as the vultures rose into the sky. Soon, I heard the crunching sound of approaching footsteps, and felt the gentle caress of breath on my ears. Forcing my eyes to open, I stared through narrow slits at a gray muzzle only inches from my eyes. An old and weathered desert burro stood over me as if coaxing me into consciousness. Seeing my movement, the burro walked a short way, and turned to stare as if beckoning. From somewhere within me I summoned the strength to rise, and on trembling legs I followed the old four-legged one.

I trailed the little desert horse through the basin and to the top of the ridge at the basin's far side. The old burro was nowhere to be seen as I stared from the top of the ridge into yet another brush choked arroyo. As I staggered downward on a well-worn trail, my world began to spin dizzily around me. I could go no farther. My legs buckled beneath me, and I slid helplessly down the side of the draw. Through creosote bushes and prickly pear cactus I tumbled, sliding finally over a small outcropping of rock.

I landed with a huge splash in a small pond that lay hidden in the brush in the bottom of the wash. I lay on my side in the water in quiet disbelief, too sick and weak to move. In a short while I struggled onto my stomach, and between my outstretched front legs, I lowered my mouth to the pond's surface and sucked its wonderful wetness into my mouth.

I lay the rest of that day and night in the coolness of the pond. When the skies began to lighten early the next morning I was able to rise at last from the water, and

93

struggle up the bank at the pond's edge. I immediately lowered my head and chewed at the abundant grass that grew on the small canyon's side surrounding the pond.

As the days passed slowly by, I became accustomed to the solitude of my lonely existence. I ranged farther and farther from my tiny oasis each day in search of yet other sources of water. I was determined to never again be trapped by a drying waterhole. During the heat of each day, I lay quietly alone in the shade of the manzanita. At night, I rested beneath the stars on the ridge above the pond.

The brutal, hot season of the growing grass was at last nearing its end. The days were not so burning hot, and the nights were cool and comfortable.

This day had been a good one. As darkness overcame the land, I lay on the ridge above the pond studying the river of stars that splashed across the inky sky. I watched the moon climb slowly from behind the mountains and bath the silent desert before me in its silvery blue light. I never again saw the old, gray desert horse that had saved my life. Many times as I drifted into slumber, I pondered the old one's unlikely appearance, and his strange vanishing.

Each night, my dreams were tormented by the frightful screams of my herd calling from the trailer as it sank in the raging water of the draw. Again and again in my sleep, I fought the raging water, and would succumb finally, to its icy grip.

Gratefully though, in my slumber this night, I was again in the darkness of our tepee, standing at the side of Talking Bear.

For six days and nights, the storm lashed at our village. In the darkness of the seventh night, all became quiet. Talking Bear, awakened by the silence, rose from his bed roll, and struggled through the drift that stood outside our tepee's opening. The wind was gone, and the sky above our village was clear. Stars twinkled brightly in the blackness above.

Entering the tepee again, he said, "We have survived the first of many battles, my friend."

Talking Bear led me from his tepee as the sun climbed above the mountains the next morning. Our village was nearly buried in snow. The sun reflected brightly from huge drifts that stood at the downwind side of each tepee. The entry to most, was little more than a cave that had been dug in the snow by the tepee's owner. Frost, falling gently from the sky, sparkled brightly in the morning sun. Steam rose from a chaotic jumble of ice stacked high from bank to bank in the great river beside our village. Only days before, the water there had run freely. Now, it was nowhere to be seen.

Talking Bear again went from tepee to tepee, digging the snow from the front of some, checking the well-being of the people within. Soon, smoke rose from the top of each tepee in our village, telling of a warming fire that burned within.

The season of renewal had seized our land. As the days slowly passed, blizzards howled through our village endlessly it seemed, and the cold was often unbearable.

The burial racks at our village's edge were now many. Ravens sat patiently in the trees at the edge of the forest awaiting their turn to feed on the frozen carcasses of my kind. Many of the people who had earlier fallen sick with the red spotted disease, though, were now growing stronger. It seemed certain some would live.

I stood one morning, long after the sun had risen, waiting for Talking Bear to step from his tepee. When the sun had climbed to a spot high overhead, the chief still had not emerged. A small group of concerned people gathered finally, at the front of Talking Bear's tepee. Having received no answer to their beckoning calls, they anxiously pulled back the flap and entered.

The people soon spilled from the tepee, their voices filled with alarm as they called excitedly to others in the village. A great crowd watched anxiously before Talking Bear's tepee when at last the healer of our people, Standing Owl, emerged. The medicine man told the nervous gathering that Talking Bear had succumbed to the red spotted sickness. He was burning with fever, and too weak to rise.

Standing Owl ordered a sweat lodge to be immediately erected. A fire was to be built, and forty rocks were to be heated in the flames. The rocks would be used in a healing ceremony that the medicine man would conduct for Talking Bear.

A group of warriors quickly gathered long willows from the edge of the frozen riverbed and stuck them in the snow forming a small circle. The willows were then bent over and tied together forming a small dome-like structure. Bison hides were then thrown over the framework, leaving only a small opening in its side through which the medicine man and two helpers could enter. A door was fastened above the opening that could be rolled down, completely sealing the tiny lodge in darkness.

Night had fallen when four warriors carried Talking Bear from his bed and placed him in the sweat lodge beside his tepee. The rocks glowing with heat, were pulled carefully from the fire with large antlers, and were placed in a small cradle dug in the center of the tiny lodge. The door of the sweat lodge was then pulled tightly down and secured. I soon heard the muffled hiss of steam as water was poured on the hot rocks, and the melodic, chanting voice of the medicine man from within.

The ceremony went long into the night. On four occasions, the door of the tiny structure was opened. Steam billowed from the lodge as Talking Bear, glistening with sweat, was carried from the structure and lay in the snow beside it. The chief groaned in misery as the helpers covered him with snow. In a short while, Talking Bear was carried again into the sweat lodge, and the door was lowered for yet another round. The sky was beginning to lighten when at last the helpers, followed by Standing Owl, carried Talking Bear from the sweat lodge. His arms draped loosely around the shoulders of the helpers, the chief stumbled to his tepee and disappeared within.

Each night for four days, the sweat lodge ceremony was held. On the morning of the fifth day, Talking Bear walked from the sweat lodge without help and trudged through the snow to his tepee.

There were no more deaths in our village. Those who had succumbed to the red spotted sickness continued to grow stronger, and were soon performing the daily chores of snow removal and caring for horses.

Talking Bear's strength quickly returned, and he shouldered his burden of leadership with such fury, it was as though he had never been touched by the terrible sickness.

The chief sent word through the village that he wished to speak to the people that night at a counsel fire that was to be lit near his tepee.

After darkness had fallen, the people gathered around the fire, filled with curiosity. Talking Bear soon appeared from his tepee and stood before them.

"Brothers and sisters," he said, "As you know, Standing Owl performed a ceremony of healing for me. For a period of four nights, he performed the ceremony of the sweat lodge. On the second night, as I lay delirious in the steamy darkness, I suddenly left my body. My spirit flew through the night and was soon above the village of our

99

brothers and sisters who traveled southward with Spotted Fox. Their village was not in the valley of the Red Rocks though. It was at the far side of the great divide. As I looked down, I could see the village was hopelessly trapped beneath the deep snows of winter. I saw no people. No smoke rose from the top of the tepees, and burial racks beside the village were many. Tomorrow, brothers and sisters, I will ride southward. I must find our imperiled people. I must help them."

When the sun had risen the next day, Talking Bear walked from his tepee. He wore fur leggings that ran from his feet to above his waist. A coat fashioned from coyote, was drawn snuggly at his neck. Fur mittens covered his arms to his elbows, and on his head, was a fur covered hat that tied beneath his chin, to protect his ears from the cold. He turned and fastened the door securely, then, stood for a moment studying the snow-covered land around him. Looking upward into the cloudless sky, his chest swelled with a huge breath. Exhaling loudly, he turned and walked toward me. After looping the bridal around my nose and passing the reins over my neck, Talking Bear stood for a long moment quietly studying me.

"Today Wakia," he said finally, "We will ride southward. It will take all the strength you have. You must carry me over the great divide, then downward into the land of Targhee. We must find our people, White One."

With that, the chief swung onto my back. With his lance held firmly upright, its adorning eagle feathers dancing in the wind, Talking Bear and three warriors rode from the village.

We toiled up the broad valley until the sun drew close to the horizon in the west. Far in the distance was a looming range of mountains that formed the great divide. Steam rising from the ice jammed river shone in the fading sun, marking its path far ahead in the valley. In the distance, the river turned, and its rising mist stood like a shimmering wall between us and the great divide.

Approaching a small stand of cottonwood trees, the chief told the others, "We will make camp here for the night. Tomorrow, brothers, we must somehow cross the ice that has gorged the river, and begin our climb to the top of the great divide."

The sun had not risen the next morning when Talking Bear swung onto my back. A pinkish glow shone from the peaks around us, as we moved steadily upward in the valley. Late in the day, we came to a place where the river turned eastward, blocking our path to the great divide.

"It is here," said Talking Bear, "That we must cross the river to continue our journey southward."

Broken shards of ice and debris filled the riverbed from bank to bank, stacked high by the driving water of the great river as it froze. Though no water could be seen, steam swirled mysteriously from hidden places in the ice jam. The far side of the river could barely be seen through the rising mist.

Talking Bear slipped from my back, and with the others, prepared for the precarious trek across the gorged river. The chief, and a brave warrior named Little Crow, each drew a long leather thong from their packs and tied securely around their chests. The other end of each tether was to be held by a man on the bank, and fed out as the two worked their way across the ice. Should Talking Bear and Little Crow become trapped in the icy gorge, the men were to pull them to safety.

Standing beside me now, Talking Bear gently stroked my neck. A soft breeze played at the hair of his fur-lined hat.

"Wakia," he whispered, "Long ago, before our journeys had become one, Yellow Tail sat in the clouds above us. He told us that with you beneath me, I would return always from battle. This may be the battle of our lives,

White One. I know though, that with your great will, and the spirit that burns within you, we will soon walk on the far side of this frozen river."

Talking Bear then swung onto my back. Looking behind us at Little Crow, he nodded silently, then, turned toward the river and looked skyward for a long moment. With Little Crow following behind, Talking Bear urged me forward onto the ice.

The footing was precarious. One foot would sink deeply in the slushy rubble, while the others would slip and slide as I fought for purchase on the uneven surface. Each of my foot tracks would quickly fill with water as we struggled forward. I could hear the strenuous gasps of Little Crow's horse, as they toiled across the icy mass behind us. The men on the bank carefully played slack into the tethers tied around the two riders as we toiled through the broken ice flow.

I often floundered and fell, as we battled toward the far side. With lungs burning, and heart pounding, I lay trembling with exhaustion in the icy rubble, my legs stuck deeply in the frozen mass beneath me. From above me though, each time, came the reassuring voice of Talking

Bear, and from somewhere within me came the strength to rise.

When nearly to the other bank, we suddenly heard a thunderous crack. With a shuddering groan, the river of ice beneath us began to rumble slowly downstream. In a thunderous roar of snapping and grating, the treacherous flow quickly gained speed. Water boiled to the surface everywhere as we were swept along in the churning rubble.

I was paralyzed for a moment, by the shock of the frigid water as we sank in the icy jumble. Barely able to breathe, my breath came only in short, ragged gasps. Above the roar of grinding ice, I heard the frantic cries of Little Crow, and the desperate squeals of his horse. The warriors on the river's far bank were dragged into the ice flow as they fought to pull the freezing warriors to safety. The tether attached to Talking Bear became entangled in the ice, and pulled him from my back as I toiled through the frozen torrent toward the river's edge. On trembling legs, I stood finally, gasping for air in the shallow water near the bank. I turned to see tumbling shards of ice sever the tether tied to Talking Bear. Clinging desperately to his lance, he held it across the surface of the ice as he sank slowly in the churning flow.

Plunging into the river, I lunged with all my strength toward the drowning chief. From beneath the surface, Talking Bear grabbed my tail as I toiled past him in the ice, and with strength I had never before known, I dragged him to the bank.

Talking Bear lay in the snow at the river's edge gasping and choking as he sought to clear his lungs. The fur on his leggings and gloves was frozen and stiff, and ice clung everywhere to the fur of his coat and hat. Slowly, he raised himself to his knees and carefully scanned the river's surging ice. Little Crow and his horse were nowhere to be seen. The two warriors on the far bank had struggled from the icy flow. Arm in arm, they labored toward the shelter of the trees.

Knowing that without fire, he had only moments to live, Talking Bear rose painfully from the snow. Near a small group of trees, he removed his sacred bundle from his chest and laid it carefully on a rock beside him. He then pulled his pack from his back. With fingers nearly frozen, he struggled to remove a small waterproof pouch from within it. Kicking the snow away from the base of a large tree, Talking Bear knelt on the ground and opened the pouch. He removed a ball of wood shavings, a rock, and a small piece of flint which he lay carefully on the ground before him. With his body and hands shaking so violently he could barely hold his flint, he struck it against the stone. Sparks flew from the rock landing in the dry ball of shavings, and soon a small flame erupted.

Groaning with effort, Talking Bear willed himself to move. On unwilling legs, he struggled through the snow gathering dry limbs from the trees around him to stack on the doubtful flame. He then removed his wet clothes, and moaning with freezing pain, hovered over the growing fire.

A trail of smoke rose from a fire on the far bank as darkness fell. I could see the silhouettes of two men against flickering flames as they sat huddled around it.

Talking Bear stood upright with his arms raised toward the sky as the flames of our fire grew larger, and when at last the ice that clung to my body began to melt, I knew we would survive.

Long after Talking Bear had dressed himself in his dry buckskins, and surrendered to slumber, I stood quietly awake in the darkness. I silently remembered our near-death crossing of the frozen river. I shuddered, as in my mind I heard again, the deafening roar of grinding ice when suddenly the river had awakened. Embraced by the warmth of our fire, the terrible exertion of the day overcame me finally. Listening to Talking Bear's measured breathing, I lowered my head and slept.

Chapter Six

I was awakened suddenly by curious cries that echoed across the desert. I listened intently for the strange sound that had drawn me from my icy dream world. The sun had just risen, and I lay beneath palo verde trees on the ridge above my waterhole.

Soon, I heard the unmistakable call of horses from far off in the desert. Rising excitedly to my feet, I scanned the desert before me. I heard the rumble of countless hooves as a herd of my kind quickly approached.

The sound grew steadily louder, until suddenly on the rise in front of me, appeared a large herd of horses running in my direction. Behind them ran a large black and white stallion. Muscles rippled beneath his glistening coat in the early morning sun as he impatiently guided his herd forward.

The stallion drove his herd past where I stood hidden in a tangle of mesquite, and stopped at the edge of my waterhole where his mares immediately began to drink. Memories of Banshee danced across my mind as I quietly studied the black-and-white stallion below me. At last, I would again know the security of the herd.

I trotted from my hiding place quivering with anticipation. The mare's heads shot from the water when they heard my approach. They stared nervously at me as I galloped excitedly toward them. The black-and-white stallion though, strutted back and forth at the pond's far side, snorting angrily. With his neck arched and prancing wildly, he suddenly charged in my direction. Sliding to a halt, I stood frozen before the stallion's on-rushing assault.

Without stopping, the big horse hit me full on with his shoulders, rolling me through the cactus in a billowing cloud of dust. I scrambled to my feet as the stallion's front feet crashed down upon my shoulder and neck knocking me once more to the ground. Immediately on his hind legs once more, his front feet crashed downward toward my head. With all my might I rolled from beneath his plunging hooves and scrambled to my feet. With him crashing angrily behind me, I bolted up the ridge and across the desert.

Having so easily defended his herd against the pitiful newcomer, the huge stallion soon stopped and watched my flight. With a final contemptuous snort, the stallion turned from my trail, and returned to his herd. On a ridge far from the raging tyrant, I watched as the great horse gathered his mares and drove them angrily out of sight.

I was covered with cactus. Blood ran from gaping wounds in my neck and shoulder, the painful result of the crashing hooves of the stallion. The sting from the fiery hooks of the cactus was excruciating, but the pain that I felt in my heart at the rejection of this herd seemed worse.

For many days, the great stallion drove his herd to my pond early in the morning and again before darkness settled. The only time I could drink safely now, was in the heat of the day. Before approaching the pond, I would climb a nearby ridge where I would read the wind for his scent, and carefully scan the area for the presence of the stallion. Certainly, I would never again test the ire of the storming leader.

Many times, I saw the angry stallion knock a disobedient mare to the ground. As he had me, the stallion punished the hapless mare beneath his flailing front feet for offenses I did not understand.

I moved slowly toward the lower regions of the desert as the days grew shorter, telling of winter's ever nearing approach. In the lower elevations of the rocky foothills, the cold was not so biting and the snows seldom lay on the ground for more than a day or two. As the days drew by, the wounds on my neck and shoulder healed, and the nauseating sickness caused by the penetration of countless cactus spines slowly diminished. The tiny wounds had festered finally, and the pus had forced the spines from my flesh. Small bumps remained, though, where spines were deeply embedded in the bones of my shoulder.

I shared my winter range with many animals. The baneful call of coyotes echoed across the desert nightly. More than once, they had attacked me. There slashing teeth had taught me quickly though, that when backed up to a ledge of rock, the lurking four-legged ones were ill prepared to attack me head on. Several of their number had died beneath my flailing front feet. The great mountain cat that stalked my desert home, however, was a deadly predator that must always be avoided. When passing beneath large trees at the arroyo's edge, or traveling on trails beneath ledges of rock, I was constantly vigilant. For in these places the great mountain cat often lay quietly waiting for its next victim.

As winter progressed, I occasionally saw the black and white stallion and his herd. The fuming leader had also chosen the protection of the desert's lower foothills for his winter home.

From my hiding place, I would watch quietly as the stallion and his mares moved slowly across the broken

111

plains before me. Nearly forgotten memories of companionship and security always flooded over me when I saw them. It was as if I were seeing again, my old herd and the great leader that had guarded us. But always, I worked in a direction away from the unfriendly stallion and his herd. Sadly, more than once, the circling of vultures led me to the body of a mare who had fallen to the wrath of his crashing hooves.

I survived the winter grazing on meager clumps of grass and the leafless branches of desert willow that lined the edges of winding arroyos. When the land again began to warm, I moved steadily across the desert toward the towering mountains that lay at its upper reaches. The hot, sultry days of summer found me at the waterhole that the old desert burro had shown me. Though I kept a wary watch for the black-and-white stallion and his great herd of mares, I did not see them again.

Four years quickly came and went. It was now the early days of spring. Winter had passed slowly, filled with howling winds and biting cold. Many animals had perished during the trials of the brutal season. The desert, though, now shown with greenness, a benefit of the heavy snows I had endured.

My strength grew steadily as I grazed on the tender new grass beneath the ever-warming sun. It was the sixth year of my life and a strange, new energy had settled over me. It was with purpose that I moved steadily onward toward the higher reaches of my desert home. I sipped water from a meager trickle in the bottom of yet another rocky arroyo, as the fading light signaled the end of another day. I lie quietly on a small rise beneath the protection of mesquite as darkness gripped the land. The jagged mountains that marked the desert's upper edge, loomed before me in the growing darkness. I knew that in one day, I would drink again, from my old waterhole.

I was drawn from my bed the next morning by a mysterious new scent that hung heavily on the early morning air. It was a scent unlike any I had ever smelled. I stood quietly on the ridge carefully studying the desert that lay before me. From deep within me, grew an urge to seek the source of this alluring smell, and I moved quickly across the desert. I came upon the trail of a large herd of my kind as I climbed the far bank of an arroyo. The herd had recently passed, and I lowered my head to their trail and breathed deeply. From their tracks rose the alluring odor that had awakened me from my sleep. Filled with a remarkable new energy, I galloped across rock strewn ridges and crashed through small canyons choked with twisted creosote brush as I followed the mares that had made this trail. Finally, I lunged to the top of the rise above my old waterhole.

Beneath me, at the water's edge was a large herd of mares. Beyond them stood my old enemy, the black-and-white stallion. The scent that came from the herd of mares was overwhelming. Without fear, I started toward them.

The black-and-white stallion recognized me immediately. Shaking his head with anger, he rose to his hind feet flailing at the air. Screaming with rage, his front feet crashed to the ground, and the storming leader thundered my way. But this time, I did not run.

When at last we met, we rose to our hind legs shrieking angrily, our front feet crashing heavily on one another. To the stallion's dismay, he did not drive me to the earth. In the years since our last battle, I had grown. My chest had become broad and thick, and my height was now far greater than his.

Beneath the fury of my crashing hooves, I drove the black-and-white stallion to the ground. As he rose, I lunged powerfully forward. Hitting the shaken leader squarely with my chest, I knocked him again from his feet, rolling him into the pond. I was immediately on my old nemesis. Again, and again I fell on him with my crashing front hooves until the stallion no longer moved. When certain he was dead, I turned from him without remorse.

Walking quickly to the mares who watched nervously from beyond the pond, I moved slowly through them, carefully learning the scent of each. With a mighty scream, I gathered my herd and drove them upward from the pond. I stopped at the ridge's crest and watched as my mares thundered through the desert before me. Turning back toward the pond, I saw the black-and-white stallion struggle to his feet, and stagger from the water. He stood with his head lowered at the pond's far edge as I turned, and followed my herd through the desert.

As I drove my mares onward, the feeling of having acquired something of such natural importance was nearly overwhelming. I had been given the answer to the question that had raged across my mind since first I had smelled the strange, new scent. From this day forward, my life would be defined by the mares that galloped before me. A sense of purpose pounded through my veins as I breathed their heady scent.

The seasons came and went quickly. Six years had passed since I had acquired my herd. Each year it seemed, was a copy of the one preceding it. Our winters were spent in the lower reaches of the desert. Then, as the days became warmer in the spring, I moved my herd to the seclusion of a small basin overlooking our winter range. Here, we stayed for a short time while my mares brought young ones into our world. When the new colts were strong enough to travel with the herd, we continued our migration toward the high desert. Our summers were spent in the broken terrain along the base of the towering mountains that defined the upper end of the high desert. Here, we battled the scorching heat and the dogged pursuit of the two-legged ones. When the days became shorter marking the end of summer, we returned once more to the lower reaches of our desert home.

The past winter had been a cold, bitter one. The snow had grown nearly to our knees in depth, and the wind drove it endlessly in great swirls across the land. Each day the sun softened the snow, and the cold of each night, froze it hard. The rear of our hooves and legs had grown raw and bled from our constant pawing through the frozen snow to find what little grass lay beneath.

But now finally, the days had at last grown warmer, and six new colts had swelled the numbers of my herd. All were a jumble of colors with the exception of one. A bit larger than the others, he was solid white in color. A mask of black, shiny hair grew from beneath his eyes to the base of his ears. When the colts were strong enough to travel, I moved my herd steadily onward through the desert. Soon, we were again in the rugged foothills at the base of the great mountains.

The days grew steadily warmer, as the months of summer drew quickly upon us. With the lengthening days, came weather that was hotter and dryer. The feeling of fulfillment within me was amazing, but my responsibility for the safety of my herd, was staggering.

With the coming of the hot months, also came the increasing presence of man. It was often now, that we saw plumes of dust rising into the air far off in the desert. These I knew, told of the movement of vehicles used by man.

As the days of summer passed, my herd and I were seen several times by the two-legged ones as we grazed through the desert. We had seen them as they sat on their horses studying us from distant ridges. Often, upon seeing us, the hunters moved slowly in our direction. Each time they did, I waited patiently until their approach dropped them from view behind a ridge or in a canyon, then I led my herd quietly away.

Early one morning after we had watered, my herd and I grazed along the side of a ridge as we moved slowly across the desert. Curiously, I heard the squeal of javelina from the brush of an arroyo that lay beneath us. A strange feeling overcame me as I turned and watched the little four-legged ones scramble from the tiny canyon.

Suddenly, a terrible explosion shattered the quiet morning stillness, and I heard the awful sound of a bullet striking flesh. Memories of the death of my mother flashed through my mind as the mare beside me crumpled to the ground with a terrible moan. Again, came the dreadful thunder, and yet another of my herd fell bleeding, to the earth. Hunters appeared from the brush of the arroyo as I drove my herd frantically across the desert away from them. Another of my herd fell to the deadly thunder as we crossed a rise and disappeared from the hunter's view.

We ran without stopping for a long while. Breathlessly, we rested finally, at the crest of a small rise. All in my herd turned nervously from side to side, scanning the desert around us for the movement of two-legged ones. Certain at last that we had left the hunters and their killing guns far behind, I walked through my herd carefully studying each of my mares. None had been wounded, but the number of my herd was fewer than when the day began. Four of our number had fallen to the guns of man.

The meat from those of my herd that had been killed by the hunters would be butchered and frozen in small mobile packing plants hidden in the desert. The meat brought top dollar at packing houses in the cities where it was sold as dog food.

As darkness settled over the land that night, I quietly scanned the desert around us from the small pinnacle upon which my herd and I now rested. As I pondered the tragic events of this day, I quietly wondered why man so ruthlessly pursued my kind. My every encounter with them had ended in either the capture, or the killing of my herd. 'Why was this two-legged one known as man, so ruthless to those around him, I wondered angrily?' The smell of creosote and mesquite hung heavily on the air around me. From distant ridges, the call of night birds rang softly through the darkness. I settled to the ground finally, and slept.

Unlike the relentless heat through which I journeyed each day in my wakeful world, in my dreams this night, I stood suddenly beside a frozen river choked with ice.

The mighty river that had nearly taken our lives, was again gorged and no longer flowing. The gray morning light shone ominously on great chunks of ice that were stacked in jumbled disarray from bank to bank. As before, steam rose from mysterious crevices between the jagged shards. Water, I knew, moved silently beneath the frozen mass. Talking Bear knelt before our blazing fire beside the clump of trees where we had taken refuge the night before. Rising from his fire, the chief turned, and quietly scanned the river.

"Wakia" he said to me finally, "The river is again choked with ice. The lives of anyone attempting to cross the frozen mass would almost certainly be lost should the river again awaken. It is only because of your great strength, White One, that I live still, to see this day. The words spoken from the sky by Yellow Tail were true. On your back, I will return always from battle."

Talking Bear turned then, and in a booming voice called to the warriors on the far side of the river. Through twisting billows of fog, we saw the two men rise from their fire and walk quickly to the far bank.

"The great river is again held fast by the icy hand of the season of renewal," shouted Talking Bear. "Passage is not possible. Return to our village, brothers. Tell the people of the brave death of Little Crow. Tell them how he lost his life in the icy waters of this great river on his journey to find our lost relatives."

"Tell our people that I will travel on," he bellowed. "I will cross the great divide, and travel into the land of Targhee. I will find the village of our lost brothers and sisters. With them, I will either live or die in this season of renewal. Should it be the will of the Great Spirit, I will lead them to our home in the Valley of Shining Mountains late in the season of ducks returning."

With his arms raised toward them, Talking Bear then shouted, "Go now brothers. May the wind be at your backs as you journey."

Talking Bear turned then, and mounted me. With his sacred bundle tied firmly across his chest, and his lance firmly in hand, we started toward the looming range of mountains that were the great divide.

The day was clear and cold. The early morning sun sparkled from frost clinging to the limbs of exposed brush, and reflected brightly from the snow's dazzling surface. With our eyes squinted against the glare, we moved steadily onward.

The broad valley became narrower as we climbed upward, and ended finally, when we reached the base of the mountains. Here, the climb would become much steeper I knew. The river, far behind us now, looked like a crooked, white scar stretching across the snowy landscape. Its ice jammed banks were still shrouded beneath a mantle of fog.

The snow became deeper as we started upward. Talking Bear wisely chose to guide me along the crest of small ridges as we went. On the higher ground, much of the snow had been swept away by the driving wind, and travel forward was possible.

What had been a steady breeze, quickly became a fierce wind when the day was half gone. Clouds of snow were driven across the snowy landscape, spiraling into the air around us as we struggled upward. The snow was soon nearly to my belly in depth, even on the tops of the small ridgelines that we followed. I proceeded now, only by lunging powerfully forward. The relentless wind formed cliffs of snow on the downwind side of the ridges as it ate away at the snow on the ridge's top. Several times, blinded by the driving snow, we ventured to close, and the cornices gave way beneath us. Rolling and tumbling from the ridge in a cloud of snow, we would gather ourselves at the ridge's base and claw our way back to the top.

As darkness gathered, the gale intensified. With eyes barely open against the stinging, wind driven snow, it was nearly impossible to see even the ground directly in front of us.

Laboring slowly upward through the blizzard, we came finally, to a stand of trees that stood at the base of a small hill. Though we were showered by a continual downpour of snow that sifted over its crest, the small knob shielded us from the driving wind.

Sliding from my back, Talking Bear said, "We will stay here for the night Wakia. There is wood for a fire, and this small hill shields us from the bite of the wind. Tomorrow White One, we will cross the great divide."

The wind raged through the night, there was no let-up in its intensity. When morning came at last, our world was totally white. It was impossible to see through the swirling rush of snow. Browsing on bark at the edge of the cottonwood trees, I was unable to see Talking Bear huddled near his fire only a short distance away. The chief appeared through the blinding wall of snow, and stood by my side in the swirling torrent. Gently patting my neck, I heard him say above the roaring wind, "Wakia, it would be foolish to attempt travel in this blinding gale. We must be patient White One. We must wait until the storm has passed.

The howling blizzard lasted for two days and two nights. In the darkness of the third night, I was awakened suddenly by the silence that had settled on our world. The wind was still, and snow was no longer driven over the crest above us. The stars that shone from the dark sky seemed so close, that where I standing at the top of the mountains that surrounded us, I was certain I would be able to touch them. I heard squeaking footsteps on the frozen snow as Talking Bear approached me in the darkness.

Patting my neck, the chief said, "At last, the storm has ended. Tomorrow, White One, we will cross the divide."

The jagged, snow-covered peaks around us shone with a purple glow in the frigid morning air, when the sky began to lighten. A short distance above our camp a huge cornice of snow had formed beneath the driving force of the wind. It loomed ominously at the crest of the hill under which we had taken shelter. As the sun rose from behind the mountains, Talking Bear swung onto my back, and coaxed me toward a small ridge that lay to the side of our camp. The gentle spine would lead us to the top of the knob under which we had taken shelter.

We heard a reverberating crack as we topped the ridge. The cornice broke under its own weight, and in a great swirl of snow crashed through the trees where we had camped. Talking Bear sat quietly on my back as he studied the snowy rubble where for three days we had taken refuge. Raising his lance to the sky, he mumbled a few words to the heavens, then urged me upward toward the crest.

The snow on the face of the mountain had been scoured and frozen by the relentless wind. Huge drifts stretched across the open face in strange sculpted designs. Behind any rock or bush large enough to slow the wind, there stood a huge drift. On most of the drifts, the snow was frozen so hard I could walk with barely leaving a track.

Far above us on the mountain, I could see a low-lying notch in the ridge line. It was through this saddle, I knew, that we would soon walk to cross the great divide. The sun hung low in the sky when at last Talking Bear and I stood at the top of the pass. On its far side stretched a vast, tree covered basin. In the distance, loomed a towering mountain named for the great chief, Targhee. Along the ridge line that continued beyond the mountain, lay another notch. In that faraway saddle, Talking Bear told me, was the pass where he had led his people many times as they journeyed to the land of the Red Rocks. Behind us for as far as we could see, stretched the broad valley up which we had journeyed. From our lofty vantage point we could easily see an odd series of plateaus that stood at the valley's sides. They stair-stepped upward toward the rugged mountains until hidden finally, by thick, green forests.

The slope on the far side of the divide was open, and mostly void of trees. Huge, winding depressions beneath the deep snow on the mountain's face, told of crooked ravines that meandered downward toward the valley's floor. With a sense of growing urgency, Talking Bear started me downward through the saddle. Though moving steeply downhill now, our trek was still grueling and strenuous. The snow's frozen surface broke often beneath us, sending me to my knees in a river of crusted snow that slid before us down the mountain. Talking Bear, though, with words of encouragement, clung steadfastly to my back.

The sun reflected from the windswept ridges around us as the sun dropped behind the mountains. A large circle of teepees appeared suddenly before us as we crested yet another ridge in the fading light. Talking Bear pulled me to a halt and sat quietly studying the lifeless scene below us. We saw no people walking between the tepees, and smoke rose from only a few. A small herd of horses stood at the edge of the village straining high into cottonwood trees for bark to eat. Everywhere at the village's edge stood the ominous forms of burial racks.

"This was the vision given me by the rock spirits White One," said Talking Bear. "It was not our village that lies in the Valley of Shining Mountains that I saw on the cliff of talking rock. It was this village. It was the village of my trapped people."

A small group of people met us as we entered the village. Yelling and screaming with great joy, they rushed forward to greet Talking Bear. The chief slid quickly from my back and embraced each one for a long moment before moving on to the next. Many of the men and women that gathered anxiously around him, he had known his entire life. With pleading eyes, they returned his stare as Talking Bear studied the face of each man, woman, and child before him. An old man named Standing Elk led Talking Bear to a teepee that had long been vacant. Its owners had fallen victim to the red spotted disease. Its walls soon glowed in the darkness from the fire that Talking Bear had kindled within the tepee. The fire's soft light shone suddenly on the snow as Talking Bear threw back the tepee's flap.

"Rest tonight in warmth," he said as he led me into the tepee. "Tomorrow our journey continues, White One."

Talking Bear went from tepee to tepee through the night. His people were elated to see him, and with new hope in their voices, told him the story of their brave fight for survival.

After crossing the great divide, they told Talking bear, the people had begun to fall ill. As they passed through the land of Tahgee, so many became ill finally, that they could not go on. Spotted Fox, they said, had fallen sick, and had died. They were unable to travel onward toward the valley of the Red Rocks. Winter had come suddenly to the land, and they were soon trapped on the banks of this frozen creek.

From daylight to darkness, all those well enough to work had gathered firewood from the surrounding forest. It was only because of the dwindling numbers of the tribe, that they still had firewood for warmth and cooking. The men who were well and strong, were gone for days on end in terrible blizzards. They hunted endlessly for the meat we knew we would need to survive. The bison and all other four-legged ones, though, had been driven from this high country by winter. Very little meat was gotten. Their food, they said, had soon run out. The creeks that had teemed with fish in summer, soon froze completely to their bottoms, and the ice on the lake at the foot of Tahgee Mountain had quickly grown too thick to break. Fish could no longer be caught.

When the blizzards came, they told Talking Bear, it was punishingly frigid for weeks at a time. The snow stacked quickly over the openings of their tepees, and the icy winds lashed relentlessly at their walls. Many of their horses had succumbed to the terrible storms, they told the chief sadly. Upon its death, each horse was butchered, and the meat was divided between the people of the village. The meat was gone now, they told him, and the bones that they now boiled for soup had been used many times. They left little taste in the water.

Late in the night, I heard the rustle of leather as Talking Bear opened the flap and entered our tepee. He knelt in the darkness as he put small pieces of wood in the circle of rocks where our fire had been. Lowering his head, he gently blew on the embers until a bright, yellow flame licked greedily at the wood.

"Wakia," he said, as he gently stroked my neck, "We have done well. We have found our lost brothers and sisters. Many though, are sick with the red spotted disease. They have run out of food and will soon starve if game cannot be found.

The chief turned from me then and sat by his fire. I could see his silhouette as he held his out stretched hands above the flames. I heard his movement as he opened his pack, and the quiet hiss of leather thongs as he opened the cover of his pipe bag. The chief rolled a ball of sage between his palms and held it to the coals of the fire to light it. Its sweet aroma soon filled the darkness of our lodge. Holding first the bowl, then the stem of his pipe over the burning sage, he carefully purified them. Clutching his pipe to his chest, he sat for a time quietly thinking.

Opening a small pouch, the chief withdrew a pinch of tobacco which he held between his finger and thumb in the air above him. Reaching toward the direction of the west, the chief gave thanks to *Wiyopaata,* the spirit that holds back the waters there. He then placed the tobacco into the bowl of his pipe. In this way, he gave thanks to *Waziata,* the spirit in the north, *Wiyohayanpaata* in the east, and finally, to *Ito Kagata* in the south. After having given thanks to each of the four winds, the chief held yet another pinch of tobacco to the earth in front of him.

"Thank you, Mother, for all you have provided us," the chief whispered. "Thank you for the meat you will soon provide for my starving people."

Holding one last pinch of tobacco high above his head, Talking Bear said finally, "Great Spirit, Wakan Tonka, thank you, that you have led me here to my lost people. Many are sick, Father, and they are near starving. Please show me the way to help them. I am the keeper of my son's soul. You have taught my people that one who carries a soul must not hunt or touch blood in any way. But Father," he continued, "Without meat, my people will die. Forgive me, I must hunt. I pray that you will give me the eyes of the eagle, as I go. Please give my horse, my sacred dog, the heart of the great bull elk as he carries me through the snow that covers our land. And I pray, Father, that you will give me the courage of the Silver Bear as I face those animals to which you will lead me. *Pilamaya,* thank you, Father, for hearing my words," he whispered finally.

Talking Bear then scooped a small ember from the fire, and held to the bowl of his pipe. I heard a soft rush, as he drew air through his pipe, and soon the tobacco in the pipe's bowl began to glow. Talking Bear quietly prayed as he blew bellows of smoke into the air around him. The alluring aroma of the chief's pipe soon filled the darkness of our tepee. When he had finished, Talking Bear sat for a long while quietly holding his pipe. Soon, I heard the chief place his pipe in its pouch and lay the leather bag near the fire. With a sigh, Talking Bear slipped into his bed roll.

131

As the heat from the fire slowly filled the tepee, I heard him say softly from the darkness, "Our people are starving, Wakia. Their horses are weak, and can no longer endure a hunt. We must go, White One. Together, we must find food for our people. Rest well," he said, "Tomorrow we begin yet another battle."

For a long time, Talking Bear lay awake in the darkness. He quietly pondered, I knew, the terrible plight of his people. I stood quietly listening until the chief's soft, even breathing told me that at last he slept.

Chapter Seven

The growing heat of the desert wrenched me from my sleep. Suddenly vanished was my dream world of blizzards and snowbound tepees.

The grim reality of my existence settled upon me as I stood from my bed. I pondered the events of the last day as I watched the sun climb over the mountains in the east. I remembered the killing of my mares by the two-legged ones.

At last, the hunters had seen me closely. They had plainly seen the mask of shiny, black hair that covered my eyes. It was the same unique blaze, the two-legged ones knew, that my father had worn. Word traveled quickly among them, that a great, white stallion now roamed the mountains of the high Nevada desert. Almost certainly, it was said, that this white horse was the son of the legendary stallion known as Banshee.

We saw more and more of the two-legged ones as the hot days of summer slowly passed. With their increasing numbers, we moved constantly along the base of the mountains to elude them. Travel through the twisting ravines and across the rock laden ridges was difficult for my herd, but was nearly impossible for the hunters who seemed always in pursuit. Hidden beneath the trees at the tops of ridges, I could see their approach long before they came close. It was here, beneath juniper and scrub oak, that we sought shelter during the heat of each day. It was only with great caution that I led my herd from the protection of the brush early and late in the day.

Man was not our only enemy in our high desert home. The long, hot days of summer had caused a scarcity of game, and animals not normally our enemy now hunted us. Late one day, we grazed slowly across a ridge as the sun dropped from the sky. Suddenly from the brush at the edge of my herd, came a terrible commotion of howling and yelping. A pack of coyotes burst suddenly from the creosote brush and cut wildly through my herd. The mayhem was short lived as the pounding hooves of the angry mares soon drove the coyotes back into the brush. But the damage had been done. The coyotes had accomplished their goal.

A young colt stood with his head down at the side of a brown and white mare. Blood ran steadily from the colt's hip where the slashing fangs had torn deeply into the flesh and severed the tendons of its leg. I gathered my herd and guided the mare and her injured colt to the top of a gentle hill. Here, I knew, I could easily defend all in my herd should the coyotes return. The colt stood beneath its mother for only a short while before it crumpled to the ground. Soon, with a quiet gasp, it died.

The mare refused my every attempt to guide her away from her fallen colt. Our only protection from the predators of our land was the constant movement of my herd. I knew that we must move on. Try as I might, though, the mare would not follow. A chorus of ghostly wails rang from the brush around us as I guided my herd down the ridge in darkness. I knew that when the coyotes returned to feast, the mare would even the score for the death of her colt.

Rain began to fall softly one evening as we grazed across the desert. As darkness fell, the rain intensified, and soon puddles begin to form everywhere in the desert. It was a welcomed relief from the terrible heat we had long endured. The pithy smell of creosote seemed tenfold stronger on the night air, the twisted brush had quickly awakened in the pouring rain. The sweet smell of saguaro and ocotillo cactus filled our senses as we grazed steadily along. The light of morning found us on a narrow shelf of land that lay at the base of the mountain range. A jagged band of rock rose steeply on the lift's upper side, forming a natural barrier to any who would try to climb upward. Below us, a winding arroyo followed the foot of the mountain. The great wash had long ago been gouged into the desert floor by water shed from the mountain's rocky slopes. When evening came, we would travel upward on the lift, and cross through a narrow pass that led to the high desert beyond.

As the day progressed, I quietly studied the desert below us as my mares lay resting beneath scrub oak and juniper. Curiously, I heard a growing rumble in the distance. I nervously scanned the sky as the ominous sound became louder. Suddenly over the ridge behind us, burst a great, thundering bird. I immediately remembered the strange craft I had seen above the wash after the terrible drowning of my captured herd years before. My mares scrambled from beneath the trees and looked breathlessly upward as the thundering craft passed directly over our heads. Its thundering voice slowly diminished as it continued upward along the mountain's base. It disappeared finally, over the pass through which we would soon travel. I knew this was yet another device used by man. The craft had not hesitated in its flight and had shown no sign that it had seen me and my herd. The mares stood nervously scanning the skies for a long while before finally lying once more beneath the scrub oak. I stood awake though, scanning the desert around us. An uneasy feeling grew steadily within me.

The rain intensified as the day drew on. The puddles that had formed around us splashed chaotically in the drenching rain, and everywhere, the water began to flow across the ground. The small gullies that fell from the sides of our narrow plateau refuge became noisy torrents as the rain soaked land shed the water ever downward. The wash beneath us was soon filled to its banks with a roaring flood of brown, churning water. Trees that had long stood at the arroyo's edge, tipped, and fell slowly into the boiling torrent as the dirt that bound their roots was washed away. A deep, ominous thunder echoed from the terrible rush as boulders tumbled and collided beneath the water, driven relentlessly downstream by the raging surge.

The day was half gone when I heard the call of desert partridge echo from the mesquite that lined the banks of the arroyo beneath us. Their cries became steadily louder until finally, the flock thundered into the air and disappeared in the desert beyond the wash. I scanned the trees below us intently now. Every nerve in my body tingled as I watched and listened for any movement. Suddenly, from somewhere below us on the lift, came the nervous whinny of a horse. Soon, I could hear their plodding footsteps. Then, I heard the muffled voice of man.

My mares bolted to their feet at the sound of my shrieking cry, and we stormed upward along the base of the rocky cliff. Far above, I could see the narrow notch through which we must pass to gain the freedom of the desert beyond. Breathlessly, we toiled upward.

As we neared the saddle, I suddenly saw a glint of light. To my dismay, I realized the two-legged ones were there. My mind was filled instantly with the memory of the terrible trap in which my father had died. I slid to a halt, looking fretfully around me, filled for a moment with uncertainty. My mares, snorting and shaking their heads, milled nervously around me. I rose to my hind feet screaming in anger. Crashing to the ground with my front feet, my mind made up, I turned and thundered downhill toward the unseen hunters I knew lurked below.

The thundering craft we had seen earlier in the day appeared suddenly above a ridge before us. Barely above our heads, it roared directly at us. Sticks and leaves and debris of all kinds were blown into the air by the terrible, roaring wings that beat the air above the craft. Horrified, I turned my herd from the path of the beast, and drove them breathlessly upward again. I tried again and again to veer from the path upon which the thundering beast drove us, but each time, its terrible thunder thwarted my efforts and turned us upward toward certain capture.

A rope fence sprang from the brush blocking our way as we entered the saddle. Hunters appeared from the brush at our sides, their lariats twirling above their heads. Raring to my hind legs, I pummeled the air in anger, then spun to meet the roaring bird that had driven us to this place of capture.

Suddenly, a blinding flash of light engulfed the world around us. A writhing line of light shot from the sky and held fast for a moment to the thundering wing of the beast. Its roaring voice became silent, and dark smoke boiled from its sides. Choking and sputtering, the craft fell from the sky. An enormous explosion shook the ground as a billowing wall of flame boiled upward from the rocks where the great bird had struck the earth. Adrenaline pounded through my body as I crashed forward leading my herd past the terrible fire. The screams and shouts of the alarmed hunters grew quickly distant as we thundered downhill away from them.

Beneath us on the mountain, I knew, were the two-legged ones that had stalked us earlier. Rounding a bend in the trail, we entered a small meadow. At the far side of the opening now stood a tall rope net. The hunters had stretched their rope fence from the band of rocks on the uphill side of our trail, to the banks of the raging arroyo below us. Our path was completely blocked. Men appeared from the brush at our sides with their lariats ready to throw. The cliffs above us blocked any possible escape uphill. The raging water in the arroyo below, blocked our path across the desert. I slid to a stop, and raised to my hind legs screaming in anger. I had allowed my herd to become trapped. I had chosen to take refuge on this narrow strip of land.

Pounding the ground angrily with my front feet, I spun, and crashed downward toward the wash. There was no other way. We must cross. I heard the excited voices of the pursuing hunters as we reached the edge of the thundering arroyo. Without hesitation, I sprang from the bank into the turbulent rush of brown water. One by one, the mares behind me leapt from the bank, and together, we were washed downstream as we fought desperately toward the arroyo's far side.

With my sides heaving, I at last dragged myself from the water and climbed the far bank. I paced nervously above the raging torrent as my mares struggled from the water and joined me. The hunters on the far side of the wash watched in awe as we turned, and stormed across the desert away from them.

When far from the hunters and the raging water of the arroyo, we stopped finally on a small hill and looked back. A dark, black cloud of smoke billowed into the sky where the thundering bird had crashed on the side of the mountain. Near the towering column of smoke lay the pass that led to the high desert beyond. I could see no hint of the two-legged ones who had attempted to capture us there.

Filled with nervous energy from our near capture, we moved steadily across the desert long after darkness had fallen. Without rest, we crossed ridges and splashed through small canyons filled with churning, brown water. The rain had long ended when at last we stopped at the crest of a small hill. The mares of my herd quickly took refuge beneath the juniper that covered the small peak's top. I walked quietly around them peering into the darkness, watching for any hint of man. Again and again I relived the horrific events of our day. I had nearly allowed the capture of my herd. I had taken refuge on a narrow shelf of land and had been trapped between the cliff at its upper side, and the raging water in the arroyo beneath. My life had been a series of learning events, most of which had nearly cost me my life. Six fewer mares now lay beneath the trees around me. The boiling water of the arroyo had taken their lives. The young ones were gone. Only the white colt still ran with my herd.

Anger welled within me as I remembered the lurking hunters. The fear that I had long felt for the two-legged ones had become an intense loathing of them. This terrible, unending anger, I knew, was hate. Staring into the darkness, I saw again the frightful twisting light as it shot from the sky and drove the thundering craft of the two-legged ones to the earth. It had been as my mother had long ago said. Indeed, the thunder beings had walked with me this day.

Exhausted, I lowered my head finally and allowed my eyes to close. Gratefully, slumber quieted my angry turmoil, and soon I was again at Talking Bear's side.

I was awakened by the movement of the chief as he rose from his bed roll. Light flooded our darkened enclosure as the he opened the tepee's flap. The bright light that shone from the snow outside, told me the sun had risen. Talking Bear led me from the tepee, and tied me to a post at its side. He then went from tepee to tepee, asking his people to gather near him. Soon, a large throng of people stood before Talking Bear's lodge.

"Brothers and sisters," said Talking Bear, "Today I will leave our village. I will hunt until I find food. But know this, my people, I will return. If it is the will of the Great Spirit that we perish during this season of renewal, then together we

142

will walk the spirit trail of stars. If we live still, when the season of ducks returning comes, it will be together that we travel to our village in the Valley of the Shining Mountains. But, brothers and sisters, know that it is together, that we will remain."

Talking Bear studied the face of each person that stood before him. He held the gaze of each for a long moment. He turned then, and walked to me. The chief swung onto my back, and with one hand firmly against his sacred bundle, he held his lance above his head with the other, as he guided me through the crowd of people and away from the ring of tepees.

Beyond the village, we turned and walked upward on the banks of the frozen creek at its side. "The great Bannock leader, Tahgee, was killed here in battle long ago Wakia," said Talking Bear as we struggled through the snow. "This creek now bears his name. If fortune is ours, White One," he continued, "We will find animals along this frozen creek. The great moose, often stays in places such as this. Their long legs enable them to travel easily in the deep snow, and they feed on the willows that grow at the creek's side.

As the day progressed, we saw no tracks of any kind. It seemed as though we were alone in these mountains, the season of renewal had driven all four-legged ones from this frozen land.

As the sun drew low in the sky, Talking Bear slid from my back beneath a large group of trees near the bank of the frozen stream. The towering forest stretched upward on the mountain at the far side of the creek. Beside a large rock, he kicked the snow away, and built a fire. I turned my attention to the bark of aspen trees that grew in small clumps among the towering fir.

The forest was quiet as darkness enveloped our camp. Not a breath of wind moved through the trees around us. Talking Bear's silhouette danced on the rock behind him, as bright, yellow flames licked at the wood he had stacked on his fire.

Sitting quietly, the chief was lost in deep thought. With both hands firmly against the sacred bundle on his chest, he spoke finally.

"Yellow Tail," he said, staring into the flames of his fire, "When the river awakened, I was trapped in the flowing ice. I thought for certain I would die. But Wakia suddenly returned to where I floated helplessly drowning. From below the water's surface, I saw the White One's legs as he lunged through the icy water toward me. Clinging to his sides, I saw

144

the buck skin-covered legs of a rider." Peering into the darkness, he whispered, "It was you, Yellow Tail, on the White One's back when he saved my life."

Talking Bear sat for a long time then, staring into his fire. With a great sigh, he laid down in his bedroll, and soon, I heard the even breathing of his slumber.

The night was completely dark. There was no moon, only stars twinkled above us in the blackness. With my head lowered, I stood quietly resting.

Far above us on the mountain, I heard the wind began to stir softly through the trees. As it moved toward us, the bluster grew in strength. Soon, the trees that stood in the wind's rushing path, began to squeak and groan as they bent before its mysterious touch. Then, as abruptly as it had begun, the gale was gone. All, was silent.

Suddenly from far off in the forest, I heard a strange, high-pitched wail. The call was like no other I had ever heard, and sent chills coursing over my body. It was like the ominous wail of a wolf, but high-pitched like the call of a bull elk. The duration though, of the eerie cry, was much longer than either. Talking Bear lay unmoving in the soft glow of his fire. Somehow, he had not heard the terrifying call.

Trembling, I nervously scanned the dark forest around me. From far off, I heard the sifting, plunging sound of heavy footsteps in the snow. A large animal moved steadily toward us. The footsteps became louder, then suddenly all was quiet. I felt a strange energy in the darkness around me, an energy I had last felt in the terrible crashing light of Yellow Tail's vision quest. Quietly, the footsteps resumed. Suddenly, barely visible in the glow of our dying fire, appeared the hulking form of a large animal. I could hear its rasping breath, and I could see the unmistakable sheen of its eyes in the firelight. The huge animal stood upright in the darkness, quietly watching our camp. Its scent was unlike any animal I had ever smelled. My heart pounded so loudly in my chest, that I was sure the great beast could hear it.

I glanced nervously toward Talking Bear. Though his eyes were open, he lay unmoving beside his fire. His breathing was deep and even, as if he still slept. Swooshing footsteps drew my attention from Talking Bear. The animal turned suddenly, and disappeared. Trembling, I listened nervously as the sound of heavy footsteps faded in the darkness. Looking again at Talking Bear, he lay unmoving still, but his eyes were now closed.

I stood fearfully awake through the night, but saw no more of the mysterious beast, nor did I again hear its frightful cry. But I stood anxiously listening for its ominous footsteps, still, as the first streaks of gray began to show in the skies the next morning.

When fully light, Talking Bear rose from his bedroll and walked to my side. The chief quietly scanned the forest around our camp, then turned to me and said,

"My people have long known that the spiritual beast called, *Sasquatch,* travels on the night wind of the mountains. Last night, in my dreams, White One, I was touched by the breath of the mountain. The great beast told me to follow."

Talking Bear's eyes grew wide with wonder when suddenly he saw the huge tracks in the snow beyond me. Bending to study the tracks, he said excitedly,

"It was not a dream, White One! It has long been known by my people that the two-legged beast is our spiritual brother," Talking Bear said to me. "Our elders have long said that Sasquatch comes to those who are pure of heart in their time of need. The huge one journeys easily between our world and the spirit land. Some, like me, have dreamed of the great beast, but he has been seen by very few."

Suddenly, from on the mountain above us, came the terrifying high-pitched wail that I had heard in the darkness. Anxiously, we stared upward toward the place from which the call had come.

The space between the tracks of the great beast was large. It had climbed the ridge with ease as it wound between the gigantic fir trees on the mountain's side.

Our progress was exhausting. The snow was so deep that with the weight of Talking Bear on my back, I was unable to climb through the deep snow on the ridge. Talking Bear dismounted finally, and holding firmly onto my tail, I struggled through the deep snow as I pulled him upward. At times the chief wallowed and crawled, but often times my upward lunges pulled him from his feet, and I dragged him through the deep snow behind me.

Talking Bear turned to me as we stood resting, and between great gasps of air, said, "My lungs burn, White One, and my legs quiver and shake with the weakness of an old man." His stomach cramping, he turned from me then, and retched in the snow.

The sun was near the far horizon when, nearly exhausted, we stood heaving and gasping at the top of the ridge. Though I was lathered with sweat, ice and snow clung to my tail and mane, and steam swirled upward from the hair on my back. Talking Bear was covered from head to foot with snow. Ice clung to his leggings, and tiny balls of snow hung from the fur of his coat and hat. In the valley far below us, we could see the beleaguered encampment of our people.

Swinging again onto my back, Talking Bear urged me forward. Laboring tirelessly through the deep snow, we followed the huge tracks of the frightful beast into a sparsely timbered basin. As we struggled across a gentle rise, suddenly in the tracks of the great beast stood a huge bison. Strangely, the tracks of Sasquatch could no longer be seen in the snow beyond the great bull. His cows stood anxiously looking our way from beneath the trees at the edge of a small meadow. The bison had been trapped in this small basin by the onslaught of winter and had somehow survived in the protection of this pocket of timber. Upon seeing us, the startled cows lunged through the snow, gathering quickly behind their enormous leader.

Talking Bear slid from my back, and stood quietly facing the bull.

"Tatanka," he said at last, "You stand in the tracks of the spiritual beast that led me here. Great bull, I know that you face me to protect your herd. Like you, great one, I must care for my herd also. My people are sick, and famished. They have grown weary from the raging storms of winter. They have become too weak to hunt. I have come here alone, huge one. On my chest, I carry the sacred bundle of my son. It is the belief of my people that one carrying a spirit cannot take the life of another. But I must. My people are starving. I must take your life, Tatanka, so that they will live."

The huge bull snorted and shook his head menacingly at Talking Bear. Pawing at the earth, it threw great billows of snow into the air above its back.

Raising his lance, Talking Bear looked skyward.

"Forgive me Great Spirit," he muttered, as he started bravely toward the bull.

As he neared the seething animal, the chief faltered, then stopped. A storm of torment welled within him, and he drew his sacred bundle tightly to his chest.

Tears streaming down his cheeks, he said, "I will not kill you great one, I cannot take the life of another with the soul of my son bound tightly to my chest. My people will die," he whispered sorrowfully.

The angry bull exploded suddenly forward. Snow boiled into the air from beneath the driving legs of the great animal as he charged. Talking Bear threw his lance into the snow at his side, and drawing himself to his full height, stared bravely into the eyes of the onrushing bull.

The bull turned as it reached Talking Bear, and with a terrible groan, plowed into the snow at the chief's side. Talking Bear watched in disbelief as the enormous animal thrashed and kicked in the snow beside him. With a final shuddering gasp, the bull rolled onto its side. Talking Bear's lance was buried in the great bison's chest. Only a small part of the lance's shaft protruded from its thick, brown hide.

Kneeling beside the bull, Talking Bear lay his trembling hands on the huge animal's shoulder.

"You have given your life that my people will live, great one. Thank you ,Tatanka," he whispered.

Talking Bear drew a bundle of sage from his pack, and rolled a handful into a small ball. With a few strokes of his flint, he soon had spirals of smoke rising from the sage. To honor and purify the great bull, he slowly passed the smoking sage over his body. Mumbling quietly to himself, Talking Bear rose and passed the smoking bundle over both himself and me. Then, with a sigh of finality, he turned, and

151

began breaking dry limbs from the surrounding trees for a fire.

Darkness had fallen when the chief at last began skinning the huge bull, and the sun was rising the next morning when he cleaned the last of the meat from his bones. Talking Bear cut two long poles from the forest. He tied one pole to each side of me with a strong leather thong that he fastened securely around my neck. He draped the bull's hide over the poles just above the place where they dragged in the snow behind me. Upon the hide, he then stacked and tied the piles of fresh meat.

The skies were fully light when Talking Bear led me from the small basin. As we moved quietly away, the skull of the great bull stared solemnly from a small prominence where Talking Bear had placed it. The load was very heavy, but the downhill drag was bearable on our previously broken trail. We toiled downward through the snow stopping often to rest. There was happiness in Talking Bear's voice as he chanted softly on our relentless downward trek.

Darkness had long gathered when we reached the tepees of our beleaguered people in the valley below us. Upon seeing us, messengers ran through the village telling all of the arrival of Talking Bear. A din of anxious voices echoed through the darkness as the news spread of our arrival. A huge crowd of people soon gathered around us, where Talking Bear stood quietly at my side. The people stared in disbelief as the chief walked to the skid behind me, and opened the buffalo hide revealing the stacks of fresh meat. A great roar of jubilant voices filled the air as the excited horde rushed forward to embrace their chief. With shaking hands, the people held slabs of bison skyward, giving thanks to the Great Spirit.

A huge fire was built in the center of the village near Talking Bear's tepee. The boisterous swarm of villagers stood with roasting sticks in hand, laughing and talking. Men, women and children of all ages gorged themselves on buffalo meat.

Talking Bear led me from the village to the trees that stood at its edge. He removed my bridal and brushed me down.

"You've done well, big friend," he said softly. "Together, we have saved our people." Talking Bear then climbed a tree near us and broke off several large, green limbs upon which I could easily feed. Eat well, White One," he said. As the chief walked away, he stopped and looked back.

"Yellow Tail," I heard him whisper, "Thank you for this sacred dog."

Talking bear then walked back to the village where I knew he joined his people in a great feast and celebration of life.

Around me, I could hear the crunching footsteps of other horses as they fed in the darkness. Remembering our amazing hunt, I pondered the appearance of the two-legged beast that had led us to the bison. Again, I saw the snow fly from the bull's powerful legs, and swirl upward over its back as it crashed toward Talking Bear. Fatigue from our arduous hunt overcame me finally, and lowering my head, I slept.

Chapter Eight

The daunting images of hulking two-legged beasts, and great bull bison faded quickly as I awakened and lifted my head from the earth. Around me, on the small knoll's top, my mares slept peacefully beneath the manzanita in the predawn light.

The crash of the great thundering bird had somehow quelled man's tireless pursuit of us, and we soon became at ease again in our desert world. The searing, hot days of summer passed without further incident, and now, in the shortest days of winter, only occasionally did we hear their rumbling devices far off in the desert. Only white scratches across the sky, left by their shining, silver birds, were daily reminders of the existence of man. I thought often about the storm that had drenched our desert world and filled the arroyos to their banks. I remembered plainly the near capture of my herd. Even the wisest of leaders, I realized, could fall victim to the whims of nature. I vowed to never again drop my guard.

When the days began to grow long beneath a warming sun, we once again traveled toward the mountains of the high desert. With the warmth, man came again to our desert land.

One morning, as we watered at our oasis, the two-legged ones appeared suddenly, thundering toward us on horses. With an anxious whinny, I gathered my mares and drove them storming across the desert away from them. Shots rang out behind us as we ran headlong through cactus and brush. Bullets whizzed angrily through the air and exploded against rocks at our sides, screeching noisily away as we ran. None in my herd fell to the bullets of the two-legged ones. Only once did a member of my herd cry out in pain, but even this wounded one did not lag, as we raced through the desert away from the hunters.

The horses ridden by the two-legged ones were well-rested and strong. They pursued us tirelessly through ravines, and across rocky ridges thick with ocotillo, and saguaro cactus. As we stormed across yet another ridge, I saw before us, a broad, sandy flat that lay at the mouth of a wide arroyo. As we thundered toward the flat, I saw bones and the skulls of my kind scattered across the sand there. Remembering long ago lessons taught by Banshee, I wheeled from the flat, and led my herd upward on the bank of the arroyo. In a short distance, well beyond the sandy deathtrap, we crossed the wash and continued our headlong flight across the desert.

The hunters, crossing the ridge behind us finally, saw that they had gained on my fleeing herd. Without hesitation, they thundered headlong across the sandy flat. The first of the hunters, screaming with fright, cart-wheeled headlong into the sand as the front legs of his racing horse sank in the watery mire. The terrified screams of man and horse filled the air as they floundered helplessly in the quicksand that had entrapped them. Only the hunters in the rear of the pack were able to slow, and turn their horses before tumbling into the deadly bog. Quickly, they dismounted, and with their lariats, worked feverishly to save their struggling brethren. The panicked screams of the hunters and the death cries of their drowning horses faded in the distance as we thundered away from them.

The hunters were able to drag all but two of their kind from the quicksand. Six of their horses were lost to the lake of death.

When at last we were far away from the hunting two-legged ones, we stopped on a ridge and looked nervously back. Their recklessness at the sea of flowing sand had ended their relentless chase. There was no sign of their pursuit.

The mare that had been struck by the bullet of the two-legged ones, stood with her head down at the side of my herd. Blood dripped slowly into the sand beneath her, and guts hung from a gaping hole in her belly. Sand and bits of earth covered the exposed entrails, and flies buzzed angrily in the air around her wound, attempting already, to lay eggs.

I led her slowly to the top of a gentle hill where she quickly lay beneath the protective cover of palo verde trees. We stayed with the mare for two days and two nights. We carefully watched for coyotes, whose torment would make the mare's dying even more agonizing. Vultures appeared in the sky on the second day. Their numbers grew as the day wore slowly on. Their keen eyes told them that soon they would feast. Coyotes called from the desert on all sides of the hill as darkness fell on the second night. They did not stalk closely though. Like the winged ones, their senses told them that their wait would not be long. As light began to grow in the sky, I heard the mare moan quietly, and then exhale in one long, shuddering breath. I knew, finally, that her suffering had ended. She had died. Softly, I called to the others, then turned and led them from the knoll. A chorus of excited calls rang from the brush as we continued into the desert. I knew that the mare would soon live again in the spirit of the coyote and vulture. The mare's circle of life would soon continue.

An air of sadness and desperation hung over my herd as we moved quietly through the desert. All knew that death was an important part of life. It was not an end, but rather a beginning. But this latest death, like so many before it, had come needlessly, at the hands of man.

In the air around us, hung the intoxicating smell of our ever-greening desert. Our world was alive with sprouting grass and myriad blooming plants as a result of a drenching rain we had endured a few days earlier. The wonderful smell of the moist desert earth, and the sweet scent of blooming cactus filled our senses as we moved steadily onward. The endless pursuit of the two-legged ones and the death of the mare was temporarily forgotten as we walked through a greening landscape filled with the coming of new life. As darkness fell on the land that night, I stood at the edge of my herd watching carefully from the crest of a tall hill. I pondered the passing of the mare earlier in the day. I knew that if somehow, I could understand death, I would better understand life.

For many days, our migration toward the upper desert was uneventful. The hunters had not followed our trail, and we drew closer by the day to the mountains that towered at the edge of our desert world. All in our herd looked forward to the shady stands of mahogany and scrub oak, beneath which we would seek shelter from the summer's sun.

Far away, in places where great numbers of the two-legged ones lived, the gruesome story of the men and their horses that had died in the sandy sea of death, was told again and again. The hunters described how the white stallion had led them on a wild chase through the desert, and fooling them finally, had led them to their death. The story was embellished each time it was told, and my fame was soon legendary in the great living places of man. The numbers of hunters who came to our land in pursuit of me and my herd, grew tenfold.

Never did we now feed in the light of day. Only late at night did we slip quietly from beneath the thick brush of our hiding place, and feed quietly across the desert. Again and again from my vantage point at the tops of hills or ridges, I would see the two-legged ones coming. Sometimes on foot, sometimes on horseback, but always it seemed they were coming. Endlessly, my herd and I stole quietly through the creosote, avoiding bullets, and the capture of man. As time passed, our senses became keener and we watched even more carefully from our hiding places in the desert. I learned new ways to hide and to escape man. I came to believe that we would never be captured.

The sweltering season of summer was nearly half gone. As the skies became light early one morning, I crossed a narrow wash and led my herd toward cover at the top of a rocky knoll. We would spend the day hidden in the concealment of brush at its top. The white colt pranced excitedly through my mares as we climbed steadily upward. The young stallion had grown, and the time had come, I realized, that he be vanquished from my herd. He would soon find mares of his own.

With my ears laid back and my head lowered, I charged angrily toward him. Confused at first, the colt darted sideways and rejoined my mares. Charging through the herd, I drove the young one from their midst. Rising to my hind legs, I brought my flailing front legs pounding against the earth, warning the young horse of my angry intentions. Charging again at the confused young stallion, I knocked him to the ground. Raring to my hind legs above him, I pawed at the air screaming furiously. The young horse, realizing finally, that his life was in danger, scrambled to his feet. With me pounding at his heels, the young stallion sprinted down the side of the hill and away through the desert. The sun was rising over the mountains as the young stallion disappeared from sight behind a wall of creosote brush. I stood watching sadly as the trail of dust kicked into the air by his hasty retreat settled slowly to the earth.

The morning stillness was shattered suddenly by a sharp explosion that echoed from the trees on the far side of the arroyo. My body shuddered in shock as the hunter's bullet struck me. The bullet passed easily through me at a place high on my neck. In blinding pain, I slumped immediately to the ground, paralyzed by the terrible blow of the projectile. The world around me spun dizzily and I fought to gain my feet, but I could not command the slightest movement from my legs. I heard the excited voices of two-legged ones as they crashed toward me from the brush. Standing above me now, they looked excitedly down.

"Nice shootin', Bob," said one of the hunters. "Looks like you got him just right!"

"By God, the white stallion is finally ours," exclaimed another excitedly!

"Yeah," said Bob sarcastically, "*Son of Banshee* don't look so smart now, does he? Get them hobbles on him quick like, before he comes fully to and kicks the heck out of us."

The hunters had temporarily paralyzed me by a well-placed bullet shot through the top of my neck. This method of capture was known by the two-legged ones, as *grazing*. If done successfully, the chosen horse was paralyzed by the terrible shock of the bullet for only a short while. It gave the hunters time to secure the wounded animal. Many of my kind, though, had been killed by the misplaced bullet of hunters attempting this feat. The two-legged ones had tried to capture me by their every method. In this most vile of ways, finally, they had been successful.

The hunters quickly buckled hobbles on both my front and rear legs. One, grabbed my ears and roughly jerked my head from the ground while others put a rope halter around my head and fastened their rawhide lariats around my neck. Beyond the hunters, I saw the young, white stallion slip quietly through the brush toward the top of the hill. Gratefully, I knew he would lead my herd down its backside, to safety.

The sun was high overhead when at last, I could again move my legs. Snorting, and squealing with anger, I fought to stand. Riders quickly guided their horses backward, drawing the lariats tightly around my neck as I gained my feet. Their rawhide nooses quickly strangled the air from my lungs. Fighting to stand, I wheezed helplessly for breath, stumbling in the clutch of lariats, and hobbles strapped on my legs.

Only once as a colt, had I endured the humiliation of man's lariats around my neck. Though I was nearly strangled, the anger that welled within me at the touch of the ropes was more than I could bear. The strangling lariats, and the pain that I felt from the wound at the base of my neck, caused my head to swim in a sea of blinding white light. The anger that welled within me now, brought a savage, angry strength that emanated from my very core. Screaming and snorting, I kicked and fought violently. With all my strength, I struggled to rear. Two of the hunter's horses, wide-eyed with fear, were pulled from their feet, their lariats snapping as I pulled them to the ground. The lariats of the other riders, though, held fast, and as the hunters drew their horses backward, the air was squeezed from my throat. Wheezing and choking, I slumped to my knees. My world spinning dizzily around me, I was subdued at last.

The hunters started me slowly across the desert, and with the fight in me now gone, I could do nothing else but to follow. The hobbles strapped to my front and rear legs caught on rocks and brush, tripping me to the earth. Hopping, and stumbling in a cloud of dust, the two-legged ones pulled me roughly along.

As the men dragged me across a small rise, I saw several trucks in the desert below. Attached to the rear of the trucks were trailers. Dragging me to the rear of one, the hunters swung the gate of the trailer open. Passing their lariats through the enclosure, they dragged me into the trailer and strapped me securely to its sides. I stood frantically looking between the narrow openings in the trailer's side as the hunters loaded their horses in the other trailers and closed the doors behind them. The long-ago memory of the capture of my herd and me, loomed in my mind as I heard the rumble of the truck's engine. With a jerk, I began to move, and I watched in horror from my enclosure, as the desert slipped swiftly by.

The sun was settling near the horizon, when my enclosure at last ground to a halt among a group of buildings. The barking of dogs, and the excited voices of man filled the air, as I was dragged backward from my trailer. Mounted riders again held me tightly from all directions as I was pulled into a small corral.

I kicked and bucked angrily at the two-legged ones who gawked at me from all sides of the enclosure. They were in disbelief that this white stallion, the one long known by them as Son of Banshee, now stood before them. The riders, drawing my nooses ever tighter, pulled me toward a small opening in the corral. Poking and jamming at my flanks with their stinging prods, the men forced me into a small, metal chute. Men working at the sides of the chute, drew it increasingly tighter to my sides. Soon, I was held fast in the grip of the enclosure, totally unable to move.

A man carrying a small black case, climbed into the corral and quickly approached where I was held fast in the metal chute. Pulling the hair of my mane this way and that, he inspected the bullet wound at the top of my neck. From the black case that lay on the ground beneath him, he drew a small container. Opening the vessel, he rubbed a foul-smelling substance on my wound. From his case, he then drew a small stick, at the end of which, appeared to be the spine of a cactus. The man stuck the device into my hip. A burning pain emanated from deep within the muscle as he held the device fast to my rump. Done at last, the man placed his tools back into his bag and quietly left. As I watched the two-legged one walk from the corral, the world around me began to darken. A strange sense of well-being drew slowly over me, and I was soon lost, deep in slumber.

Crunching footsteps in the frozen snow filled my dream world. The morning skies had not yet begun to lighten. To my nose came the smell of smoke and dried meat. It was the scent, I knew, of Talking Bear. Walking

166

quietly to my side, the chief placed one arm under my neck while he rubbed my ears and back with the other. "Are you ready, White One," he asked? "Are you ready to continue the journey that is ours?" Talking Bear put my bridal over my head, and led me toward the village.

When the skies had become light, the men of the village gathered before Talking Bear's tepee. With their stomach's full, and fear of starving gone, their mood was one of lightheartedness and banter. They stood happily talking to one another as they awaited their chief. The warriors fell silent when Talking Bear emerged from his tepee and stood before them.

"Brothers," he said, pointing to the towering ridge that lay beyond the village, "Today we will climb the mountain. In a small basin, high on the mountain's flank, we will kill and butcher a small herd of bison. They will give us their lives so that our people will live. Their great leader has given his life already. We will follow the tracks made by Wakia and me. Brothers," he said, "I was led to the bison by the sacred one known as *Sasquatch*."

A murmur of excitement rumbled through the gathering at Talking Bear's mention of the great beast. The chief stood quietly before his warriors then. He looked slowly from man to man looking into the eyes of each for a moment. Certain that the warriors understood the importance of the story he was about to share, Talking Bear continued.

"In the darkness of night," he said, "The spiritual one came. The huge one stood unmoving, barely visible in the soft glow of my fire. Then, as suddenly as he had appeared, he was gone. My horse carried me tirelessly upward on his trail for nearly a day. As we crossed a small rise, the trail of Sasquatch ended. In his tracks stood *Tatanka*, the great bull bison. Sasquatch had vanished."

"I do not understand, brothers, all that happened on the mountain that morning. But when my hunt had ended, the great bull lay dead before me. Tatanka had given his life so that my people could live."

Talking Bear and his warriors stood quietly in thought, for a bit. Then, drawing in a great breath, Talking Bear said, "Go now, and prepare yourselves to hunt. Bring your best bows and lances. Bring two of your sharpest knives. Their stone blades will be brittle from the bite of winter and the bones of Tatanka are large and heavy. Knives will easily be broken. Wear the warmest of your furs and the tallest of your boots. When you return here to my tepee, I will choose the strongest and best prepared among you, to accompany me on our hunt."

Talking Bear knew that sickness and near starvation had badly weakened many of his warriors. Not all could make such a climb as would be necessary to hunt the bison hidden in the basin far above.

When the warriors returned, Talking Bear chose twenty of the best prepared men before him. "Brothers," he said, "Go now, and return with two of your strongest horses. Bring your warmest bedroll and a spool of leather strapping.

The return to the mountain seemed harder than when Talking Bear and I first climbed it. On our second day, the chief rode me steadily upward on the trail that we had broken only three days before. Though there had been no fresh snow, the arduous hunt and packing of meat we had undertaken then, had robbed my legs of their strength. I fought the searing burn in my legs as I carried Talking Bear upward. From the trail behind me, came the labored sound of both horses and man as they struggled upward in the snow.

The day was half gone when finally, we neared the basin. Talking Bear raised his arm and silently stopped our laboring procession. Steam billowed from the nostrils of the wheezing horses behind me, and rose from their backs and heaving sides. The warriors, covered from head to foot in snow and ice, stood quietly waiting for Talking Bear's further commands.

The chief crept slowly over the ridge and in a short while returned. The smile on his face and the upward pointing fingers of both hands told the warriors of the many bison he had found. With a wave of his arm he signaled the warriors to follow. Beneath the trees at the far edge of a meadow, stood the small herd of bison we had found on our previous hunt. At the chief's signal, all horses were tied, and weapons were made ready for the hunt.

During our upward climb, storm clouds had begun to gather, and now a cold, biting wind grew steadily from the north. Snow began to swirl from the sky as Talking Bear huddled in the midst of his warriors quietly whispering final instructions for the kill.

Talking Bear knew that in this bitter cold, only a few bison could be killed at a time. If too many were killed, the bodies of some, would freeze before the meat could be cut from their bones and placed on skids for travel.

It was normally the custom that the warriors charged forward on their horses and killed the bison at close quarters with their lances. But the snow here was too deep. Were the bison to turn and charge the mounted hunters, the horses would be unable to evade their deadly horns. Bows and arrows would be used.

In an ever-thickening wall of snow, the warriors crept silently from tree to tree at the edge of the meadow behind Talking Bear. When the distance between them and the bison was small, the warriors drew their bows and let their arrows fly. The huge animals quivered as the arrows struck them behind the shoulder, but they did not run. They only walked slowly away, as if unaware they had been struck. Bleeding profusely from the wound where only the feathered end of the arrow shaft protruded, they stood for a moment before staggering and toppling into the snow.

Four bison at a time were killed in this way. After the animals had fallen, the warriors would move quickly forward. They would kneel before the animal, and with a burning ball of sage, pass purifying smoke over its body. They would give thanks to the bison for having given its life so that their people would live. Then, the warriors would begin skinning and boning before the huge carcasses could freeze. When the meat had been placed on skids and ready for travel, more bison were killed.

The storm steadily worsened and the wind roared angrily through the trees around us. The warriors could barely be seen through swirling billows of snow as they worked feverishly to bone the carcasses of the bison, and put the meat on skids before it froze

A large warming fire was built near where the skids of frozen meat had been made ready for travel. The warriors stood by the fire only briefly as they came and went with meat. They knew that to stand too long by the fire would cause the snow and ice that was caked to their garments to melt. To become wet in a storm such as this, would bring certain death.

For two days, the hunters worked through darkness and light, as they processed the meat of the bison and readied it for travel to the village. As was the custom of the keeper of a spirit, Talking Bear did not participate in the killing or handling of the meat. He watched quietly from beneath a tree as his warriors worked without rest in the frigid storm. In honor of their disregard for the swirling snow and biting wind, Talking Bear had no fire. Once, through the swirling blizzard, I was certain that I saw Yellow Tail sitting beside him in the snow.

As it became light on the third day, the wind howled endlessly still, and snow swirled dizzily across the meadow. The warriors were nearly exhausted as they dragged meat to the fire and lashed it to the remaining skids. Twenty-one bison had been killed and butchered. Seven bison watched stoically from beneath the trees at the far side of the meadow.

Talking Bear stood from beneath his tree and walked into the opening. Raising his arm, he said in a loud voice so that all could hear, "I am humbled, brothers, by your strength and will. Our hunt is over. We have what we came for. Our people will live."

His warriors gathered around him in a large circle. Opening his pack, the chief withdrew his pipe whose bowl had been loaded with prayers before their departure from the village. Removing the small ball of sage that sealed its bowl, Talking Bear lit the pipe with an ember from the warming fire and drew deeply on its stem. He blew smoke into the air in each of the four directions, then held his pipe skyward and gave thanks to the Great Spirit for the lives of the bison they had taken. He asked that the Great Mystery give his warriors and their horses the strength to carry the meat to the village of our people. He then passed his pipe to the man standing beside him, who drew a puff of smoke from the pipe and blew it into the air before passing the pipe on. In this way, each man in the circle drew from the pipe and mumbled a few words of prayer before passing it on. When the pipe returned finally, to Talking Bear, the chief smoked it until the tobacco was gone, then quietly replaced it in his pack.

Then, looking from man to man, Talking Bear said, "You have done well. We have taken twenty-one bison. I am proud to say that we are brothers. It is time now to finish our journey."

The warriors quickly fastened the skids behind their horses. When all were ready, Talking Bear signaled the warriors with a wave of his arm and led me forward into the storm. From behind me, came the anxious snorts and calls of the heavily laden horses as the warriors started them forward. Only the skeletons of the last bison that we killed could be seen above the deepening snow. All others had long been covered.

When we reached the edge of the basin, Talking Bear turned, and held his lance into the air. Staring upward, the chief asked that the seven bison that still lived, be given the strength to again see the season of the growing grass. The remaining bison watched from the far side of the meadow as we walked across the ridge and started downward.

Our trail had been completely covered by the storm. The snow was past my belly in depth, and even though it was downhill, I lunged with all my might to move my heavy burden forward. The horses behind me, snorted and groaned as their winter weakened bodies strained against their heavy drags.

We struggled endlessly downward through clouds of billowing snow blown into our faces by a relentless wind. The men and horses at the rear of our procession were hidden behind the wall of falling snow. As we lunged and wallowed downward, the snow beneath us often gave way. With a loud crack, the snow would slide from between our legs, and in a boiling mass of whiteness, hiss slowly down the mountain before us.

When I was nearly exhausted, Talking Bear drew me to a stop, and motioned the others to pass. When the last of the long line of horses had passed, Talking Bear started me forward again at their rear.

"We work through this deep snow as do the elk when they migrate, White One," he said. "When the leader becomes weary, they step to the side and let all behind them pass. Then, they assume a place in the back of the line. In this way, the elk save their energy, and all in the herd have their turn at breaking trail."

At the bottom of the mountain, the snow was so deep that we could move forward only a few lunges at a time before we had to stop and rest. Snowshoes were fashioned from buffalo hide and willow, and two men were sent ahead to the village. They were to return with all people and horses strong enough to help in the packing of the bison meat. As our laboring line of horses struggled on into the night, the storm abated, and the skies cleared. Stars shone brightly, and the moon appeared from behind retreating clouds to bathe the snow in a bright, blue light. The moon's light was so bright that we cast shadows on the sparkling snow before us as we struggled forward along the creek.

When the skies began to lighten the next morning, we suddenly heard voices in the distance. Soon we saw the shadowy forms of people moving slowly toward us in the early morning light. Upon seeing us, they struggled forward in the deep snow with newfound energy. Yelling and laughing joyfully, the people embraced the chief and all the successful hunters. The villagers drew suddenly quiet, as in awe, they studied the skids of meat tied behind weary horses whose mains and tail were tangled with ice.

With fresh horses, and more people to help, we moved steadily forward toward the village. The air was filled with the sound of barking dogs and the happy drone of laughter and talk. We emerged from the canyon of Targhee when the sun was high overhead. Before us, at last, was our village.

Fires were quickly made in the village's center. Men, women, and children surrounded each blaze. Laughing and singing, they held roasting sticks laden with buffalo meat into the flames.

Darkness was falling when Talking Bear rose and stood before them. The laughter and talking slowly ceased, and the people fell silent. In a loud voice, Talking Bear told his people how the Great Mystery had sent the two-legged spirit known as Sasquatch, to him. He told them how the beast had led him to the bison. He told of the bravery of his hunters. How they had worked nonstop in the terrible storm to fill their skids with buffalo meat. The people sat in silence long after Talking Bear had finished speaking. They were thinking about the wonder of our world, and the Great Spirit who cared for them.

The villagers were still happily celebrating when Talking Bear led me from the village toward the aspen forest at its side. He stroked my ears and rubbed my neck and back for a long while before speaking. "White One," he said at last, "We have done well. Our prayers have been answered. The Great Spirit chose that our people should live. Within you, White One, indeed beats the heart of the bull elk. Thank you, sacred dog, that you share my journey. Eat well, Wakia," he said, as he turned and walked toward the village.

The snows that had come while we were on our hunt, made it easy to reach the fresh bark on the aspens. All in the herd were able to eat. With my belly full at last, the deep weariness that had grown within me, drew me quickly into sleep.

Chapter Nine

My dream of quiet solitude in the snowy aspen forest beside my village vanished suddenly as I awakened. Strangely, I realized, the sun had drawn to a place fully overhead.

The stinging pain of the white man's cactus stick had caused the night to be very long. Slowly, I realized I was held immobile still, in the small metal enclosure in which I had been placed after my capture. Around it, was still a tall, round corral. Panic overcame me as I remembered my brutal capture and my frightful journey to this place of man. I sprang forward with all my might, but was held fast by chains and leather straps. My herd was nowhere to be seen, and pain shot through my neck at my every movement.

Suddenly, beyond the walls of the corral I heard the voices of two-legged ones as they approached. Stepping onto the lower rail of the surrounding corral, several men stood looking and pointing at me. Anger welled within me at the sight of the two-legged ones. Snorting and kicking, I lunged at them, pounding my restraints against the sides of the metal chute as I surged forward with all my might.

Startled, the men jumped from the side of the corral and cowered backward, away from my enclosure.

Throughout the day, two-legged ones continued to come. They talked quietly as they looked and pointed toward where I stood helplessly bound in the metal stall. With my head lowered, and my ears laid flatly back against my head, my eyes shone with the hatred that I felt for them. The men stayed respectfully back from my corral.

When the sun drew near the far horizon, I heard the crunching footsteps of several two-legged ones as they approached the corral from a barn that stood at its side. A large gate squeaked loudly as it swung open, and two men approached my chute from behind. Each man carried a black case. I recognized one of them as the man who had stuck me with the cactus stick the night before. Blinding pain filled my head as I lunged and kicked at them in anger. Manipulating levers at the sides of my small enclosure, they drew the sides of the metal chute quickly against me. Soon, I stood helplessly trapped, held fast between the walls of the metal stall.

As he had the night before, the man carefully inspected the wound in my neck, and rubbed his foul-smelling substance into my injury. The man then drew the cactus tipped stick from his case and stuck in my hip. Soon, I was no longer able to summon the slightest movement from my legs. Though fully awake, I was unable to move as the other man now approached me. Bending to the ground at my front feet, the two-legged one worked carefully on my right foot. I watched frightfully, as the man etched strange figures into my hoof.

The two-legged ones had put what their kind called, a *brand,* on my foot. It had long been illegal to shoot or capture wild horses on government land in the desert. The hunters had knowingly broken the law when they captured and took me from my desert home. Now, they had hired this man to put this brand on my hoof. Though illegal, the brand and fraudulent bill of sale they created, would enable the men to move me across state lines. Soon, I would be sold at their auction.

Over the coming days, the two-legged one who carried the strange black bag, came often. Each time he came, he trapped me tightly in the metal chute, then inspected my wound, and applied his foul-smelling liquid to the injury. As the days drew slowly by, the terrible pain that throbbed from the wound slowly eased. I could at last move my head from side to side without pain.

One day the man with the black bag came, but this time, only looked at the wound on my neck. He did not put his foul-smelling liquid on my injury, nor did he stick me with his strange cactus stick. He merely inspected the wound, then patted me on the neck and said, "You are a tough horse, White One. You are ready to go."

The next day, the two-legged ones appeared in the corral next to my metal enclosure. They quickly tightened the walls of the chute against my sides until I could no longer move. With all my might, I fought them as they strapped hobbles to my front and rear feet, then placed the nooses of their rawhide lariats around my neck. Mounted riders at all sides held me fast as I was led from the metal chute. Kicking and bucking, I fought my captors as they shocked me with their prods and drug me into a trailer. Fastened securely from all sides, I stood anxiously watching as the engine of the truck rumbled to life, and with a jerk, my trailer started forward.

For a short while, we bounced along in the dust, but soon we came to a smooth, black trail where we moved much faster. As we moved steadily through the day, the trails upon which rode, became wider. To my horror, on these wide black trails, other trucks both large and small, rushed by us on either side. Some roared ominously as they rumbled past, others passed with only the sound of rushing wind. The smell that came from the vehicles around us, was putrid. In all the land that I had traveled, I had never smelled such foul odors. The wind lashed at the sides of my enclosure as we rumbled along. The trees and hills at our sides, passed at a rate I had never before seen.

Soon, I began to see many buildings, and even more vehicles flashed by in all directions. We slowed, and turned onto another trail, and then drew alongside a large building and came to a stop. With lariats, mounted riders drug me from the rear of the trailer. Hopping and stumbling, I fought, as the riders dragged me into an enormous barn. An arena, surrounded by a tall wooden fence, nearly filled the inside of the structure. Stalls at the far end of the huge building were the only exception. I was dragged quickly across the arena in a cloud of dust, and fighting still, was forced into a stall at the barn's far end. A small pile of hay lay at the side of the stall, and a tiny pool of water shone from a metal container at its rear.

As the day passed slowly by, many other horses were led through the arena and put into stalls beside mine. As darkness fell, I suddenly heard the tormented scream of a horse I knew well. Peering between the slats of my stall, I watched in disbelief as mounted riders dragged an old black and white stallion across the arena's floor. They placed the storming horse in a stall at the arena's far side. It was the stallion whose herd I had taken years before in my desert land. The old horse had fallen captive to illegal hunters as had I. Our trails had crossed once more, in this most unlikely of places.

Far into the night, I listened carefully to the sounds that emanated from this strange place in which I was now captive. Above me in the rafters, I heard the occasional cooing of pigeons, and from somewhere in the darkness came the call of owl. From outside the barn, came the far-off roar of the vehicles of man, as they raced by on the huge, black trail of the two-legged ones. Shivers ran through me, as twice, I heard the angry scream of my old foe from the arena's far side. Often in the night, came the nervous whinny of horses as they called to one another somewhere in the darkness. All, wondered anxiously, I was certain, what daylight would bring.

The strange world in which I was now a prisoner, grew active as the skies lightened the next morning. The machines of man, rumbled everywhere it seemed. Some toted hay, while others turned in dusty circles, smoothing the arena's floor.

As the morning drew on, the numbers of two-legged ones walking past my stall steadily grew. The people often stopped and peered at me between the slats of my enclosure. They would nod their heads approvingly as they carefully studied me. Angrily, I would lay my ears flatly against my head and lunge at them. The chains that bound me, though, would halt my attack as they rattled loudly against my stall. Frightened, the people would move quickly on.

More and more of the two-legged ones came as the day passed. It seemed that they were everywhere in the arena. I no longer lunged in anger at the ones who peered between the slats of my stall. Now, I stood quietly in contempt, glaring at them with hatred in my eyes.

When the day was half done, a man and woman quietly approached my stall, and stopped in front of it as many others had done. They talked quietly to one another as they studied me carefully. The woman slowly walked closer to the door of my stall, and staring into my eyes, spoke to me in words I did not understand. Her voice was soft and soothing. Strangely, the anger that I had felt for the other two-legged ones, did not well within me.

Suddenly, a man with a booming voice spoke from a raised platform at the far end of the arena. The man and woman turned from my stall and quickly joined the horde of two-legged ones who had gathered there. For the remainder of the day, there was a great deal of excitement among the crowd as the man on the platform yelled to them in his strange, booming voice. Only occasionally, when the man struck a small block of wood with the resounding clap of his wooden hammer, did his booming voice rest. Strangely, each time he did this, calls of joy came from some of those gathered before him.

The men who had captured me, had taken me to auction. Now, with many other horses, both domestic and wild, I would be sold.

After a long while, the booming voice of the man on the platform, quieted. I watched nervously from my stall as he climbed from his perch above the others. The excited voices of the people that had been gathered before him, slowly dwindled as they turned, and left the arena. The man and woman who had stood before my stall earlier, suddenly appeared before me once more. Together, they approached the door of my stall. For a short while they talked to me in hushed tones, then turned and left the arena.

As the day passed, some horses around me were taken from the stalls in which they had been kept. Many, like myself, were left chained in their stalls. As darkness fell, I stood nervously waiting for what was to come.

When the skies became light the next morning, more of the horses were taken from the stalls around me and led from the barn. Suddenly from across the arena, I heard the snort and angry cry of the old stallion as he was pulled from his stall. Bucking and fighting, mounted riders pulled him through the arena where he disappeared through the large opening at the end of the barn.

Nearly all the horses were gone, when finally, I heard the steady plod of horses as mounted riders moved in my direction. The gate to my stall swung suddenly open and lariats were placed around my neck. The hobbles that had been fastened to my front and rear feet two days earlier, were still firmly in place. The chains that held me securely to the sides of the stall were removed, and the riders pulled me from the enclosure. Their horses staggered and lurched against my raging tirade, as they pulled me through the opening of the barn. Blinking against the sudden brightness of sunshine, I saw before me, a long, white trailer fastened behind a shiny truck. The riders pulled me roughly into the trailer. I was quickly fastened to its sides, and the lariats

187

were removed from my neck. With a screech, the door was closed and fastened behind me. In front of me, was a large metal door through which I could not see. The occasional snort and stomping of feet, told me that another horse stood captive on its far side.

Outside the trailer, I heard the voice of the lady who had twice stood before my stall in the barn. I heard her crunching footsteps as she approached the trailer. Looking nervously through the slats on the trailer's side, I watched as she spoke to the horse in the stall before me. Moving slowly toward me, she stopped and looked in.

"May our journey together be good, White One," she said. She turned then, and walked toward the truck. I heard the doors of the truck close as she entered, and soon we lurched forward as our journey began.

For the rest of that day and far into the night, we rumbled onward on a wide, smooth trail. The skies were dark still, when we slowed and turned from the black trail. For a time, we banged along on a winding, dirt trail, then came to a grinding halt amongst a small group of buildings. The door of the trailer opened behind me, and two riders, holding the chains of my bridal from either side, led me away from the trailer. The men drew me into a stall at the far side of a large corral where both my hobbles, and the chains on my halter were removed. I heard the steps of the other horse in the darkness, as he too, was led into the corral and placed into a stall across from me.

As the day grew light the next morning, the sun shone from a murky, white sky. The air in this new place smelled like smoke, and still, I smelled the foul odor of the wide, black trail. But on the air also, was the alluring smell of trees and flowers, the kind I had never smelled before. Dogs barked in the distance, and occasionally I heard the far-off voice of man. The soft thunder of the two-legged one's black trail rumbled from somewhere far away, and the voice of the shining crafts that carried man through the skies, rumbled above me.

The buildings around me were painted the glistening color of snow. Their roofs were the color of the brightest of sunsets. For the first time since my capture, I wore only a halter over my head. The hobbles that had been lashed to my front and rear legs and the chains that bound me at my sides, were now gone. The wooden sides of my stall were tall and stout, only narrow openings between the boards allowed me to see out. A large wooden trough at my stall's far end was filled to its top with bright, green hay, and a metal container beside it, shimmered with water.

A high-pitched squeal reminded me of the horse that occupied the stall on the far side of the corral. With disbelieving eyes, I stared between the slats of my stall. Across from me, glaring angrily from a stall at the corral's far edge, stood my old nemesis, the black-and-white stallion.

When the sun was high overhead, the woman, my apparent new owner, appeared at the edge of the corral. She walked first to the old stallion, where she stood and talked quietly for a short time. Then, she turned and walked to me. Her eyes were bright and kind, and her voice was soft and comforting when she spoke. Though I did not understand what she said, I listened carefully as she talked. Her words somehow lessened the nervousness within me.

Later in the day, the lady appeared again. She led a small colt from the barn, and opening the gate at the far side of the corral, led the young one into the arena. Attaching a long rope to the halter on its head, she ran the colt in circles around her. The little horse nickered proudly as it pranced in circles at the end of her rope. Across from me in his stall, the old stallion snorted and stomped with anger at the sound of the colt's joyful calls.

Summer had long passed, and now even the shortest days of winter were behind me. On the lonely nights when I stood in the darkness of my stall, I often wondered upon which knob my herd had taken shelter this night.

'Was it the young, white stallion that now led my mares,' I wondered, 'or had some other stallion taken possession of my herd?'

Early each morning, the lady would appear again, in the corral. She would fill both my, and the old stallion's troughs with hay and water. Then, she would lead her colt from the barn and run it in circles around her in the corral. Only occasionally, the man would appear with the woman. When he did, he sat in the shade at the edge of the corral, and quietly watched her as she trained her colt. My old nemesis often screamed in anger from the far side of the arena as she trained the young one.

One day while the woman was training the young colt, the old stallion stomped and snorted angrily in his stall across from me. But this day, the ire of the old one seemed much worse. As the young colt pranced in circles in the corral before him, the old horse became increasingly angry. Raising to his hind legs, the old stallion pawed at the gate of his stall as he screamed with rage at the young horse.

Charging suddenly forward, the stallion leapt into the air and crashed into the boards on the top of the gate. With a loud crack, the top two rungs on the gate snapped, and the stallion crashed into the arena. Both the lady and the colt stood frozen with fear, as the stallion charged toward them.

The old horse hit the colt at full stride, knocking it from its feet. Before the young one could rise, the stallion fell upon it with its front feet. The lady, screaming in terror, whipped at the rearing stallion with the loose end of her rope. Fitfully, she pulled at the end attached to the colt's halter in a futile attempt to save him.

The death screams of the dying colt, and the terrified shrieks of the woman born in me in anger I had not often felt. With all my might, I sprang at the door of my stall smashing its wooden slats to bits. Charging across the arena, I hit the old stallion as his front feet crashed down on the lady. The stallion flew from his feet and rolled through the dirt with a mighty groan. Rearing to my hind legs, I sprang forward again, but the old one remembered me well. He rolled to his feet and bolted toward his stall.

Clearing the broken gate with a mighty lunge, the old stallion cowered at the stall's far corner as I snorted angrily at him from the arena. Knowing that he was no longer a threat, I turned and walked to where the woman and colt lay motionless in the dirt. Lowering my nose, I breathed deeply of their scent. Both the colt and the woman, were dead.

Suddenly the man burst into the corral. Yelling and screaming, he chased me from their side. Kneeling beside his wife, he drew her into his arms. Rocking back and forth in grief, he carefully brushed the hair from her face as he cradled her limp body. Slowly, his eyes fell upon the lifeless body of the colt that lay near him in the dirt. Shaking his head in disbelief, he raised his head and stared into my eyes.

"You have killed them," he said. "You have killed them both."

Slowly, he scanned the corral around him. He saw the broken rungs on the gate of the old stallion's stall.

"He nearly killed you too, old man," he said.

Rising to his feet, his eyes filled with anger, he turned again to me. "You have taken the life of my wife," he said. "Now, White One, I will take yours."

Later in the day, I watched from my stall as men entered the corral. Dressed in white, they quietly approached where the woman lay in the dirt. They carefully covered her with a blanket, placed her on a stretcher, and without a word, carried her from the corral. As the sun drew low in the sky, men came and dragged the lifeless body of the colt from the corral. The old horse stood across from me in his stall, his eyes filled with hatred as he watched.

As darkness fell, I heard the creak of the gate at the corral's far end. Slowly, the man entered the corral and walked my way. In his hands was a rifle. Stopping in front of my stall, his face etched with pain, he stood quietly glaring at me.

"White One," he said, his voice cracking with grief, "You have taken the life of my partner, my wife, and you have killed her colt. "Now, he said, as he leveled the rifle at my chest, "I will take your life."

Staring into his angry eyes, I waited for the explosion that I knew would soon come. The man's shoulders slumped, and he began to sob as he lowered the rifle toward the ground.

"I cannot shoot you," he moaned. "I cannot take your life. But make no mistake, White One, I will see to it that your life is ended." He turned from me then and walked from the corral.

Long into the night, I pondered the remarkable events that had been my life. I stood quietly staring at the old stallion's stall on the far side of the corral. I thought again about the killing of the woman and the young colt, and wondered at the terrible anger that consumed the old horse. By the strangest of chance, our trails had once again crossed. And through his brutal killing of the woman and her colt, my old nemesis, without his knowing, had reaped his mighty revenge upon me.

Drawing a deep breath, I closed my eyes and slowly lowered my head. The smell of campfires and roasting meat filled the night when finally, I slept.

Drying racks full of meat soon stood on snowdrifts in the bright sunshine throughout my village. Hope had suddenly grown in my people. The sound of singing and laughter was often heard from within the tepees, and the sound of children playing in the snow was commonplace now. The shortest days of winter had passed. Each day grew in length, as the sun traveled higher in the sky on its daily journey. The sun's heat grew in intensity, and each day was warmer. The creek that ran at the edge of our village, no longer slept. It could be heard gurgling beneath the snow and ice that covered it. Soon, open water began to show at the mouth of each creek where they entered the lake at the foot of Targhee Mountain. Fish teemed in the open water of each, as they began their age-old journey upward in the creeks, to spawn. The bright, red meat of fish soon appeared on the drying racks next to the dark, thick strips of bison meat.

As the snow began to recede, evidence could be seen telling of the terrible struggle the people had endured with the red spotted disease, and the terrible storms of winter. Beyond the village, burial platforms began to show from beneath huge drifts of snow. In places, groups of the ominous structures stood closely set, a grim reminder of an entire family that had passed. Throughout the forest of aspen, many bodies of my kind began to appear from the receding snow. These were ones who had succumbed to raging storms and were covered beneath the snow before the people could butcher them or the black winged ones could ravage their carcasses.

In the open beyond the tepees, matted yellow grass from the previous year began to appear between the melting drifts of snow. At the bases of some huge rocks where the reflected heat of the sun had melted the snow, green grass began to rise from the earth.

This day had been sunny and calm. Though the sun had long ago fallen behind the mountain, the night was warm, and moonlight filled the valley around me. To the north, I could see a towering mountain range still covered in snow. The great divide, I knew, lay at its top. As I lay in the grass near a huge boulder, I remembered the journey Talking Bear and I had made as we struggled across those peaks in search of this village. I knew that soon we would retrace the steps of that perilous journey. Our trek would be easier now, in this season of ducks returning. The numbers of the herd that lay resting around me were few. Most had starved or frozen to death during the season of renewal, but the ones who lived still were quickly becoming healthy and strong again. Some had only oddly shaped holes in their head where ears, or the sensitive tissue of their noses had been. These grotesque reminders of the freezing cold they had endured, were a badge of courage worn by these hearty survivors.

The day came finally, when Talking Bear sat astride my back facing his people. Waiting anxiously before him were the men, women, and children whose lives he had saved. Skids, heaped with provisions, were lashed to what few horses they had. A day that many had doubted would ever come, was finally upon them. Their chief would proudly lead them northward to the Valley of Shining Mountains. In seven day's travel, Talking Bear's people would at last, be reunited.

Without speaking, Talking Bear raised his lance into the air above his head. The sun gleamed from its tip as he lowered his arm, pointing at the mountains ahead. He turned me then, and our procession started forward.

The tepees of those who had succumbed to sickness stood deserted around us as we walked from the encampment. A howling gust of wind swirled suddenly through the village. From within the wind came the anguished cry of a hundred people. Dust from the earth rose whirling into the air from around the deserted tepees. "Welcome brothers and sisters," said Talking Bear as the cloud of dust overtook our procession.

An ominous hush settled over the people as we walked through the field beyond the village. Quiet chanting and wails of grief were heard often as the villagers passed the death scaffold bearing the remains of a loved one. Saddest of all, were the tiny platforms beneath which no worldly possessions lay. Only a ragged, leather doll hung swaying in the wind.

The somber mood of the people slowly changed as we began to climb upward, away from the land of Targhee. When the sun was near the western horizon, our tribe stood finally in the narrow gap at the top of the great divide.

Quietly, the people turned and studied the land in which they had been trapped. In the bottom of the huge basin was the lake that lay just beyond the place where the tribe had built their makeshift village. Its surface, now void of ice, shimmered in the setting sun. At the lake's far side stood the towering mountain of Targhee. Releasing troubled memories, the people turned one by one, and followed Talking Bear downward.

Our tribe slept that night at the edge of the aspen grove where Talking Bear and I had taken refuge during the terrible storm on our journey upward. Talking Bear sat quietly leaning against a tree as darkness overcame the land. Flames outlined the deep creases in his face as he stared quietly into his small fire. His thoughts, I knew, were of the fire that had burned within that same ring of rocks during the terrible blizzard that had stranded us here.

The people readied the skids and lashed them to the horses the next morning as the sun shone above the mountains to the east. All were anxious to continue our northward journey.

Talking Bear pulled me to a halt often, as we descended the great divide. He sat quietly each time, while he slowly scanned our surroundings and remembered.

199

The sun drew low in the sky when at last we stood on the bank of the River of Spirits. At our feet in the grass, were the blackened coals of the fire that had saved our lives after our imperiled crossing. Talking Bear sat quietly astride my back remembering the treacherous ordeal. It seemed impossible now. The river moved peacefully along before us, its soft, chortling sounds bringing confidence to even the most wary of those who would cross.

The sun, even though low on the horizon, still glowed warmly. Riding through the throng of people gathered on the riverbank behind him, he told them to ready themselves and secure their skids. We would cross now. He turned and guided me into the water.

Unlike our icy crossing of the previous season, this crossing was uneventful. When all the people were safely on the far side, Talking Bear gave the order to make camp. Soon, smoke from cooking fires filled the air. The mood was one of jubilance. Happy chatter and laughter filled the air. Dogs barked and children screamed with laughter as they ran playfully through camp.

Talking Bear walked to my side where I grazed near the river's edge.

"White One," he said, there is a small journey we must make." He swung onto my back and we slowly followed the river downward from our makeshift village.

Fish splashed from the surface of the river, and birds rose from the tall grass as we moved along. Soon we came to a slight bend in the river where logs and other debris had been stacked by the driving ice of winter. Talking Bear suddenly drew me to a halt and dismounted. Sitting amongst the logs as if waiting for us, was the fully clothed skeleton of the brave warrior who had drowned in our deadly crossing of the past winter.

"Thank you, Little Crow, for being my friend," said Talking Bear. "You were a brave man. You gave your life to save our people. You have waited here for me, Little Crow. How did you know I would return? We are here now, Little Crow, all of us. The Great Mystery led me to our lost people. We will pass this way tomorrow. We will honor you, my friend."

As we passed the silent form of Little Crow the next day, Talking Bear dismounted, and stood quietly beside his deceased friend. All in the tribe mumbled their silent prayer of thanks as they passed slowly by.

For two days, we moved steadily downward on the banks of the Spirit River. The familiar benches of land that lay on either side of the river told me we would soon arrive at our village. Long before we came to the encampment, we saw clouds of signal smoke billow into the air at both sides of the valley. They were soon answered by rising clouds of smoke farther down. It was the place, I knew, where the main encampment of our people lay.

Our arrival was met with yelling and screams of disbelief. There was much laughter and tears of joy as we entered the encampment. The people hugged and cried and danced. There was much happiness. Tales were excitedly told. Looks of disbelief filled the faces of the listeners, as those thought to be forever lost, told of the season of renewal that had imprisoned them in the land of Targhee. Many sad remembrances were shared. The villagers wailed and cried together with the mention of each loved one lost to the violent storms and sickness.

When the horses had been put in the field to eat, and the tepees of the returning people had been erected, fires were quickly made. Soon, the smell of roasting meat hung heavily on the air. The feast lasted long into the night. Laughter and joy filled the air as all in the tribe celebrated the reunion of our people.

I was tied beside Talking Bear's tepee where the chief sat cross-legged on the ground before a small fire. His eyes sparkled and a faint smile played at the corners of his mouth as he quietly watched his tribe rejoice. All in the tribe knew of the bravery of their great chief. They knew that it was because of his undying resolve to find his lost people that they now lived.

Around many blazing fires, the new arrivals told in detail the harrowing challenges that they had faced at the foot of Targhee. Again, the villagers cried at each account of those who had died from the red spotted sickness, and the many others who had starved and succumbed to the frigid winds of the terrible winter. An elder stood before the flickering light of a huge bonfire and told how Talking Bear had climbed the mountain that lay beside the creek named for the great warrior, Targhee. Shared looks of amazement and a soft murmur came from the people when the old man told how Sasquatch had come to their chief and led him to a small herd of bison. "The meat had saved the people," he said.

Man and woman alike stood in turn before the dancing flames of the bonfire and related their story of the perilous winter in the land of Targhee. The first streaks of light were beginning to show in the sky when at last, the fires were allowed to die, and the great feast ended.

A counsel fire was built early the next day before the tepee of Talking Bear. I stood quietly to the side, as the chief sat cross-legged on the ground before the flames. His leaders flanked him on either side, forming a circle around the fire. They told Talking Bear that two full moons ago the Crow had come in the night to steal horses. Our guard that night, they told him, was a young warrior named Broken Knife. Though outnumbered, he had refused to yield and fought bravely to save our horses. His battle cries had awakened the encampment, and our warriors soon repelled the Crow. Broken Knife's bravery had saved our horses, but the young warrior had been killed. Only his horse with the white, blazing star on its chest, had been stolen, they said.

Talking Bear sat quietly listening. His face was expressionless, his eyes were cast downward to the ground in front of him. It was but one year ago, that Yellow Tail's best friend, Broken Knife, had become a warrior. Upon earning the rite of manhood, Talking Bear had given Broken Knife the black horse with the blazing white star.

After a long while, Talking Bear raised his head and met the eyes of each of the warriors around him. In a low, grumbling voice quivering with anger, he said, "Vengeance will be had. But it must wait. There is something I must do."

That night after darkness had settled, Talking Bear led me from my spot beside his tepee. I followed him to the deep grass at the edge of the river where he turned finally and patted me on the neck.

"Eat well, White One," he said, "Tomorrow we will ride. We will set free, finally, the soul of Yellow Tail."

I stood quietly listening to the night, long after Talking Bear's footsteps had faded in the distance. Indiscernible voices, and muffled laughter echoed occasionally from the village. At times, a swirl of sparks floated suddenly into the night above the tepees. Another log had been thrown onto a fire of celebration there. The moon climbed silently from the mountains across the river and shone on its churning surface. I thought about the buckskin bundle that Talking Bear had carried bound tightly to his chest for more than a year. As was the custom, Talking Bear had watched as his warriors killed and butchered the bison that saved his people from starvation. He had not participated in their killing. But now, with the Crow's killing of Broken Knife, he could no longer watch. Now, he knew, he must touch blood.

After setting Yellow Tail's spirit free, he would lead his warriors against their old enemy. I knew that in a way, the release of Yellow Tail's soul would set free also, the soul of Talking Bear. With my hunger appeased finally, I lowered myself to the grass.

Chapter Ten

The terrible sound of a truck drew me from my slumber. Wresting myself from the shelter of my dream world, I watched nervously as a truck and trailer pulled into the driveway beside the barn.

In a short while, my owner led the truck driver into the corral. The driver's eyes immediately grew wide with amazement when he saw me. He walked quickly forward and stood for a long while before my stall as he carefully studied me.

"Do you know what you have here?" he asked my owner excitedly. "Half the cowboys in the west chased this horse all over the state of Nevada," he said excitedly. "This is the stallion known as Son of Banshee."

"It doesn't matter now," said the man flatly. "This horse must die. Load the horse in your trailer, and take him back to Carson City with you. I have sold him to your company for processing. He will be dog food by the end of the week."

He turned then, and left the corral.

Men soon appeared, and with horses, dragged me from my stall. Fighting for my life, I bucked and squealed, but I was helpless against their choking ropes as they drug me from the corral and into the waiting trailer. Appearing once more outside my trailer, my owner gave the driver a large, yellow envelope.

"Here is the bill of sale for the horse and the papers you will need to transport him. He is yours now," said my owner. "Make the trip a quick one," he added, as he pushed a wad of green paper into the driver's hand.

The two shook hands, and the driver turned and entered his truck. The engine rumbled to life, and we began to move forward. I watched between the slats of the trailer as the white buildings fell behind me in the distance.

Soon, I was again on the black trail of the two-legged ones. As before, cars, and trucks rushed by my enclosure in all directions. In a short while, my trailer slowed, and we turned from the trail. My trailer ground to a halt, and I heard the squeak of the truck's door in front of me. I heard the sound of approaching footsteps, and the driver appeared outside of my trailer. Again, the two-legged one studied me quietly.

"So," he said finally, "You are the old desert ghost that made a fool of half the cowboys in this land. I wish I could see the things you've seen and done in your life. I have heard the stories about you, White One, and now I see that you are as magnificent as they all said."

"Your owner sold you to the cannery in Carson City. He even paid me extra to get you there quick," he said. "You killed his wife, and he wants you to die. Dog food," the driver whispered, "He wants you to be dog food. Well, White One, I'm going to deliver you all right, but it won't be to no cannery in Carson City. I reckon I'll make a few bucks out of this deal for myself," he said, as he turned and walked back to his truck.

Ahead of me, I heard the truck's engine roar, and we lurched forward.

As the day passed, my trailer turned onto many different trails. Each trail it seemed, was a bit narrower and rougher than the one before it.

At one place, the driver pulled from the trail and entered a barn that was open on both ends. Two men in uniforms walk around my trailer peering carefully in at me. They looked at the brand on my foot, then, carefully studied the papers that the driver had presented to them. Nodding their approval, they scratched their design at the bottom of the papers, and handed them back to the driver. The driver, visibly relieved, entered his truck, and we started forward.

As the sun grew low in sky, we turned from the black trail and bounced along on a narrow, dusty one. The sun was dropping below the mountains when we pulled into a small ranch. Anxiously, I studied the surroundings. On one side of my trailer stood several buildings of varying size. On the other, stood a huge barn surrounded by a large array of corrals. In the corrals stood horses of all sizes and colors. Some stood silently watching my arrival. Others, with ears forward and nostrils flared, whinnied and nickered in my direction.

I heard the door of the truck open, and watched as the driver walked quickly into one of the buildings. He returned with several men who quickly saddled horses, and drew me from the rear of the trailer with lariats. I fought them as they dragged me into one of the corrals. The other horses eyed me nervously from their enclosures as I snorted and stomped angrily at the edge of mine. The cowboys and driver stood outside my corral watching me.

"With his size and build, he looks like he'll make a right fine saddle bronc," said one of the men to the driver.

"Wow," exclaimed another, Look at them muscles in his shoulders and hips!"

"Glad you decided to bring him here," said the other, as he drew a role of green paper from his pocket and handed to the driver.

The men led an old white horse from a corral on the far side of the barn, and loaded it into the trailer where I had been.

"The slaughterhouse will never know the difference," said the driver as he shook hands with the cowboys.

Darkness was overtaking the land as the driver and old white horse rumbled away from the ranch.

I stood nervously awake through the night, listening to the sounds of this strange new place. Any horse that came near me in the darkness, I sent crashing away beneath a flurry of striking front feet, and gashing teeth. It became quickly known by all those around me that any horse foolish enough to approach would be met with the wrath of my terrible fury. Occasionally, from somewhere in the darkness would come a sudden outburst of squealing horses and thundering hooves, as others fought somewhere near me in the night.

The air was filled with dust, churned by the myriad feet of the horses around me. But in the darkness of night also drifted the pungent smell of creosote and the sweet smell of cactus. I knew that I was once again in my desert land.

Early the next day, four mounted riders appeared at the far side of my corral. They opened the gate and quickly drove me into the corral's corner. Lassos twirling above their heads, they soon had me roped. The cowboys dragged me from my corral into yet another, in the center of which was a small metal stall. Screaming and kicking I fought them, but with others poking and prodding me with stinging sticks, the cowboys soon had me inside the enclosure.

The sides of the stall were drawn in until I was held fast. I squealed and bit at the men as they strapped a halter over my head and attached it to the sides of the stall. I watched with fright as the men held a strange rod in the flames of a roaring fire. When its end was glowing red, one of the cowboys pulled the rod from the fire and approached me. Helplessly, I fought the confining walls of the metal chute as the two-legged one jammed the rod against my hip. Searing pain shot through my rump as smoke and the smell of burning flesh filled the air around me.

"There," said one, "He's got our brand."

"Yeah," said the other, "And he's got a new name too. The boss says his new name is *Ghost*. As far as everyone knows, the stallion known as Son of Banshee died in the slaughterhouse in Carson City. The boss says the brand inspector owes him a favor or two, and he'll have the bill of sale on Ghost made up in a day or so. We'll have all the papers we need to pass brand inspection in any state we enter. We will be able to take him to anywhere we want."

Replacing their ropes around my neck, the cowboys drew the walls of the chute a short way from my sides. Able to move at last, I bucked and kicked, fighting desperately for freedom, but the choking lariats and the chains on my halter held me fast.

To my dismay, a cowboy wearing leather chaps, and a red bandanna around his neck, approached me from across the corral. In his hands, he carried a saddle. I stood helplessly gasping for air, as the two-legged one climbed the side of my stall. With the help of another, the cowboy reached forward and snapped a bucking rope to the halter on my head. I lunged and kicked when I felt the sudden weight of the saddle slam onto my back, and I screamed with rage as I felt the cinch tightened around my chest.

Never before had I been so constrained, and I fought with all my heart to free myself.

Climbing the outside of the chute, the cowboy took the rope attached to my halter in one hand, and slid quickly into the saddle on my back. The sudden weight of the two-legged one filled me with an anger I had never before known. The cowboys quickly removed the chains that held me fast to the sides of the stall, and removing their lariats, threw open the stall's door.

I exploded from the chute with all my might. Launching myself into the air, I twisted and turned. Landing with a jolt on all four feet, I spun and lunged powerfully into the air in the opposite direction. I shook my head from side to side, and twisted my body in midair until my belly nearly pointed to the sky. The rider stayed on my back for only three bounds. As I twisted again in the air, the rider flipped from the saddle and landed awkwardly in the dirt beneath me. The two-legged one did not move. The mounted riders quickly surrounded me and forced me into a stall at the corral's far side. I stood angrily bucking and fighting against the saddle as others entered the corral and carried the injured cowboy to a waiting truck. In a cloud of dust, it rumbled from view on the dirt trail leaving the ranch.

Soon, the mounted riders approached me once more. Throwing their ropes around my neck, they held me fast as two men stripped the saddle from my back. They replaced the hobbles on my front and rear legs and placed me alone in a corral.

A man with a fat belly, and a dark, smoking stick in his mouth, turned to another, as they studied me from the side of the corral.

"Looks like we got a winner here, Jeb," he said, "This stallion is going to make us some money."

"Yes," agreed Jeb, "You made a shrewd purchase when you got this one."

The next day, the two-legged ones again roped me, and drew me into the small metal stall. They removed my hobbles and attached my halter securely to the sides of the stall. Instantly, the anger boiled within me, as two cowboys placed a saddle on my back, and clipped a bucking rope to my halter. They then strapped what they called a bucking rig around my belly, just in front of my rear legs. The humiliation I felt at the weight of the saddle and the pinch of this strange strap around my belly grew an anger in me that nearly made me blind.

A cowboy slowly climbed the outside of my stall. His face was ashen in color and drawn in fear as he drew the bucking rope into his hand and slid carefully into my saddle. The chains on my halter were removed, and at his signal, the gate in front of me was swung suddenly open. I lunged from the stall in a burst of anger. The rider stayed on my back for only two bounds before flipping end over end through the air. Again, the mounted riders guided me into a stall at the corral's far side, while others helped the shaken rider from the arena.

The fat man clung to the outside of the corral watching excitedly as the cowboys stripped the saddle from my back. "Yep," said my apparent owner, the cigar still in his mouth, "I got a winner here."

Word of the white stallion, known as Ghost, spread quickly through the ranches of the desert land. The two-legged ones who now owned me, had unwittingly given me the name long ago used to describe my father, Banshee.

More cowboys came to the ranch each day, and stood in wonder on the far side of my corral as they quietly studied me.   Screaming with rage, shaking my head angrily, I would explode suddenly toward them, sending them jumping fearfully away from me. My handling by the two-

216

legged ones known as man, fueled a rage within me that grew more intense with each day.

The days grew steadily hotter as summer drew upon the land. Day after day, I stood beneath a cloudless sky, held captive in my small corral. Dust from the movement of the horses around me, billowed through the corral on a ceaseless wind. The only relief from the blistering heat came in the darkness of night. As had been the case for what seemed countless days, I stood quietly alone in my corral as darkness fell. I watched as the moon climbed above the mountains to the east, and savored a soft breeze that washed gently over me.

My unrest was finally quieted by my growing weariness. Fatigue drew my head slowly downward, and I was soon in a dream world filled with the earthy smell of green grass and cottonwood trees.

The moon shone brightly still when I heard footsteps approaching. I rose from the grass with my ears erect and nostrils flared. The familiar scent of Talking Bear came to my nose. Walking to my side, he reached beneath my neck and drew me to him as he gently rubbed its far side.

"This day that I have both prayed for and dreaded has come finally, Wakia," he said, as he placed the leather bridle over my head. "Carry me to the mountains now, White One. I must release the soul of Yellow Tail."

Grabbing my mane, Talking Bear swung onto my back, and clutching his leather bundle to his chest, guided me across the river. The moon was nearing the horizon as we reached the river's far side. Behind us, the tepees of the village shone in the soft blue light of the moon. The encampment stood in stark contrast to the dark mountains that towered behind them at the valley's far side.

The sky showed only the first hint of gray when Talking Bear guided me upward on a dim trail at the valley's west side. The scent of juniper and pine filled the air as we climbed steadily through the ever-thickening forest. Deer and elk crashed away into the timber as we entered grassy meadows lined with aspen.

The sun was dropping toward the horizon when at last we walked through a narrow pass at the mountain's top. In growing darkness, Talking Bear guided me downward toward the Valley of Shiny Stones, on its far side. Working carefully between rocky outcroppings, we moved ever downward through the trees toward the valley's floor. The moon was climbing steadily above the mountain behind us when we started across the open valley. At each hill or rise,

Talking Bear dismounted and crept slowly forward. Peering over the top, Talking Bear carefully scanned the moonlit valley ahead. Upon seeing no danger, the chief mounted me once more, and guided me onward.

"We must be very careful, White One, he whispered, breaking the silence. "In the warm seasons, the Crow come here often to hunt bison. To elude them, we must cross this valley in the cover of darkness."

The acrid smell of smoldering campfires touched my nose as we approached one ridge. Talking Bear, smelling it also, dismounted and crept carefully forward. On the far side of the rise stood a group of tepees. The design of the dwellings, and the symbols painted on their walls told Talking Bear that it was a Crow hunting party that camped along a small river below us. The many horses staked around the tepees told of their large numbers.

Talking Bear led me away from the ridge, then swung again onto my back. Angling away from the enemy camp, we continued across the valley. We were far above the place where the Crow hunters had camped when at last we reached the valley's far side. The first streaks of light began to show in the sky when we entered a smaller canyon at its side. The canyon climbed crookedly away, between rolling hills lined with jagged rock. A creek hidden by gigantic sagebrush coursed downward in the small canyon. The smell of wet earth, and the tangy smell of willow floated in the air as Talking Bear started me along a faint trail in the canyon's bottom. The sagebrush became ever thicker as we moved upward. The pungent smell of the sage was nearly overwhelming as the twisted giants clawed at my sides, covering me with their silver-green leaves and pollen as we passed.

The sun was dropping beneath the horizon when we stood before the small mountain whose rocky top formed the head and face of Yellow Tail. Talking Bear slid from my back and stood beside me in silence. His eyes were filled with wonder. Though we had been here before, it was as if he were seeing for the first time the likeness of his son in the cliffs above us. Talking Bear stood quietly clutching the buckskin bundle to his heart as the sun dropped from view.

As if waking from a dream, the chief took a deep breath finally and led me from the trail. We crossed the creek and continued through the giant sage brush as we had done long ago. When we had circled to the back of the mountain, Talking Bear threw my reins over my neck. Rather than mounting me, he began climbing the mountain on foot. In failing light, I followed quietly behind.

Darkness had settled, when the chief sat quietly beside a small fire at the top of the mountain, among the rocks that were Yellow Tail. At times, the dancing flames shone upon a face filled with happiness. But, at other times, his face was etched with grief. Talking Bear fed the fire through the night. He sat quietly bathed in the dancing yellow light, reliving the journey he had known with Yellow Tail

When the new day began at last to break, Talking Bear stood and turned to face that place in the sky where the sun would soon rise. With both arms extended to the heavens, Talking Bear began to chant quietly. After the sun had fully risen, Talking Bear begin gathering large rocks and stacked them at the cliff's edge.

The day was half gone when the chief stood finally before a spire of rocks whose base was as wide as his outstretched arms and was as tall as he.

"This monument, Yellow Tail," said Talking Bear, "Reaches upward toward the Great Mystery. It will hold the prayer ties I will soon offer Him." Opening his pack, he removed four rabbit pelts. From a small pouch, he drew a handful of tobacco, then held it to his heart and prayed softly. When his prayer was done, he placed the tobacco in the center of the first pelt. He twisted the hide around the tobacco and secured it in place with a narrow leather thong, forming a ball with a flowing skirt of rabbit hide beneath it. He then secured the prayer flag to his spire of rocks. This, he repeated with the three remaining pelts. In this way, Talking Bear honored each of the four sacred directions. Drawing a great breath, and exhaling with an air of determination, Talking Bear removed the buckskin bundle from his chest and placed it at the foot of the spire. Standing before his monument, he drew his eagle bone whistle from his pack, and placed it in his mouth. Slowly, Talking Bear began to dance in place. With each step, he blew shrill notes from his whistle.

For the remainder of the day, the chief danced before his rock spire and prayer flags at the edge of the cliff. From above us, came the piercing cry of an eagle as the sun drew low in the sky. Answering the call of Talking Bear's whistle, the great, white-headed bird circled in the sky above us.

"Yellow Tail has joined us, Wakia," he said, as the chief watched the huge bird above us. When the sun sat on the horizon, the eagle turned suddenly, and flew to the south.

"Yes, Yellow Tail, it is time," said Talking Bear as he watched the great bird disappear. "You have flown in the direction of the Spirit Land."

Kneeling slowly at the base of the tiny monument, Talking Bear loosened the straps binding his sacred bundle. With shaking hands, he drew Yellow Tail's long locks of hair from their buckskin wrapping. Standing at the edge of the cliff, he raised his treasure skyward. Slowly, he opened his hand.

His voice choking with emotion, he cried as loudly as he could, "Be free my son, be free!"

A gentle gust of wind drew the hair from Talking Bear's hand. With tears streaming down his cheeks, he watched as the spirit of Yellow Tail danced upward and disappeared.

Slowly, Talking Bear sank to his knees before the small spire of rock. Raising his eyes to the heavens he said, "Oh, Great Mystery, I am a spiritual man. I know that the spirit of my son, Yellow Tail, stands beside me even now. But for all the seasons of this past year, I have felt his mortal weight bound to my chest. Now that I have freed his remains, I feel more alone than ever before."

"What have I done, Yellow Tail, oh, what have I done?" He pleaded. Talking Bear lowered his head, and wept.

A cloud rapidly approached as the sun dipped from view. Overhead now, glowing in the fading light, was the silhouette of a great silver bear. His head lowered in grief, Talking Bear did not see it.

When the skies began to brighten the next morning, Talking Bear rose from his bed roll at the foot of the small rock spire. He stood quietly facing the prayer flags he had tied at its top. Quietly he said, "Together, Yellow Tail, we stood atop this mountain many times. When the time came to descend, I always turned to you and said, lead the way, big man. With a smile in your eyes, and an air of importance about you, you would turn, and lead me downward. But now, big man," he said with a troubled voice, "Who will show me the way?"

Talking Bear turned sadly from the monument and walked to my side. He gathered my reins, and led me downward. We had only walked a short distance when Talking Bear stopped suddenly, and knelt in the trail before us. In the soft earth, were the tracks of a huge grizzly. The great silver bear had walked downward on the trail in the darkness of last night. Nowhere did we see evidence of its climb. Talking Bear ran his fingers gently over the huge track. Standing, he looked back toward the rocky spire at the mountain's top. The prayer flags moved gently in the wind.

"You have come one last time, Yellow Tail," he muttered, "To show me the way."

Talking Bear turned then, and we followed the great bear's tracks downward. We wound our way through the giant sage at the mountain's base, and having crossed the creek, stopped on the trail below its rocky summit. The spire of rocks he had stacked in the cliffs, was visible from where we stood.

"It seems that the journey shared by Yellow Tail and I was short," he said, facing the tiny monument far above. "And already, it seems, the time since his parting has been long."

Talking Bear swung onto my back, and we started downward toward the Valley of Shiny Stones.

As we neared the valley, six Crow warriors suddenly appeared on the far side of a small rise. The warriors instantly recognized Talking Bear, the great chief of the Sioux. Studying the men before him, Talking Bear's eyes came to rest on a warrior who sat astride a black horse with a large, white star emblazoned on its chest. It was the horse of Broken Knife's.

"Thank you, Father, for showing me the way," he muttered. Then, looking skyward, he screamed, "Hoka hey! It is a good day to die!"

His heels digging into my sides, we charged toward the Crow warriors. The riders, surprised by our sudden charge, tried to spin away from Talking Bear as we crashed forward. One horse and rider was driven to the ground as we stormed screaming into their midst. Pressure from Talking Bear's knees turned me whirling toward the warrior astride the horse called Star. Talking Bear ducked the warrior's war club as we charged past. Whirling, we thundered toward the warrior once more.

Talking Bear deflected the warrior's lance with his own, as the two men met, its tip slicing the flesh of the chief's cheek. The lance in the outstretched arm of Talking Bear, though, did not miss. Its obsidian tip pierced the warrior's chest just below his neck, and with a guttural groan, the rider tumbled backward from Star. Once more I whirled, and as we thundered past, Talking Bear grabbed the reins of the riderless horse.

Shrieking battle cries filled the air behind us as we stormed from the mouth of the canyon into the Valley of Shiny Stones. Below us, was a series of short cliffs. Above us at the valley's edge, rolling hills climbed upward to meet the towering mountains on its west side. The horses of the Crow were not nearly as strong and fast as was I, but with the frightened horse dragging at my heels, the screaming warriors drew slowly closer. Arrows whizzed through the air around us. More than once, searing pain exploded in my flank at the sound of my cutting flesh. Above me, the gasping moan of Talking Bear told me a Crow's arrow had found its mark.

As we stormed across the top of yet another sage covered ridge, suddenly below us in a gentle canyon was a large herd of bison. Without hesitation, we crashed into the feeding behemoths. Lunging with all my might against the bodies of the feeding bison, Talking Bear guided me feverishly toward the herd's far side. The Crow warriors, sensing imminent victory, entered the herd behind us without hesitation. Their hideous war cries, and misguided arrows frightened the feeding bison, and in a giant sea of brown, the great animals sprang forward. The thunder from countless hooves hid the sounds of the Crow's deadly pursuit. No longer did their arrows sizzle through the air around us.

Hidden in boiling clouds of dust, we were drawn downward in the canyon, trapped in the herd of rampaging animals. Barely visible through the dust, the flat, even horizon ahead, told of the cliff that lay at the canyon's end.

With all my strength, I crashed against the lunging bodies at my side, working feverishly toward the edge of the stampeding herd. We sprang from the herd as the first of the bison lunged helplessly over the cliff, pushed by panic stricken animals behind them. We climbed the rise at the far side of the canyon and turned to watch. Horrific grunts filled the air as the lunging bodies tumbled from view. When at last the carnage ended, the Crow warriors that had so doggedly pursued us were gone.

Talking Bear slid from my back and tied Star to a juniper at our side. He then walked forward and stood by my head. A deep wound ran jaggedly across his cheek, evidence, I knew, of the near fatal blow from the lance of the Crow warrior. An arrow protruded from his arm. Stroking my neck, he said, "Again, White One, you have saved my life. Yellow Tail's words were true. Upon your back, Wakia, I will always return from battle."

Talking Bear walked to my rear where two arrows hung loosely from my hide. Carefully, he removed each.

Then, gripping the arrow that protruded from his arm, he took a mighty breath and pulled. With disgust, he threw the dislodged shaft to the ground.

Darkness was gathering as we climbed upward through the forest at the valleys far side, and the sun had long been overhead when, at last, we started downward. The River of Spirits beckoned enticingly from far below us in the valley's floor. Grassy hills at the valley's lower end, I knew, hid the encampment of our people.

Billows of smoke rose from a small hill at the far side of the valley as we walked steadily onward. In reply, similar signals rose from beyond a gentle ridge ahead of us, where I knew our village lay.

We were met by a jubilant swarm of people as we entered the encampment. The people grew immediately quiet, though, as Talking Bear continued past them. They saw his wounds, and his blood-soaked shirt. The horse he led, they quickly realized, was the one known as Star. The death of Broken Knife had been avenged.

Broken Knife's father waited quietly before the opening of his tepee. Talking Bear swung from my back and led the horse to where the old man stood.

"This was taken from your son, Broken Knife," said

229

the chief. Handing him the reins, he said, "It is yours once more."

The word of Talking Bear's arrival and his obvious punishment of the Crow, had spread quickly through our encampment. All the people of the village now stood quietly waiting before their chief.

Turning to them, Talking Bear said, "I have traveled to a sacred mountain two day's ride from our village. There, I released the soul of my son, Yellow Tail. I have met our enemies in battle many times. Never have I cried out in pain at the strike of their war clubs, or the slash of their knives. But, the pain that I felt at releasing his mortal remains caused me to weep as if I were a child.

The people parted as Talking Bear led me through their midst. Each gave words of thanks as we passed. When we arrived at Talking Bear's tepee, he threw open the flap, and led me inside. Long after he had doctored the wounds we had suffered at the hands of the Crow, the chief sat quietly staring into a small fire before him. The frightful cries of Crow warriors echoed through my mind as I stood quietly beside him in the darkness.

Chapter Eleven

The daunting image of stampeding bison and screaming warriors was suddenly gone when I was awakened by the voices of approaching men. Struggling from my dream world, I watched nervously as two men approached my corral.

Leaning on the fence, they studied me carefully. Snorting with contempt, I moved to the corral's far side.

"Looks like his new brand has healed nicely," said my owner carefully studying the new design on my hip. "The brand they had on his hoof is completely grown out and gone now. No one will question the origin of Ghost."

"Yeah," said the other man, "As far as anyone knows, the white stallion known as Son of Banshee met his fate at the slaughterhouse in Carson City."

"Yep, exactly," said my owner. "Next week," he continued, "We'll take Ghost to the show in Las Vegas. It's the biggest bucking horse sale in the west. Some of the best rodeo cowboys around, will be on hand to ride them. All the stock suppliers for the big rodeos will be there. If this horse bucks in Vegas like he has for us here, one of them buyers will snap him up, and he'll be bucking on the rodeo circuit within a month. Maybe I'll make a few bucks on this old mustang."

The two men studied me admiringly for a while, then turned and walked away.

My days became a torment of repetition, each day was as monotonous as the one preceding it. My spirit grew ever darker as the days went by. The horses around me had soon learned I was better left alone. With my striking front feet, I had pummeled several to the ground, injuring them severely. The two-legged ones, realizing finally, the terrible anger that simmered within me, placed me in a corral apart from the other horses.

One day as the sun rose above the horizon, two riders approached my corral. The men quickly roped me, and fighting and kicking, I was forced into the back of a trailer. They fastened me securely to its front, then, closed the door behind me.

As the two cowboys walked past my trailer toward the truck, one peered into my enclosure and said, "You ready fer yer first rodeo, Ghost?"

"See ya in Las Vegas, White One," said the other, as he sauntered past. I heard the doors of the truck slam as the cowboys entered, and soon, I was racing across the desert on the two-legged one's black trail.

The sun was drawing low in the sky when at last we slowed, and turned from the trail. At a much slower pace, we proceeded forward on a smaller trail where tall buildings stood at all sides. I stared in wonder as we moved steadily through this place of man.

Soon, we turned from the trail and stopped beside a sprawling structure. The building was round in shape, and had no roof. Beyond us, were other trucks and trailers like ours, parked side-by-side in long, even rows. At the edge of the structure stretched a rambling set of corrals where countless horses stood watching our approach. I heard the doors of the truck in front of me squeak as they opened, and heard the footsteps of the cowboys as they approached my trailer.

"Well, big guy," said one, as he peered in at me, "This here's the rodeo arena. I reckon we're gonna find out what you're made of, in the next couple days. If you're half the saddle bronc the boss thinks you are, you'll be going home with a new owner."

I heard the plodding footsteps of horses as riders approached the two men standing outside of my enclosure.

233

Sunlight suddenly flooded my trailer as the men swung the door open behind me. They unfastened my halter from the front of the trailer, and lariats were placed around my neck. The riders pulled me from the trailer, and holding me securely, led me into a corral. I glared angrily at the cowboys as they closed the gate of my enclosure and disappeared.

The horses in the corrals around me, paced, and milled nervously as the sun dropped beneath the horizon. The dust that hovered above the corrals, shone with a reddish glow in the retreating sun.

I stood nervously watching as darkness settled over the land. The anxious cries of horses filled the night as like me, they wondered what tomorrow would bring.

I quietly watched the moon as it rose slowly above the horizon. It cast an eerie purple light on the huge structure that the cowboys had called a rodeo arena. Small groups of cowboys passed by my corral as the night drew on. One group stopped before me and talked excitedly while studying me carefully.

"There's that big white stallion from up on the Bar-N-Ranch," said one burly cowboy. "It sure don't look it, but they say he's a mustang. They claim he's a real man hater."

"Yeah, nearly killed the first cowboy that tried to ride 'im," said another. "The boys that's seen 'im buck, say this horse won't never be rode. I reckon if a man's lucky enough to draw this horse on the last day, he'd be right likely to take home the money if he can ride 'im to the buzzer," he said.

The men around him grunted in agreement as they quietly watched me.

I stood anxiously as daylight came the next morning. When the sun was nearly overhead, the sound of cars and trucks rumbled at all sides of the arena. Soon, long lines of them were parked side-by-side in the open area near the structure, and a steady stream of men and women walked toward the stadium. The clamor of their collective voices from within the structure grew steadily louder as more and more people entered. Already, I had seen many times more two-legged ones than I knew existed in all of the land.

When the sun was high overhead, mounted riders entered the corrals around me and began to drive the excited horses through gates at their far sides. Whooping and hollering, they drove fully one hundred horses thundering into the arena. Amid the howls and cheers of the chaotic crowd above them in the stands, they drove the anxious herd across the floor of the arena, and placed them

235

in holding pens at its far edge. Some horses, like me though, were pulled from the corrals by two or more mounted riders. Amid a deafening roar from the stands, we were dragged, kicking and bucking, across the arena and placed in the holding pens with the others.

Immediately in front of the holding pens was a long row of short, narrow, chutes that stood beneath the stands at the arena's edge.

"Load the bucking chutes," yelled one cowboy, as a group of men entered the rear of the holding pens. Poking and jabbing with their stinging prods, the cowboys moved the unwilling horses forward until all the bucking chutes at the arena's edge were full. There, halters were placed over the heads of the anxious horses, and they were quickly saddled. From small boxes mounted above all sides of the stadium, suddenly came a booming voice. The two-legged one who talked, could not be seen, only his resounding voice could be heard from the boxes.

The roar of the crowd quieted as the booming voice spoke suddenly again. At the unseen one's command, the people in the stands rose to their feet and removed their hats. They turned then and faced a flag at the arena's far side as they listened quietly to music. The calm was short-lived though, and a deafening roar shook the arena when the music abruptly ended. Terrified, I watched the bizarre antics of the howling two-legged ones in the stands above me.

The voice of the hidden two-legged one thundered once more from the talking boxes above us. My attention was drawn suddenly to the movement of cowboys near the bucking chutes ahead of me. I watched nervously as one slowly climbed the outside of a stall in which stood a fidgeting, anxious horse. When at the chute's top, the cowboy reached down and drew the horse's halter rope into one of his buckskin covered hands. Steadying himself with the other, he slid into the saddle on the horses back. With a nod of his head, the door of the chute burst suddenly open.

With a mighty grunt of exertion, the horse exploded from the chute. Amid booming cheers and applause from above them in the stands, the horse and rider bound twisting, and bucking across the arena. The rider fanned frantically in the air above his head with one hand, while clinging desperately to the horse's halter rope with the other. Pitted in a terrible battle, the stallion fought to throw the cowboy from his back, while the rider raked his spurs at the horse's shoulders at each mighty lunge. A loud buzzer sounded suddenly from somewhere in the arena, and horsemen galloped to each side of the tiring horse and swept the cowboy from its back.

Again and again, the doors of the bucking chutes slammed open, and horses and riders crashed through the arena in a cloud of dust. Often, the riders were thrown from the backs of the raging horses to land in the dirt at their feet. Other cowboys though, were pulled from the backs of the brawling horses by the mounted riders after the buzzer had sounded. One by one, the horses around me were driven into the bucking chutes and saddled, then crashed through the arena in a battle with the two-legged ones.

I stood alone in the holding pens as the sun dropped low in the sky. I glared angrily at mounted riders as they entered my corral. Working carefully together, the cowboys forced me toward the open door of a bucking chute. Once inside, the door behind me slammed shut, and my halter was quickly fastened to the sides of the stall.

I heard the nervous talk of two-legged ones, as they climbed the side of my chute. I kicked and fought against the chains that held me as a saddle was dropped onto my back and its cinch was quickly tightened around my chest. I snorted with anger as a man reached through the sides of my stall and placed a bucking strap around my stomach.

Rage pounded through my body as I felt a rider settle into the saddle on my back. I quivered with anticipation as the cowboy drew my lead rope into his hand.

I screamed and kicked at the sides of the chute as the chains that bound me were removed. Blinded by rage, I sprang from the stall when the door before me swung suddenly open. The roar of the crowd was deafening as I lurched and twisted across the arena before them. Above their thunderous cries, I heard the labored grunts of the cowboy that rode me, and the thundering fall of my hooves as they struck the ground. Twisting and shaking, I sprang again and again into the air. On one great hop, I spun and twisted my belly skyward. With a groan, the cowboy flew from my back and landed on the earth beneath me. I felt the crunch of his breaking bones as my feet struck him, and I saw the dull look in his eyes as I spun away. I charged onward across the arena, bucking and spinning, trying to loosen the saddle and the terrible bucking rig that still bound me.

Riders herded me into the corner of the arena where an open gate led me back into the holding pens. From my corral, I glared angrily across the arena as men rushed forward toward the motionless body of the one who had attempted to ride me. The men placed the cowboy on a stretcher, and carried him from the arena. They placed him into a truck with a flashing light at its top, and with a loud whining sound, the truck roared away.

I stood anxiously awake the next morning as the skies began to lighten. In holding pens around me, other horses milled aimlessly back and forth in the near light. Their nervous calls to others told of the uneasiness that they too felt.

The rumble from the machines of man, began as the sun rose above the mountains. Beyond the bucking chutes, the two-legged ones drove slowly along on tractors. They carefully smoothed the earth that had been torn and gouged the previous day by the pounding hooves of bucking horses. Many other men crept through the stands, cleaning and preparing for the crowds of people that would soon appear.

When the sun had drawn high overhead, trucks and cars again filled the area beyond our holding pens. Hordes of men and women climbed from them, laughing and calling excitedly to one another as they walked toward the arena. As time drew slowly on, their numbers increased. Now, the two-legged ones walked from all directions it seemed. Long lines formed at the arena's entrance and the constant chatter of people grew louder as they waited impatiently to enter. Soon, the stands could hold no more.

Mounted riders entered the holding pens behind the horses and began herding them toward the bucking chutes at the arena's edge. I watched nervously alone from a pen at its side as the horses were moved forward and placed in the bucking chutes. They bucked and snorted, kicking at the sides of the metal chutes as the doors were closed behind them. The clamor of voices from the stands grew louder as cowboys fought to saddle the unruly horses. There were even more people screaming from the stands, I was sure, than there had been the day before.

As it had yesterday, the booming voice echoed suddenly from the talking boxes above the stands. The chaotic din immediately quieted as the two-legged ones rose to their feet and listened quietly to their music. The earsplitting roar that erupted when their music ended though, was nearly overwhelming. The thunderous voice echoed again from the talking boxes, and the rodeo began.

With a resounding bang, the first bucking chute flew open, and a large, black horse sprang into the arena. The roar from the crowd was deafening as horse and rider lurched through the stadium beneath them. Dirt and dust was kicked into the air by its pounding hooves as it bucked and twisted, fighting violently to throw the flailing rider from its back. In only moments, a loud buzzer sounded, and as they had yesterday, riders swept alongside the bucking horse and pulled the successful cowboy from its back.

Again and again horses sprang from the open gates of the bucking chutes, man and beast pitted against one another in a battle for survival.

The sun was dropping from the sky when the last of the horses in the holding pen were driven forward and loaded into the bucking chutes. I stood alone in my pen and watched in the fading light, as the last of the bucking horses exploded into the arena amid the thunderous applause of the two-legged ones.

The crowd fell silent when the booming voice again echoed throughout the arena. Lights above all sides of the stands came suddenly on, bathing the arena in light as bright as day. After my wild performance of yesterday, I had been selected by the two-legged ones to buck last.

I drew my ears flatly back and stomped my feet angrily against the earth as mounted cowboys entered my pen. Thunderous cheers erupted from the stands as the multitudes of men and women applauded the riders as they drove me from my pen into the open door of a bucking chute. The door slammed behind me, cowboys quickly strapped a saddle on my back, and fastened a bucking rig around my belly.

A hush fell over the crowd as a cowboy climbed the side of my chute. I smelled the scent of his fear as he settled into the saddle on my back. Nervously, he took my lead rope into his hand, and at his signal, the door to the chute flew open. Fire flashed through my head as the rage within me exploded. Rearing to my hind legs, I burst from the chute and crashed across the arena in a cloud of dust. I sprang into the air with my hind legs kicking so high behind me that my body was nearly vertical when my front legs hit the earth. I launched into the air and spun, landing on all four legs, only to explode again, in the opposite direction. The cowboy rode me for only three bounds. Flying awkwardly through the air, he flipped backwards over my rump and landed in a crumpled heap in the dirt behind me.

Riders quickly surrounded me on their horses and herded me toward an open gate at the arena's edge. Stomping and snorting, I watched sullenly, as cowboys stormed toward my would-be rider who lay unmoving in the dirt. In a short while, the cowboys helped the shaken rider to his feet, and steadied him as he stumbled from the arena.

Men soon entered my pen, and held me fast with lariats as others stripped the saddle and bucking rig from my back.

For a short while, the thundering voice blared throughout the arena. When the talking boxes were at last silent, the two-legged ones began to rise from their seats. I glared angrily from my pen as I watched the throngs of people climb from the stands, and walk slowly from the arena. Beyond my pen, the cars and trucks began to rumble to life. My anger began to subside as I watched a long line of taillights move slowly away, the headlights before them, shining dimly through clouds of dust. The rodeo was at last over.

Nearly all the two-legged ones were gone when the fat man that I had come to know as my owner, appeared at the side of my pen. He stood unmoving, with a cigar in his mouth, as he quietly studied me.

"Yer a helluva bucking horse," he said finally, taking the cigar from his mouth. But there's no place in rodeo for a one-horse owner like me. I sold you, Ghost," he said softly. "I wish I could keep you, and enter you in rodeos myself. It ain't possible though, it's a big business now. All the bucking horses at the big rodeos are supplied by a single owner.

The big boys got it all sewed up," he said sadly, as he turned to go.

As he walked away, he stopped and turned back to face me. "I ain't never heard of a mustang that could buck like you, White One," he said. He turned then and walked away.

Early the next day, horsemen entered my pen. With my ears laid-back in anger I glared hostilely at them from its corner. Throwing their lariats over my head, they drug me from the pen and into the rear of a waiting trailer. Soon, I thundered down the wide trail of the two-legged ones, pulled behind yet another truck of man.

I had come to believe finally, that the end that had been my father's, or even the terrible fate suffered by my mother, would be preferable to this life that had come to be mine.

The light was fading when we slowed and turned from the black trail onto a narrow dusty one. We moved slowly along for a bit, then ground finally to a halt.

On one side of my trailer stood a jumble of buildings of various sizes. On the other, was a huge barn surrounded by corrals. Horses of all colors and sizes milled nervously watching from the pens. The calls of horses filled the air, as they strained to see this new horse whose scent they now detected. A small group of cowboys gathered around my trailer, peering curiously at me through the openings in its sides. The door of the trailer was drawn open, and lariats were again placed around my neck. When the chains connected to my halter were removed, two mounted cowboys drew me backward from the trailer. Grunts, and mumbled sounds of approval came from the ragtag group of cowboys that surrounded me, when at last, I stood before them.

"Look at his lines!" exclaimed one.

"Yeah, and look at them muscles," said another.

"His color is amazing," said yet another, "And that black mask around his eyes and ears is incredible! This sure as heck don't look like no mustang," he said.

"Put him in a corral by himself," said the leader of the men. "This horse is a mean one. I think he would kill anything around him. I think he even hates himself. But you ought to see this horse buck!"

The two riders, holding me fast from opposite sides, worked me toward the open gate of a corral, and drew me inside. Tightening their ropes, they held me fast while two men put hobbles on my front and rear legs. The riders loosened their lariats, and flipped them over my head. Kicking and snorting, I glared at the cowboys as they left my corral.

As darkness fell, two men approached where I stood quietly in my enclosure. They walked back and forth along the corral, as they studied me.

"Look at his lines and the size of this horse," said my new owner. "He's big and strong! He'll sure make a good saddle bronc!"

"Yes," said the other man. "I have never seen a mustang with the musculature and the size of this horse. And I sure as heck never heard of a mustang that can buck the way this one does. If I hadn't seen it with my own eyes, I wouldn't believe it."

"I think this horse will make me a lot of money on the rodeo circuit," said my owner, "I think he might just be a winner."

"Yeah, but he needs to buck in at least eight shows in order to qualify for the national finals up in Cheyenne," said the other man. "We ain't got much time. That's a lot of rodeos with no rest in between. That's a lot to ask of a bucking horse."

"Yeah, but he's a mustang," said my owner, "They're tougher than nails. Besides, I ain't got much invested in him, I got nothing to lose. We got a big rodeo here, in Santa Fe next week," he continued. "We'll enter him with the rest of our bucking stock. We'll see what he's got when he bucks with the real cowboys. Tell the trainer to feed him plenty of alfalfa, and double him up on grain. It'll make him mean, and edgy," he said, as he turned to leave.

"Mean and edgy?" asked the other man "I reckon he's plenty rank enough now," he said, looking into my glaring eyes.

He turned then and followed his boss into the darkness.

I stood for a long while staring sullenly into the direction where the two men had gone. I had again been taken to a place not of my choosing, and yet another man claimed ownership of me. How could these two-legged ones not understand that I was every bit their equal. I could not be owned by them, or any of their kind. But yet, I knew deep inside that indeed, I was owned. I was owned by my unrelenting quest for freedom.

Filled with anger, I stood long into the night in the confinement of my corral. I watched quietly as the stars crept across the heavens, and the moon rose slowly in the sky. I thought about my herd of mares, and wondered if it was the young white stallion that now guarded them.

As the night drew on, slumber mercifully quieted my thoughts, and the images that seemed always present in my nighttime journeys, suddenly filled my dreams.

Our tribe moved often during the hot seasons of the growing grass and ripening berries. Our new camps though, were always in the Valley of Shining Mountains, where the grass was green and deep, and afforded good feed for our tribe's many horses. For safety, our encampment was always located on a rise near the river. From these elevated places we could see for great distances in all directions, and the nearly constant winds there, kept the biting insects at bay.

The season of the growing grass had long been over, and the time of the ripening berries was now halfway gone. Talking Bear sent word through the village, telling all, that the time had come for a great bison hunt. That night, a fire was built before the tepee of Talking Bear. The dancing flames of the counsel fire reflected from the eager faces of Talking Bear's leaders as they sat around the fire facing him. The bison hunt was always a time of great excitement for everyone in the village. Everyone, except the very young or very old, participated in some way. I stood quietly watching from the shadows where Talking Bear had tied me earlier.

The buzz of friendly chatter halted immediately when finally Talking Bear spoke. "It is time, he said, "That we fill our meat racks for the coming season of renewal. The hot sun that now graces our land will heat our drying racks, and quickly cure the meat. If our hunt is successful, we will have much wasna when it is again time to travel southward to the Valley of Red Rocks."

He instructed his leaders to have all hunters and gatherers begin immediate preparation for the upcoming hunt.

"Send four men to the hill," he said. "When they return with their grand vision of our hunt, we will depart. Go now, prepare the sweat lodges for the purification of those chosen to seek vision."

The men chosen would be gone for four days. As Yellow Tail had done so long ago, they would stand alone atop a remote mountain and prayerfully plead for guidance for our impending bison hunt. The vision quest was a very important ceremony in the lives of our people. The vision quest was always performed before any grand undertaking such as war, the migration of our tribe, and certainly the bison hunt. The men chosen to perform this rite were known to have strong ties to the sacred one known as the Great Mystery. The guidance that the hunters would receive in their visions would enable the tribe to find the bison and have a successful hunt.

Late on the fourth day, puffs of billowing smoke at the far side of the valley announced the return of the four warriors. A counsel fire was quickly built in front of Talking Bear's tepee. Soon, the four vision questers sat cross legged near the fire, facing Talking Bear and his leaders.

Each of the four men sent to the mountain stood one at a time and related to Talking Bear the vision they had received.

The first man told of a great herd of bison he had seen grazing along the bluffs in the upper valley far above our encampment. The second warrior, standing then, told Talking Bear that the bison he had seen in his vision, were too many to count. Like the first warrior, he had seen them in the upper valley. They were two days ride from our village, he told the chief.

The third man, standing now, told of the many bison he had seen fall to the arrows of our stealthy hunters.

Scores more, he told Talking Bear, were driven over a steep cliff where the women of our village began the rendering of the great beasts.

The fourth warrior, visibly troubled, stood slowly and faced Talking Bear. His look was grim, his face was etched with worry as he met the gaze of Talking Bear.

Like the others, the warrior said the Creator had shown him untold numbers of bison in the valley far above us. He had seen meat racks straining beneath the weight of curing bison meat. But, on the fourth day of his quest, as the sun dropped beneath the mountain, a far different vision had appeared suddenly before him. He had seen a great band of Crow warriors moving stealthily through the juniper toward our unsuspecting people. A great battle had ensued. His vision, though, had grown dark, and he hadn't seen the battle's outcome.

Talking Bear and his leaders sat quietly for a long while staring into the flames of the counsel fire before them. Each of the men that had been sent to seek a vision had seen huge herds of buffalo. Each, had seen a successful hunt. But Talking Bear was troubled by this last vision of sneaking warriors and conflict.

Looking up from the fire finally, Talking Bear said, "Tell the people of the visions seen by each of our men. Tell them to prepare for a successful hunt. But tell them also, we must be extra vigilant. The spirits have warned us of the presence of enemies."

The next morning, scores of hunters formed a huge circle around a fire burning in the center of our encampment. The women and children that would accompany the hunters on our great excursion surrounded them. At the head of the circle stood Talking Bear, his sacred pipe cradled in the crook of his arm. He held it carefully over his heart.

"Brothers and sisters, today we will depart and travel upward in the valley along the River of Spirits. The Great Mystery has shown our vision seekers scores of bison feeding there, on the bluffs above the river. We will fill my pipe now with prayers of well-being and success for this great hunt.

Talking Bear drew open a small leather pouch of tobacco, and drawing a pinch of the mixture between finger and thumb, held it skyward and prayed silently. When his prayer was done, he placed the pinch of tobacco in the bowl of his pipe and passed it to the man on his left. Each of the hunters in the circle drew a few grains of tobacco from the leather pouch, held it skyward, and prayed silently before placing the tobacco in the pipe and passing it onward. After holding his tobacco skyward in prayer, a warrior named Rides the Sky, looked at Talking Bear and grinned as he placed his prayer into the pipe. His teeth were broken and crooked. His name, and his crooked smile, I knew, had been earned from the times he'd flown through the air, thrown from the backs of horses he was breaking. He winked knowingly at the chief as he passed the pipe to the next man.

When the pipe returned to Talking Bear, he rolled a small ball of sage in his hand and placed it in the bowl of the pipe over the tobacco. With his thumbs, he then pressed a small ball of tallow over the sage, sealing the prayers in the bowl of his pipe. Placing his pipe carefully in his pack, he looked from person to person standing around him. In a loud voice, he said, "Our prayers have been made. When our hunt is done, we will smoke my pipe and send our prayers of thanks to the Creator."

Shouldering his pack, Talking Bear grabbed my reins and swung onto my back. "It is time now, brothers and sisters," he said, "That we hunt. May our steps be strong and firm as we go."

Horses snorted and grunted restlessly as the warriors mounted them. The clamor of countless hooves filled the air behind us as scores of warriors followed Talking Bear from the village. The garble of happy chatter and the nervous barking of dogs came from the huge throng of women and children that followed.

The very young and those too old to endure the rigors of the hunt would stay behind. Twelve of our best warriors would stay to guard them and the encampment. All others would follow Talking Bear and his warriors on the hunt. For when the hunt was over, the help of all able bodies in the tribe would be needed to render the animals and dry the meat for transport back to our village.

For two days, our tribe traveled upward along the River of Spirits. As the sun was setting at the end of the second day, scouts dispatched earlier by Talking Bear, briskly approached our marching tribe. Excitedly, they reported to Talking Bear that at a half days ride ahead, at the far side of steep breaks, was an enormous herd of bison.

The day had only begun to lighten when Talking Bear and his legion of hunters watched quietly from the rocks at the top of a small hill. Carefully, they studied the sea of brown bodies feeding at the edge of the valley beneath them. Beyond the grazing animals, near the edge of the river, was a steep drop. A gentle breeze blew at our backs. It was decided that a line of fire would be set in the dry grass at the valley's edge. If fortune was with the hunters, the bison would stampede toward the cliffs. Many of the great animals would tumble to their death. Talking Bear summoned the *fire hunters*.

The fire hunters were the most experienced hunters in our tribe. Their daunting task was to conceal themselves beneath the hides of bison, then creep stealthily forward in a broad line toward the unsuspecting herd. When as close as possible to the bison, they would ignite a line of grass fires with flint and rock. When the panicked animals began to run, the fire hunters would spring from beneath their hides, and with their bows and arrows, kill as many of the mighty animals as they could. There buckskin leggings and moccasins, were always covered with black ash upon their return.

The sun moved steadily higher in the sky as Talking Bear led the hunters carefully downward toward the valley floor. When in the sagebrush at the valley's edge, the chief dispatched the fire hunters. Concealed beneath their hides of bison, the brave men crawled slowly forward on hands and knees. When they drew very near the edge of the herd, their hide draped bodies disappeared. Lying in the tall grass, they struck their flints, then huddled over the tiny flames protecting them from the wind as they grew. The fire hunters rose slowly and crossed their newly set fire-line hidden beneath their bison hides and growing billows of smoke from the fire behind them. The bison's shaggy heads shot from the grass when at last, they sensed the approaching fire. Their eyes shone black and shiny in the morning sun as they stared nervously at the rapidly growing flames. Knowing the time had come, the fire hunters sprang from beneath their hides and charged toward the bison, shooting their arrows as they ran. When their arrows were gone, they wrapped themselves in their hides for protection against the advancing flames, and raced to safety at the fire's edge.

At the sudden movement of the herd, Talking Bear sprang onto my back yelling, "Hoka Hey! It is a good day to die, brothers, may your arrows fly true."

With a swarm of screaming warriors at our either side, Talking Bear drove me feverishly across the valley floor toward the fleeing bison.

Dust boiled from beneath the pounding hooves of the great animals, their surging bodies barely discernible through clouds of torn earth and pulverized sage. The musky, wild smell of bison filled the air. Above the deafening thunder of their hooves, were the grunts and groans of the stampeding giants. From within the terrible din of surging bodies, often came the death cry of calves who had lost their footing and fallen beneath the pounding hooves of the stampeding animals.

The lines of charging hunters quickly closed at both sides of the fleeing herd. The goal of each man was to draw near the side of a chosen animal, then, with his bow, shoot and obsidian-tipped arrow deep into the flesh behind its shoulder. Only the bravest of the hunters would draw so closely to a charging bull, that he would kill the great animal with only his lance. Many brave men had been killed having been unwittingly surrounded by the stampeding herd. The horse of the trapped warrior was nearly always knocked from its feet by the storming bison, the warrior then met his death beneath the hooves of the charging giants. Sometimes, trapped within the herd, the horse and rider were driven over the cliff with the stampeding bison.

A huge bull near the leading edge of the herd, caught Talking Bears eye. His bow in one hand, his lance held above his head with the other, Talking Bear guided me ever closer to the charging animal. As we drew alongside the enormous bull, Talking Bear thrust his lance with all his might into the flesh behind its shoulder. His eyes wide with rage, the mighty animal whirled immediately toward us. Feeling the guidance from Talking Bear's knees, I spun from the path of the enraged bull. Blood gushing from its side, the great animal tipped its head and lunged toward us once more. Again, Talking Bear sank his lance into the side of the wild-eyed bull as he turned me from its path. With blood gushing from its chest, the great bull stumbled and fell beneath the thundering wall of bison.

A terrified scream from beyond us in the dust tore Talking Bear's attention from the great beast. Ahead of us, the one known as Rides the Sky, was trapped in the herd of charging animals. The chief dug his heels into my sides urging me into the herd of lunging bodies. As we neared the struggling hunter, his horse fell, and Rides the Sky tumbled to the ground beneath the stampeding bison. As we surged past the place we had last seen the hunter, Talking Bear leaned from my side and reached toward the ground. Their hands met as we passed, their powerful grips clinging desperately to one another as the bison pushed us recklessly on. As Talking Bear drew Rides the Sky from the ground, a bull lunged recklessly sideways and tore him from the chief's grip. The warrior vanished beneath the sea of

259

lunging bodies as the stampeding bison pushed us relentlessly on.

With all my strength, I pushed against the charging bodies, parting them one by one, until at last we were free. A blood-curdling cry came from behind us in the sea of lunging bodies. We watched in amazement as Rides the Sky, grabbed the wiry shoulder hair of a passing bull and swung himself onto the back of the mighty animal. Yelling and screaming, his fist held high in triumph, the warrior disappeared over the cliff on his surging mount.

The mighty herd split as it reached the cliff. A great number of bison turned suddenly away from their certain death. A cloud of dust rose from the valley floor marking their fleeing path. Talking Bear quickly gathered his warriors, and led them along the crest of the cliff away from the advancing flames of the grass fire. From a small rise at the edge of the drop, the hunters talked and laughed, celebrating their hunt as they watched the flames subside below them.

The women, having watched the hunt from the foothills above the prairie, had seen the warriors drive the bison over the cliff. Some had already started butchering the bison that had fallen to the bows and lances on the plains behind us. Many others were climbing carefully downward through narrow gaps of rock toward the foot of the cliff where ten-fold more lay dead.

Talking Bear sat quietly on my back watching from the edge of the cliff as the butchering began below. In places, groups of women crept through the brush below the workers, dispatching animals that had not died from their fall.

Suddenly, shouts of alarm erupted from below. Talking Bear guided me quickly along the cliff where we entered a narrow canyon and lunged recklessly downward in loose shale rock. Sliding to a halt amidst tumbling rock and debris, Talking Bear sprang from my back. In a tangle of small juniper trees, a group of women knelt in a circle around Rides the Sky. Their mournful cries told of his apparent demise. Parting the women, Talking Bear knelt by his friend. Rides the Sky lay with one arm and leg folded awkwardly beneath his body. From his other leg, a jagged tip of ivory bone protruded from a tear in his buckskin leggings. A pool of blood had soaked the area around the hole. His other arm, broken also, lay crookedly in the brush above his head. A short, dead juniper tree had broken his terrible fall. Its twisted trunk had pierced his back, its gnarly tip now protruded from his belly. The warrior's chest heaved sporadically as he fought for breath.

Pulling his water pouch from around his neck, Talking Bear filled the palm of his hand and patted the wet surface gently on Rides the Sky's lips. The warrior's eyelids fluttered, and slowly opened. His crooked smile slowly filled his face when he recognized Talking Bear. "I rode the sky, Talking Bear," he whispered.

His body shuddered, and his eyes slowly closed.

"Yes, my friend," said Talking Bear. "You rode the sky."

It had long been dark, when Talking Bear sat quietly on my back near the bank of the River of Spirits. We watched as the moon rose slowly above the mountains and shone on the pole scaffold upon which lie, Rides the Sky. Talking Bear thought quietly about the successful hunt, and the excitement that now filled his people. They knew now, they had plenty of meat for winter. But he thought also, about his friend, Rides the Sky, and the warrior's grieving mate.

Chapter Twelve

I awakened and slowly raised my head from the ground. The vision of moonlit rivers and the thundering roar of stampeding bison faded quickly away as my dream world vanished.

Fully awake now, I sullenly studied the prison that had become my home. Beyond the walls of my corral were countless stalls like mine. Horses stood captive in the wooden enclosures for as far as I could see.

Resentfully, I endured the daily routine of my new home. Shortly after dawn each day, a cowboy would appear on one of the rumbling machines used by man. From a bucket on its front, he would take armfuls of bright, green alfalfa and dump into a feeding trough at my corral's far end. Beside the manger was a metal trough that the cowboy then filled with fresh water. A small bucket attached to the side of my corral was filled with grain. Above that end of the corral stood a wide awning that afforded me shade as I ate or drank. Several horses were forced to share each of the other corrals around me. I was the only horse that stood alone in his own corral.

The season of summer had begun, and the days in this new place were long and hot. It was as hot it seemed, as were the sweltering days spent long ago beneath the palo verde and mesquite trees of my desert home. In the distance stood tall, barren mountains, and on the breeze were the familiar smells of the desert. Dust floated constantly around me, churned from the corral floor by the restless horses that shared this terrible place of confinement.

My mood was dark, and my stomach churned and ached from my new feed called, alfalfa. From the grain fed me by the two-legged ones, grew a terrible energy. I paced endlessly at the edges of my enclosure.

Early one morning, a group of cowboys appeared before my corral. With their horses, they pulled me from my stall and drew me into a trailer. Soon, I banged along in the dust behind a rumbling truck. This journey though, unlike my others, was a short one. Before long, we turned from the trail and drove slowly through yet another place of man. At our sides, hordes of people walked on narrow concrete trails beneath rows of towering buildings. We soon came to a halt beside an immense rodeo arena. At one side of the arena was a row of bucking chutes, and a huge array of corrals lay behind them. I remembered the place where not long ago, the two-legged ones had tried to ride me.

Large areas of land stood vacant around the arena. Its surface was black, and rows of white lines were drawn everywhere on it. The doors of the truck ahead of me opened, and cowboys appeared at the sides of my trailer. With ropes, mounted riders dragged me from the trailer and placed me in a corral near the bucking chutes.

As the day progressed, many horses were unloaded from trailers. Most were led into the holding pens and released. Some though, were dragged screaming from the trailers by mounted riders and pulled into pens. The horses here, seemed different from the ones I had seen at the last rodeo. These, stood sullenly quiet as they studied the horses around them. Their eyes glowered with hostility.

I was awake throughout the night, filled with the pounding energy given me by my diet of alfalfa and grain. The darkness was filled with the sound of plodding footsteps as countless horses paced relentlessly in their enclosures.

When the sun rose the next morning, the machines of man rumbled to life at all sides of the stadium. Small tractors groomed the arena's floor, and men worked busily everywhere throughout the stands. Men carried boxes into small buildings throughout the arena, and the strange odor of the two-legged one's food soon floated everywhere on the air.

When the sun was high overhead, cars and trucks began to fill the open area beyond the arena. Long lines of them were soon parked for as far as I could see. Doors squeaked and slammed as people climbed from them and walked toward the stadium. Their chatter filled the air as they entered the arena and climbed into the stands. Their numbers quickly grew, and their excited voices soon became a deafening roar.

The booming voice of an unseen two-legged one blared suddenly from the talking boxes at all sides of the arena. The people in the stands grew silent as doors at its far end opened, and three mounted horsemen appeared. Above each of the rider's heads was carried a flag affixed to the end of a long pole. Behind them, was a large wagon pulled by six white horses. In the wagon, sat many two-legged ones. A line of horses pranced four abreast behind the wagon, their riders all dressed in colorful garb. The procession circled the arena and came to a stop finally, in its center.

A two-legged one climbed from the wagon, and stood before the horseman that carried the forward-most flag. All the people in the stands rose, and held their hats over their chests as the two-legged one began to sing. Her voice, like the voice of the unseen speaker, blared from the talking boxes at all sides of the stadium. As the woman finished singing, a group of low-flying aircraft thundered through the sky above the stadium. The people in the stands roared in approval as the jets disappeared in the sky.

When the terrible voice of the aircraft could no longer be heard, the riders turned their horses and disappeared through the opening where they had first appeared.

Cowboys entered the holding pens and began moving horses forward into the bucking chutes. I stood with my head lowered, glaring angrily at them.

"This one's lookin' mean," said one rider. "If he bucks as hard as his attitude is bad, we'll be using him in the championship round on the last day."

The cowboys roped me and pulled me forward into an open chute. I bristled with anger as they slammed the door behind me.

Around the holding pens, cowboys stood in small groups quietly talking. Some sat on saddles they had placed on the ground. Holding one arm into the air, they rocked back and forth on them, as if riding some unseen bronc.

Other cowboys sat quietly on the ground, leaned against the outside of the holding pens. Their hats were drawn low over their eyes as they prepared inwardly for their upcoming ride.

Their hands were covered with buckskin gloves, and on their legs, they wore a thick leather garment that they called chaps. Both their gloves and chaps were covered with a sticky substance called, rosin. The rosin, they said, helped them to stick to the saddle when they made their ride. "Glue in their britches," they called it.

Small groups of pretty, young women chattered happily as they walked past the holding pens. They glanced shyly at the cowboys as they passed. The riders, thinking of their upcoming ride, pretended not to notice.

The voice again blared from the talking boxes, and the rodeo suddenly began.

I watched anxiously as a cowboy climbed the side of a chute beyond me. He settled nervously into the saddle strapped on the back of the squirming horse that stood within it. The door thundered open, and the horse and rider crashed across the arena before me. The cowboy's flailing arm slashed at the air above his head, and his legs pumped, raking at the shoulders of the horse with his spurs. The horse spun and twisted, fighting violently to shake the rider.

Just before the buzzer sounded, the cowboy flew from the back of the horse and landed in the dirt. The cowboy rose pounding angrily at the dirt on his pants as the horse lunged across the arena. Snatching his hat from the ground, he strode indignantly toward the edge of the arena.

Gate after gate popped open, and horses crashed through the arena as the afternoon wore on. Some of the bucking horses were ridden to the buzzer, while others threw their adversaries crashing to the earth.

I flinched as the chute beside mine crashed open, and I watched nervously as the horse and rider fought across the arena before me. I quivered with anticipation when their ride was done, and the horse had been run into the gate at the corner of the arena. I knew my battle would come soon.

I heard the scuff of boots against the side of my chute as a rider climbed the stall in which I stood. Anger flared within me as he spoke.

"Let's see what ya got, White One," he said, as he settled into the saddle on my back. His voice kindled a terrible rage boiling within me. The cowboy nodded his head, and the door in front of me crashed open. I sprang from the chute with an explosive lunge. Stiff legged, I bound across the arena spinning and kicking. At times, I leaped far

269

above the ground with both my front and hind legs extended in a mighty kick. I would land then, and explode immediately in the other direction. The rider stayed on my back for no more than three bounds. Flipping end over end through the air, he landed in a cloud of dust on the arena's floor. As I crashed onward, I saw him struggle to his feet behind me. Leaving his hat in the dirt, he staggered to the arena's edge.

Standing again in the pens, I glared back at the arena, wondering about the words that the two-legged one had spoken.

In amazement, I watched as cowboys began suddenly to herd huge animals from the pens behind me. The animals, known as *bulls* by the two-legged ones, resembled the mighty bison I had seen in my dreams. The bulls were fuming, and nearly uncontrollable. Clearly, they resented their handling by the two-legged ones. They kicked and snorted, tossing their heads angrily as the cowboys drove them into the bucking chutes at the arena's edge.

The talking boxes blared, and the first of the mighty animals thundered from the bucking chutes. With cowboys clinging desperately to their backs, they snorted and grunted as they spun and lunged powerfully through the air. Oftentimes the bulls turned angrily on the helpless cowboy they had thrown from their backs. Men dressed in strange clothing immediately ran to the aid of the thrown rider. Ducking and darting, slapping at the bull with their hands, they tried desperately to distract the seething animal from the downed rider.

When the last of the bulls had crashed from the chutes, the two-legged one spoke for a short time from the talking boxes. Clapping their hands and screaming their approval, the crowd rose from the stands and slowly walked from the stadium. The sun was still far above the horizon when the last of the cars and trucks had left the parking area.

As twilight settled, a group of cowboys appeared before the holding pens. Pointing at me, and a few others, the leader of the group said,

"Put those horses in the *hot* pen tonight. They were the hardest buckers today. We will use them as *eliminators* in the champion round on Sunday," he said. The men entered the holding pens and herded me and four others into a set of separate corrals.

The next day, I watched anxiously from what the two-legged ones had called the hot pen. One by one, horses again exploded from bucking chutes trying desperately to throw there would-be riders. When at last the day ended, no two-legged one had attempted to ride me.

That night, the cowboys came again to he holding pens. They herded thirteen more horses into the enclosure they called the hot pen. Now eighteen horses stood in these special pens around me.

When the sun was fully overhead the next day, the cars and trucks of man quickly filled the area around the stadium. As the chaotic din grew ever louder in the stands, riders appeared near my pen and began to move the horses around me into the bucking chutes. When the flags and the singing of the two-legged ones was done, the rodeo began.

One by one, bucking horses sprang from the chutes. Most of the storming horses threw their riders into the dirt beneath them, but some of the cowboys rode to the buzzer and were pulled from their backs by the pickup men.

When all the horses had bucked, cowboys entered my pen and drove me forward into a bucking chute. A saddle and bucking strap were quickly secured on my back. The two-legged ones had saved me for last.

The voice of the unseen one blared from the talking boxes, and a hush fell over the stadium. I heard the rattle of my stall as a cowboy climbed its side. Slowly, he reached down and grabbed the rope attached to my halter. With his other hand, he steadied himself against the side of the chute as he settled into the saddle on my back. The cowboy jerked my halter rope violently backward, slamming my head into the side of the stall as the gate before me sprang suddenly open. Reeling from the blow, I fell to my knees as I spun from the chute. Dirt and dust flew as I fought angrily to my feet and crashed across the arena in a wild, headlong rant. Moaning and grunting, the two-legged one raked his spurs against my shoulders as he clung desperately to my back. Leaping from the ground, I shook my head from side to side in growing rage. Kicking and spinning, I wrenched my belly skyward and threw the cowboy to the earth beneath me. I heard his painful cry as my hind leg struck him and saw him struggle to his feet as I crashed away. Grimacing with pain, the cowboy staggered to the arena's side before falling to his knees and rolling onto his side. With glowering eyes, I watched from the holding pens as others loaded him on a stretcher and carried him from view.

When the bulls were finished bucking, the voice blared from the talking boxes, and a thunderous cheer erupted from the people at all sides of the arena. When the applause quieted at last, the two-legged ones rose from their seats and began to leave the stadium.

The rumble of departing cars had not yet quieted when a group of cowboys approached where I stood in the holding pens. Standing before me, the men studied me in quiet amazement.

"I have never seen a horse that could buck like you, Ghost," said my owner, breaking the silence.

"Yeah," said another, "I've heard of 'em, but I ain't never seen a horse that could *sunfish,* when they bucked. Man, he twisted so hard, his belly was almost pointin' at the moon when he threw that last rider."

"Yeah," said my owner, "This is a special bronc." Then, looking me in the eye, he said as if to himself, "I don't know if this horse will ever be ridden."

My return trip to the ranch was short and uneventful. I paced anxiously in my corral as darkness gathered slowly around me. My thirst now quenched and my belly full, I pondered the strange event that the two-legged ones called rodeo. Anger welled within me as I remembered the cowboys who had tried to ride me. Their attempts to conquer me had failed. My loathing of the two-legged ones was now greater than ever before.

Embraced by the comfort of darkness, my endless walking ceased at last, and I stood quietly in the corner of my corral staring into the night. Fatigue from the mighty battle I had fought with the two-legged ones settled over me as I stared into the night.

Slowly, I lowered my head to the ground. The rich smell of green grass and the musty smell of the River of Spirits filled my senses as I surrendered gratefully to my dreams.

For ten days, our tribe worked from dawn until sunset butchering the bison and preparing the meat for return to our village. Drying racks were made, and now strained beneath the weight of drying bison meat. The mood of the people was joyous. All knew that now there would be plentiful meat for the long, cold days of the season of renewal. There was much singing and laughter.

The drone of buzzing flies filled the air on the small prairie below the cliff where scores of women knelt working by the mighty carcasses. The narrow strips of meat that they cut from the bison were given to children who carried it to the drying racks and hung it carefully to dry. Many knelt in the grass scraping the flesh from the hides, while still others scoured the hides with brains, tanning them for tepee walls. Some worked diligently collecting bones that would later be tooled and shaped into utensils for daily use.

The people who had stayed behind ran joyfully toward us as we approached our village. Talking Bear saw immediately that the herd of horses normally grazing in the grass beside our encampment was gone. The welcoming villagers became quiet as Talking Bear led our tribe of hunters into the village. Ten of the warriors he had left to protect the people stood quietly assembled beside Talking Bear's tepee in the center of the village. Some stood erect, anxiously waiting, others sat painfully on the ground, their demeanor telling of the pain that wracked their bodies. Fresh wounds could be seen on many.

The warriors told Talking Bear about a Crow war party that had attacked our village. Two of our warriors had been killed. Most of our horses had been taken, they said.

Talking Bear sat quietly at the head of a counsel fire as the sun drew toward the horizon. His leaders sat at his sides. All of the warriors and villagers drew close as the men who had fought the Crow stood before the chief. Anxiously, the brave warriors recounted the story of their battle.

They told Talking Bear that the enemy had crept across the valley in darkness. At the sun's first light, they had attacked. The numbers of Crow were huge, but somehow, the Sioux warriors had beaten the enemy. None of the villagers had been injured or killed, but all the horses had been taken. Two of our best warriors had fallen to the arrows of the Crow.

Talking Bear's eyes burned with anger, as he sat quietly thinking. The vision seen before their great hunt had indeed come true. The enemy though, had not stalked the hunters. The battle had taken place at our village. Talking Bear knew that the Crow were fierce warriors. The large number described by his warriors should have easily overpowered them. The Crow war party could have easily killed all the people in the village.

"Why had the Crow retreated, stealing only the horses not taken by his warriors on the bison hunt?" he wondered.

In a short while, Talking Bear looked up from the fire. The anger that had filled his eyes was gone, in its place was a cold, steely look of resolve. He had decided.

The chief looked from man to man, staring into the eyes of each, as he stood.

"Prepare immediately for battle" he told his warriors loudly. "Bring as many arrows as your quivers will hold. Bring your best war lance, and carry your war club on a strong leather thong around your shoulder.

277

"We will leave before darkness settles. The tracks left by the Crow as they drive our horses, will be easily followed beneath the light of the moon. Carry your war totems, and paint in a pouch. Tonight, in darkness, we will paint our bodies, and emblazon our horses for war. Go now," he said! "Fill your pipes with strong prayer. Ready yourselves for battle! When the sun rises tomorrow, we will put an end to the murderous doings of the Crow. Hoka hey!" he screamed!

Talking Bear summoned six of his best warriors. He told them they were to stay behind to protect the women and children. He told the warriors that they must follow his words exactly.

He instructed them that after dark, they were to lead all the people from the village. Even the youngest and the sick must follow them. The warriors were to lead the people south along the river. They must travel in total darkness, without sake of torch to light their way. When they had traveled seven miles, they were to hide the people in the willows along the bank. There was to be no movement. They must sit quietly even when the light came again in the morning. They were to stay hidden in this way, until messengers were sent to get them.

The sun was dropping low in the sky when Talking Bear led his enormous band of warriors from the village. His headdress of white eagle feathers floated in the breeze far behind my rump as we crashed across the river and moved quickly toward the foothills at the valley's west side. The tangy smells of juniper and sage hung heavily in the air as we moved upward in failing light. Darkness had nearly consumed us, when finally Talking Bear raised his arm and stopped our mighty band of warriors.

Confusion drew across their shadowy faces when he turned me toward them and in a loud voice said, "We will travel no further. It is here that we will spend the night. No man among us will start a fire," he continued, "The eyes of our enemy watch carefully for any sign in the darkness that we are near. I am certain, brothers, that the Crow have set a trap for our people. They have long dreamed of our nation's defeat. They are strong and fierce warriors, but they are also cunning. They know well the ferocity with which a badger fights when defending its den. But they know also that when the fearless one is lured away from its home, its young can be easily taken. The mighty badger having lost all, loses its will to fight, and the savage one is easily taken also.

"When the sun brings its light to our land tomorrow, the Crow will attack our village," said Talking Bear. A soft murmur erupted from the hundreds of warriors huddled in the darkness around him.

"They know," he continued, "That to kill our women and take our children would destroy our great nation. At last, they believe that they will defeat the mighty Sioux.

"From a hiding place in the hills at the north side of our valley, I am certain their war party watched as we left our village in pursuit of them. They knew we would follow the trail they had purposely left behind. Were we to follow that trail to its end, we would find only our horses that they had taken, and the few young boys who drove them. For our women and children, it would be too late.

"But, brothers," continued Talking Bear, "I have set a trap of my own. The Crow will not attack our village at night. They know to do so would anger the spirits. At first light, they will come. We will wait for them beneath the benches of land that lay at our valley's edge. When the Crow enter our village, it will be vacant. I have instructed the warriors that I left behind to lead our people upstream in the darkness of this night. Like a fox trapped in the bottom of an empty burrow, for the Crow it will be too late. Because, like the badger, our attack will be ferocious.

"Go now. Paint your faces and tie the feathers of the great winged one in the manes and tails of your horses. Paint them with your emblems of war. Ready yourselves to die, brothers, for tomorrow we will battle the Crow," said the chief.

From in the darkness came the rasp of leather thongs as pouches were opened, and the soft hiss of feathers, as they were tied firmly in the long hair of war horses. Prayers for strength floated quietly through the night as the warriors painted their faces with totems of strength, and emblazoned their horses with symbols of war. The ghostly sound of Hinhan, the spirit bird, owl, floated through the forest around us. But this was not the soft hooting call made normally by the great night bird. Its rasping screech on this night was meant to scare its prey into flight as it stalked the darkness. The terrifying calls of owl somehow readied the warriors for what was soon to come.

When the night was half gone, Talking Bear summoned a warrior known as Two Faces. Quietly, the two men sat in the darkness near me and talked. Talking Bear instructed the man to gather half the warriors and return on the trail upon which they had just come. Two Faces listened intently as the chief told him to travel past the village in darkness, and conceal themselves at the foot of the bluff that lay beyond the village.

"When the Crow enter our village at first light, I will attack," said Talking Bear. "When your lookouts see me attack from the west side of our valley, charge from your hiding place in the east. We will encircle the village and trap the Crow. Tomorrow," said Talking Bear, "We will defeat our old enemy, forever."

The sound of Two Face's war party was fading in the darkness when Talking Bear walked to my side.

"It is time, Wakia," he said. "We must prepare now for battle."

From small pouches, Talking Bear dipped various colors of paint. On my rump, he painted the crashing likeness of the spotted eagle. On my front shoulders, he painted bold, slashing lines of yellow. These were the sign, I knew, of the Thunder Beings. Talking Bear chanted softly as he drew dark lines of paint across his forehead. He encircled both eyes with the color of darkness. His nose and mouth were encased with white. Across his heart, he drew a wavering line of yellow that ended in an upward swoop. The sign of Yellow Tail would ride with us in battle.

Talking Bear drew a long, red sash from his leather pack and tied it firmly around his waist. He had long been a member of the redshirt society, the bravest of all warriors. In battle, the redshirt warriors staked one end of their red sash firmly to the ground with their lances. For them, there was no retreat. They would either be victorious in battle, or die where they stood.

When the first streaks of light appeared in the sky, Talking Bear donned his flowing headdress of white eagle feathers.

"It is time, White One," he said, as he swung onto my back. With a quavering whistle, Talking Bear signaled his waiting warriors, and in a rush of movement, they mounted their horses and followed us downward in the darkness.

Long before it was light, Talking Bear stopped his huge war party in a broad ravine at the edge of the valley. Here, we were hidden from view. Just beyond the rise in front of us was the River of Spirits. Beyond that, lay the encampment of our people. Talking Bear dispatched two scouts to conceal themselves in the brush at the top of the rise. They were to alert Talking Bear when the Crow war party appeared. The succulent smell of willow and moist earth drifted from the great river on the early morning air, and horses snorted and stomped nervously in the darkness around me.

Slowly, the valley around us emerged from the darkness. Ducks and geese called from beyond the rise as they flew unhurriedly along the river, unaware, apparently, of the impending battle. As the sun's pulsing edge started above the mountains, the lookouts scrambled down the rise toward Talking Bear. His eyes cold and staring, his face an emotionless mask, Talking Bear swung onto my back. In the distance, I could hear a growing thunder. Soon, above the sound of thundering hooves, I could hear the terrifying war cries of the Crow.

With a wave of his lance, Talking Bear signaled his warriors. Amidst shrieking war cries and the thunder of hooves behind us, we crashed upward across the crest.

The last of the Crow war party had entered the village when at full speed we crashed into the river at its edge. Sunlight sparkled from the watery explosion of driving hooves as we lunged toward the far bank. Two Faces had seen our attack begin, and his howling band of warriors was nearing the village from its east side.

The deafening cries of war and agonizing screams of death were bone chilling as we collided in battle with our age-old enemy, the Crow. Warriors everywhere around us were locked in battle as Talking Bear drove me onward to the center of the village. He sprang from my back as we reached his tepee. Talking Bear raised his lance into the air and drove it into the ground beside him, staking his red shawl firmly to the earth. I stood by his side as he glared angrily at the Crow warriors before him, daring any to come near.

Their hideous cry was entrenched forever in my mind, when suddenly the Crow warriors surrounding us charged forward. Talking Bear ducked and dodged the lances and war clubs of the oncoming Crow. His war club, though, did not miss. Dust filled the air as the fighting intensified. The tepees around us stood like strange mountains rising from the brown murk. The ghostlike shadows of fighting warriors darted everywhere between them.

The sun was nearly overhead when the terrible battle quieted finally. Turning nervously from side to side, his war club held high above his head, Talking Bear stood crouched and ready for the next charging Crow warrior. But there were none. The battle was over. Talking Bear slowly lowered his war club, and stood erect. He jerked his lance from the ground freeing his red shawl, and turning slowly, held the lance above his head in victory. The sun danced from the lance's gleaming black tip, shining brilliantly through its translucent seam of yellow. The stony mask of anger that had ruled his face slowly softened as the enormity of the moment settled upon him.

Quietly, Talking Bear studied the encampment around him that only one day ago had been his peaceful village. Eleven Crow warriors lay dead on the ground at his feet. Bodies lay everywhere between the tepees. Abandoned horses snorted nervously as they wandered through the village, their riders now mysteriously gone. Only sporadic outcries at our encampment's edge marked the place where yet another enemy warrior was found and killed. Talking Bear's trap had worked perfectly. The enormous Crow war party had been killed, to a man.

A sudden commotion from the tepees near us drew Talking Bear from his trance. A young Crow warrior, kicking and screaming, was dragged from a tepee near us and thrown to the ground at Talking Bear's feet. Bending downward, the chief clutched the man by his buckskin shirt and drew the Crow warrior to his feet. Screaming words in a tongue that I did not know, he spat at Talking Bear. With a mighty blow, the chief knocked the man to the dirt at his feet. With one foot pressing firmly on the back of the squirming warrior's neck, Talking Bear bent, and with his knife, slashed a long, wide strip of hair from the howling man's scalp. He then dragged the bleeding warrior to his feet.

"I would gladly kill you," hissed Talking Bear through clenched teeth, "But instead, you will be my messenger. Go, tell your people of this battle. Tell them that if ever again they enter our land, we will hunt them down and finish the battle that your people started here today." The warriors threw the man on a horse and watched as the Crow warrior thundered from our village.

Twelve of our warriors had been killed in the great battle. Those who had been wounded were now helped to a large tepee in the center of our village where our medicine man, Standing Owl, was helping them.

Our warriors walked quietly from body to body counting coup on the Crow warriors they had killed. As Talking Bear had done, they cut a wide strip of hair from the scalp of each.

Talking Bear sent runners to find the women and children who were hidden along the river in the upper valley. Soon, we could hear the wailing of the approaching women. They had been told of the great battle that had taken place. Already, they grieved for the lives they knew surely had been lost. Upon entering the village, the women scurried between the tepees in a desperate search to find their men. Joyous shouts of happiness erupted throughout the village with each reunion. But amidst the rejoicing were mournful screams of angst when the lifeless body of one's mate was found.

Burial platforms for our warriors who had been killed in the battle were erected beyond the village near the edge of the river. The wife of each brave man knelt grieving on the ground beneath her lost mate. Most had cut the hair from their head. Some had slashed fingers from their hands in grief. On the ground beneath each warrior's platform were placed their bows, lances, and all personal items needed for their spiritual journey. Twelve times, I heard the pitiful death cry of horses as each warrior's mount was led to their burial platform and killed. The warrior would need his best horse to carry him on his spiritual journey in the Southland. The horses of the dead Crow warriors were not taken by our people. Though the warriors had been our enemy in life, they had fought and died honorably. They too, would need their horse in the Spirit Land.

Talking Bear ordered all tepees to be taken down and made ready to travel. He knew that we could no longer stay in this place of death. The chief sent a war party to track down the herd of horses that the Crow had taken from us.

He knew there would be no battle. He was certain the herd would be found abandoned.

As the sun drew low in the sky, the long procession of our people moved upward in the valley along the River of Spirits. On a rise beyond where our village had stood, Talking Bear turned me and pulled me to a stop. In the distance, feathers fluttered from the burial platforms where our dead warriors lay near the river's edge. The faint sound of the grieving women beneath them floated eerily on the breeze. The bodies of the dead Crow warriors lay still where they had fallen in the huge, trampled circle where our village had stood.

"The wolves will eat well tonight, Wakia," muttered Talking Bear sadly. He turned me and we walked from the rise.

Chapter Thirteen

I was drawn from my daunting dreams of battle by the sting of driving sand. Hideous war cries turned slowly to the howl of lashing wind around me, as my world slowly focused.

The rising sun shone on billowing clouds of dust, driven skyward from the corrals by a hot, relentless wind. Though the sun was barely above the horizon, its heat forced me to rise from my bed, and seek shelter beneath the awning at the far end of my corral. The scent carried by the terrible, dry wind, told of the desert's thirst for water. The high desert land where I had roamed with my herd was often as hot as this, but unlike here in this life of captivity, the freedom to wander made the blistering heat somehow bearable. The choking dust, and hopelessness of this prison in which I now lived made even the terrible rigors of the rodeo seem a welcomed reprieve.

Since my return from the rodeo, cowboys came often to my corral. Sometimes alone, sometimes in groups, they stood before my enclosure looking. Always, I stood in its far corner staring sullenly at them as they talked excitedly about my incredible feats in the place they called, Santa Fe.

In only a few days, the cowboys loaded me once more, and I was pulled behind a truck on man's black trail for a day and a half. As the sun was dropping from the sky, I arrived in a land the cowboys called Texas. We turned from the black trail, finally, and stopped beside an enormous arena.

As in the last place, many holding pens stood at its side, and beyond them were a long line of bucking chutes. My handlers helped mounted riders pull me from the trailer, and place me alone, in a holding pen. They had learned that to do otherwise, meant certain injury to the horses who shared my corral.

When the sun rose the next day, I watched anxiously as men prepared the arena for what I now knew would come. The heat became blistering as the sun climbed higher in the sky. Unlike my corral back at Santa Fe, this one had no shade, and I was given very little water. The cowboys said water hindered a horse's ability to buck.

I stood sweltering, as cars and trucks began to fill the vacant area at all sides of the stadium. As before, the excited voices of untold numbers, soon thundered from the stands around the arena. After my humbling of the two-legged ones at the rodeo in Santa Fe, my fame had spread among both riders and spectators. More people than ever before, now filled the stands in this place called Lubbock.

Each of my torturous days for the next three, were the same. Men would prepare the arena when the sun first rose into the sky. Then, crowds of people would fill the stands. After the two-legged ones had carried their flags and sung their song, broncs were loaded into the bucking chutes. The terrible battle between man and horse, would then begin.

The two-legged ones, unlike the horses who shared my corral, were slow learners. They tried again and again to conquer me. Each time, I punished them grievously. One cowboy, on the final day of the rodeo, climbed the side of my bucking chute and settled nervously onto my back. But before he nodded his head to the gate man, his courage failed him. To the disdain of the audience, he scrambled from the saddle on my back and jumped to the ground.

I paced nervously in my pen as darkness settled over the rodeo grounds at the end of the third day. The gut-wrenching event had long since ended, and the cars and trucks of the two-legged ones had left the parking area. I knew that soon my handlers would appear, and again, I would be rushing along the black trail of man.

I heard crunching footsteps in the gravel beyond my pen, and soon a man stood alone before me. He was not tall, but his build was stocky and the color of his skin was dark. The man stood for a long while without speaking. His gaze was different than any of the two-legged ones I had known. In a short while the man stepped forward and stood near my corral. His voice was deep and soft when finally, he spoke.

"White One," he said, "I know who you are. Your name is not Ghost. You are the horse known as, *Son of Banshee*. You once led the wild horses in the high desert of Nevada. For many years, you defied all attempts of capture by man.

"My home, White One, is in the desert land where you once lived. It has long been known by the people there, that the one known as Son of Banshee, was stolen from his desert land. It is believed that you are dead. But, when I heard of the amazing feats of the untamable white horse in the rodeo, I was certain that the stallion so talked about, must be, Son of Banshee. Now, having seen you, your size, your lines, and the black mask of hair around your eyes, I know that it's true. Indeed, you are, Son of Banshee. How your journey brought you to this place, I do not know. But,

White One, I know that you do not belong here. Freedom must be yours.

"White One," he whispered, "I will free you. I will find a way."

He stood for a moment looking into my eyes, then turned and was gone. I stood for a long while in the darkness pondering the appearance of the two-legged one. Never before had I felt calmness in the presence of a man.

Throughout the blistering season of summer, my handlers loaded me often into the trailer. I no longer bucked and kicked at the cowboys who loaded me, but still I was loaded only by mounted riders with lariats tearing at my neck.

Behind the truck of the two-legged ones, I traveled the black trail to places the cowboys called, Houston, Dallas, and Denver. Again and again, cowboys tried to ride me, and each time, the riders paid the price. Some were carried from the arena on stretchers, others merely limped to the side of the arena in pain. Oddly, at the end of each rodeo, the dark-skinned man with the soothing voice waited quietly for my return near the side of my pen.

With each rodeo and with each saddling and attempted ride, my loathing of man grew. But no longer did I snort and scream and crash at them when they stood near my corral. Now, I stood quietly, glaring at them from its corner, daring them to enter.

The dark-skinned man stood next to my pen at the end of the rodeo in a place known by the two-legged ones as Witchita. My owner and a small group of cowboys suddenly appeared, walking toward my corral.

"Quite a horse you have here, Mr. Smith," the dark-skinned man said, when my owner at last stood before him. "I've never seen one like him."

"Yeah," said my owner, "He's making quite a splash on the rodeo circuit these days. I've seen you by Ghost's pen at the last few rodeos," he continued. "What's your name, friend? What do you do?"

"My name is Alan Williams," said the dark-skinned man, "I am a horse trainer from Nevada. Remarkable horses like this one have always drawn my interest."

"A trainer, huh," said my owner. "It so happens I'm looking for a handler to care for Ghost at the ranch and travel with him to each rodeo. You seem to be at each one anyway, are you interested in the job?"

Looking toward me, Alan, said, "Yeah, I'd like that, Mr. Smith. I'd like that a lot."

My owner hired the dark-skinned one known as Alan Williams, and he moved to the ranch to be my trainer. He traveled in the truck each time my trailer was pulled down the black trail. At the ranch, he fed and watered me. After each rodeo, he studied my movements carefully as I walked through my corral. Alan made certain that I had not been injured and had no lingering effects from my battles of bucking.

One day, Alan extended his arm between the rungs of my corral. In his outstretched hand, was a small morsel of food. For reasons that I do not know, I stepped forward. I breathed deeply of his scent as I pressed my nose against his open hand, drawing the pellet into my mouth. I stood with my eyes nearly shut, quietly savoring the wonderful taste in my mouth. There had been no time in my life before now, that I had felt at peace with man.

The next day, my owner stood beside Alan at my corral.

"This horse has done an amazing job," my owner said to him. "Give him plenty of alfalfa tonight, Alan, and double his oats. He's gonna need all the fire he's got this weekend in Arizona. He's entered in the Navajo Nations rodeo over in Window Rock. It's a wild one for sure, and the riders there are tougher than nails. So, have 'im ready," he said.

Early the next day, horsemen drew me into a trailer, and for a day and night, I was pulled down the black trail.

My arrival at the rodeo grounds in the place called Window Rock was the same as the many other rodeos before it. I was quickly pulled from my trailer and placed in a holding pen at the arena's edge. Like the other places I had been, the hot dusty air here was filled with the scent of angry horses and bulls. I paced broodingly back and forth in my enclosure as darkness fell. I knew what the next three days would bring.

Early the next morning, cowboys entered the pens and drove the horses into the bucking chutes at the arena's edge. Two riders entered my stall and drove me into the eliminator's pen. My reputation as a rank, angry bronc had become widely known. I would be saved for the rodeo's last day.

I watched on both the first and second day, as horses and bulls bucked frantically through the arena. The two-legged ones did not attempt to ride me on either day. I waited angrily in the eliminator's pen for the battle that I knew would come.

When the rodeo ended on the second day, the sky was overcast and threatening. As darkness gathered, rain began to fall. Soon, lightning streaked through the sky, and from everywhere came the soft rumble of rain as it pummeled the ground. The horses in the holding pens around me stood with their heads lowered, braced against sheets of driving rain. I heard the bulls in corrals beyond me, snorting and blowing in the darkness as they became increasingly ill-tempered in the growing storm. It rained hard through the night, and when daylight came, the ground was wet and soggy. Huge puddles of water stood everywhere throughout the arena.

When the final day began at last, I watched as horses leaped from the chutes, bucking and twisting in great splashes of water and mud. Some spun and crow-hopped awkwardly avoiding the puddles, as they sought to throw the riders from their backs.

I stood alone in the eliminator's pen at the end of the third day, watching as the last of the horses bucked. My ire quickly grew when cowboys entered my pen and prodded me forward into the open gate of a bucking chute. Quickly, I was fitted with a saddle and bucking strap.

After the booming voice of the hidden one blared from the talking boxes, the crowd became quiet. I tensed as a cowboy climbed the side of my chute. My eyes grew wide with fury as I felt him settle into the saddle on my back. I exploded into the arena when the gate before me flew suddenly open. Soggy earth flew in all directions as I kicked and spun, venting the terrible rage within me. On one mighty leap, the cowboy flew from my saddle, and twisting through the air, landed in a great splash of mud beneath me. The mounted riders quickly herded me toward an open gate at the arena's edge.

Before I could enter the gate, a bull, crazed from the relentless storm, crashed through the side of his pen and thundered into the arena. Shaking his mighty head, the enraged bull lunged toward me. Caught by surprise, I attempted to spin away from the great animal, but its horn caught me in the hip, rolling me awkwardly to the ground. I sprang to my feet as the bull spun and crashed toward me once more. As the collision became imminent, I sprang to the side and the bull stormed harmlessly by. He spun again and shook his head in anger at having been fooled by a mere horse. Again, the behemoth rumbled toward me and again I sprang to the side at the last moment.

The crowd in the stands above us roared their approval as they watched the unlikely duel in disbelief. Snorting and blowing in anger, the bull glared toward where I stood in the middle of the arena. Long strings of drool hung from the jowls of the enormous animal. Once more, the bull charged forward, but again I wheeled to the side as he thundered harmlessly by. Frustrated finally, the bull ran toward the corner of the arena where the strangely dressed cowboys chased him through an open gate and back into his holding pen.

The roar of the crowd was deafening as all in the stands stood clapping their hands, while riders herded me from the arena toward my holding pen.

I watched from my pen as the last of the cars and trucks rumbled from the parking area at the end of the day. Again, the two-legged ones had failed in their attempt to ride me.

My back and hips began to ache on the long return trip from Window Rock. When at last I was pulled from the trailer at the ranch in Santa Fe, the pain had become excruciating. I stood quietly in my corral as the sun neared the far horizon. The bull that had struck me had injured my back.

My owner and Alan approached my corral as darkness fell.

"Keep a close eye on him for the next day or so Alan," said my owner. "He's bound to be a little sore, but let's see how he moves in a few days."

"He needs rest, said Alan. "He needs time to heal."

"He has to buck in Wyoming next week," said my owner. "We have to show the Association that he wasn't injured by that bull in Window Rock. We need their votes to get Ghost into the national finals. Give him plenty of alfalfa and grain, he'll be fine."

Alan stood for a long while quietly staring in the direction my owner had taken when finally, he had walked away. With a sigh, he turned at last to me.

"White One," he said after a long while, "I saw your vision. As I slept last night, you were suddenly in my dream. You stood in a terrifying storm at the top of a mountain. Beside you, a young Indian brave wailed to the heavens at the cliff's edge. I saw the white stallion that crashed through the raging skies above you. Around its eyes and ears, the great horse wore a black mask. It was you who battled the rider for freedom in the stormy sky of your vision. I will free you, Son of Banshee. I will help you find the freedom that you sought that night in the raging sky."

Alan turned then and walked into the darkness.

I was now in the summer of my fourteenth season. My years of battle with the two-legged ones had at last begun to wear me down. My capture and imprisonment, and now, the rodeos in which I bucked week after week, were slowly taking my life. Without rest, I had fought the best riders in the land. None had ridden me, but each ride had taken its toll. I did not know how much longer I would live with the hatred and rage that grew within me with each passing day. But this thing that was taking my life, I realized strangely, was giving me the strength to go on. The hatred that grew within me with each ride, filled me with the resolve to punish even more severely the next one who sat on my back. With each rider that I threw to the dirt, and each time I heard the bones of the two-legged one's crunch beneath my pounding feet, it somehow cooled the seething rage that burned within me. I knew, though, that the only thing that would quell my storming anger finally, was freedom.

As darkness swallowed the world around me, I stood quietly thinking about the many two-legged ones who had attempted to ride me. I thought again, about the mighty bull that had struck me at Window Rock.

Lowering my head, I drifted slowly into slumber, and soon, the freedom of the night filled my dreams. With Talking Bear on my back, we ran suddenly, again, in a herd of thundering bison. But none were quick enough to gore me.

The remainder of the warm seasons of yellowing grass, and ripening berries, were uneventful. The sadness, however, that had settled on our people lingered still. Everyone in our village still mourned the many warriors that had died in the great battle with the Crow. Seven of the women who had stayed behind to grieve the loss of their mates, rejoined our tribe during the season of ripening berries. Five others who had stayed behind at the burial platforms, were never seen again.

When the season of falling leaves came, Talking Bear sent word through the village that the time had come for our people to begin our southward journey. The people, anxious for change, welcomed the call to move onward. The tepees were soon taken down and strapped to the travois.

Our huge procession started southward as the sun rose above the mountain the next day.

Though Talking Bear was certain that the Crow had been soundly defeated, he sent scouts ahead and to all sides of our tribe as we moved southward. In two days travel, we climbed the great divide and descended into the land of Targhee. Talking Bear stopped our procession often as we traveled, to permit the passing of spirits he felt to be present. All the people stood respectfully quiet as the unseen ones passed.

Talking Bear drew our people to a halt as we came to the banks of the small stream named for the great chief, Targhee. Beyond the creek was the opening in which the village of our trapped people had long ago been. In places across the great opening, gray, sagging polls still leaned precariously against one another where tepees had once stood. The burial platforms that had surrounded the village were nowhere to be seen. They had long ago fallen. Their sacred burdens had returned to the earth. Now, the grass on the small plain, was deep and golden, and there was no evidence of the strife our people had endured here. Only the tattered remains of tepee poles stood as grim reminders.

The people were silent as we started past the place of the old encampment. The sound of plodding hooves, and the shuffling footsteps of the people were the only sounds to be heard. Gone even, was the nervous call of a horse or the bark of a dog. The animals too, felt the sadness here.

We followed the creek downward past the lake that lay below the mountain named for chief Targhee. The lower reaches of the mountain were dotted with the fiery colors of turning aspen leaves among the forest of pine and fir. We climbed a small mountain range that lay beyond, and passed through a low-lying saddle. A huge valley stretched endlessly beyond. The valley was covered with deep golden grass and small lakes shimmered from places in its bottom. It was the valley where our people would spend the season of renewal. It was the land of the Red Rock.

As the season of renewal slowly passed, the grief our people felt for our fallen warriors slowly diminished. When the season of ducks returning came, our people were happy again and anxious to return to our far-away home along the banks of the Spirit River. When the snow had receded to all but the highest of the peaks around us, we began our journey northward.

This migration between our beloved Valley of Shining Mountains and the land of the Red Rocks was repeated many times. Always, Talking Bear led our people with unwavering vigilance on our journeys.

It was now the waning days of the season of growing grass. The time would soon come to celebrate the ceremony of the Sundance. This most sacred of all rites was the most grueling and challenging ceremony celebrated by the Sioux people.

The Sundance was always performed in the hottest season. It would take place soon, during the time of the full moon in the season of yellowing grass. For four days, without food or water, the bravest and strongest of our warriors would dance in the heat of the sun. To the thundering beat of drums, the men would dance around a sacred tree that had been specially chosen and placed in the center of a small, round area. The dance area was surrounded by a shade arbor under which all the people in the village stood as they sang and prayed, encouraging the men as they danced. When the sun dropped from the sky on the fourth day, the ceremony ended. The people then gathered before a huge fire in the center of the village, and an enormous feast was had. The people were always very grateful for the health and strength that their brave dancers had brought to our tribe for the coming year. They honored them for their strength and commitment to the tribe.

As in years past, Standing Owl would lead the dancers. Talking Bear was the intercessor of the sacred rite. It was his job to stay in the darkness of his tepee and listen quietly for unspoken words given him by the Great Spirit. He was a channel between the Great Mystery and the ones performing the sacred rite. He alone controlled the things done during the four-day ceremony.

Twenty-one warriors had come to Talking Bear and requested permission to dance in the upcoming ceremony. Each warrior chosen to dance was required to go into the mountains, and without food or water, seek vision for this most challenging of trials. The vision quest would last for a period of four days.

Talking Bear led me into the grass near the edge of the village as the sun fell from the sky. Patting my neck, he said, "Tomorrow, Wakia, we will ride from our village. We will lead our brave warriors to the mountains to seek vision. You and I, White One," he continued, "Will ride to the wall of talking rock, where we too, will seek vision."

Long before the slightest hint of light the next morning, Talking Bear and his twenty-one sun dancers emerged, purified, from sweat lodges at the edge of the village. With quiet purpose, the warriors mounted their horses and splashed across the river behind their chief. The sun had begun to rise above the mountains as they followed Talking Bear upward on the mountain through stands of juniper and white bark pine.

Seven of our band had turned from our group and gone their own way when at last we reached the top of the mountain range. In the saddle overlooking the Valley of Shiny Stones, four more sun dancers turned from our party. Our numbers continued to dwindle as Talking Bear guided me downward toward the valley. The chief and I walked alone when we reached the valley's far side. Together, we traveled onward to the towering cliff of talking rock.

A great roar of approval rose from the people when Talking Bear and I entered the village. They were certain that their chief had received the vision he had sought. The twenty-one warriors that had followed us into the mountains had each completed their vision quest and had returned.

A huge gathering of people surrounded us when Talking Bear slid from my back before his tepee. Staring into the anxious faces around him, he said finally, "I have been given a great vision. I have been shown a world where all people in our land live together in harmony. The spirits have shown me also, the terrifying bird that will end it all, should we do otherwise. We must go to our enemy, the Crow," he continued, "We must tell them of the mighty vision I have received. We must bring peace to our land."

Talking Bear sent messengers to the Crow. They were to tell chief Iron Belly that Talking Bear had received a great vision. The messengers were instructed to tell Iron Belly of our impending Sundance and of Talking Bear's wish to share his great vision with him.

In the coming days, the Sundance grounds were made ready. A large area of grass at the edge of the village was trampled down, and an arbor was erected around it. A large, forked cottonwood tree was cut and placed in the center of the arbor.

Early the next morning, scouts excitedly approached Talking Bears tepee. They told him of the arrival of a Crow war party. Iron Belly and twenty-four warriors, they said, were just beyond the river.

Talking Bear stood solemnly before his tepee as the Crow chief and his warriors entered the village. In a gesture of friendship, Talking Bear raised his right hand into the air welcoming Iron Belly and his men as they stopped before his tepee.

That night, before a great fire, the twenty-one warriors chosen to Sundance for our tribe, stood one at a time and told the people of the vision they had received. Talking Bear sat cross-legged on the ground before his tepee and quietly listened. Chief Iron belly and his warriors sat on the ground at his side. All the people in the village encircled them.

When the last of our warriors had shared their vision, Talking Bear stood and faced Iron Belly and his men.

"Brothers," he said, "I have been given a vision that must be shared with all the people of our land. Seven days past, I went to a sacred place long used by our leaders to seek vision. For four days I stood before a towering wall of rock.

"As darkness fell on the third day of my quest, a bird began to sing in the great tree above me. Strangely, its singing call did not end when darkness came. As the night passed, others joined in the small bird's song. Soon, the darkness was filled with the calls of animals of all kinds. As the night passed, even more animals joined the great symphony of life. The scent of rooted ones that I had never before smelled floated heavily on the night air.

"The earth beneath my feet began to tremble as the sun rose on the fourth day of my quest. On the ledge before me, suddenly grew an immense, towering tree. In its limbs appeared all the living things in our land. Four-legged ones, flying ones, swimming ones, creeping crawlers, and all the rooted ones were there. Beside them in the tree, sat two-legged ones from all the tribes in our land.

"As I watched, they slowly descended the great tree's trunk.

"At the base of the tree, both plant and animal joined hands in a great circle. Brothers and sisters," said Talking Bear, "All the living things in our land danced before me in harmony. No longer enemies, they danced hand-in-hand in oneness."

"Above them in the air," he continued, "Were flying ones large and small, and at the great tree's base, moved all kinds of swimming ones. The tiniest of deer danced without fear beside the greatest of bears. Everywhere, elk and mighty bison danced together."

"But from somewhere above," continued the chief, "I heard the thunder of a great storm. An enormous bird appeared suddenly from the west. Its body shimmered like the calm surface of a lake. Its voice was the sound of endless thunder, and it flew toward me on gigantic wings that did not move. Behind the fearful creature were long, white gouges in the sky that marked its passing. As the mighty bird drew overhead, from its belly dropped an ominous black egg. Tumbling earthward, the screeching orb struck the ground at the foot of the great tree. I was knocked to the ground by a deafening explosion. Flames raged immediately upward in a horrific ball of fire. When at last the terrible fire was gone, the great tree and all beneath it had vanished. An enormous mushroom-shaped cloud in the sky above the cliff was all that remained."

Turning to Iron Belly, the chief said, "Your people and mine have fought as bitter enemies for many generations. This vision I have been given shows clearly the oneness with which all living things in our land are meant to live. Our land is fertile and teeming with life. The bison that live on the plains around us are countless. The grass is tall and plentiful, and our horses are fat and strong. There is enough for all of us. The vision given me by the rock spirits clearly shows that our fighting must end.

Slowly, Iron Belly rose and faced Talking Bear. Drawing himself to his full height, Iron Belly said finally, "Your eyes have become clouded, and your words, Talking

Bear, are those of an old woman. You talk as though your courage has left you."

The color drained from Talking Bear's face as he stood quietly before the Crow war chief. The look in his eyes was that of death. The muscles in his cheeks and temples twitched with rage.

His words were slow and measured, when at last, Talking Bear spoke.

"Is it the will of your people, Iron Belly, that forever they fight and die in battle with my people," he asked? "Or is it the will of Iron Belly?"

Talking Bear's arm shot suddenly forward, and he grabbed Iron Belly firmly by the throat. The Crow chief choked and gagged, clawing at Talking Bear's hand. Iron Belly's warriors started forward.

"There will be no battle during this time of sacred ceremony," growled Talking Bear. "Go, Iron Belly, sit in silence on the mountain. Quiet the raging warrior within you. Remember carefully the words given you by this old woman. Do this, before it is too late for us all," said the chief.

Pushing the Crow chief to the ground, Talking Bear said, "Go now from my village, Iron Belly."

Our Sundance was powerful. The visions given our warriors had been strong, and they danced with great strength and determination. All in our tribe knew it would bring great strength and wellness to the people. A great celebration was held at the end of the Sundance ceremony.

Late in the night when the feast had ended, I heard Talking Bear approach in the darkness. Standing beside me where I was tethered beside his tepee, he rubbed my neck and forehead gently.

"Our Sundance was good," he said. "Our men danced bravely for our people. All in our tribe will receive much power. But I am troubled, Wakia," he continued, "The words of anger spoken between me and Iron Belly were not good for our people."

The chief turned from me then, and entered his tepee. I heard the rustle of his bedroll, and his gentle sigh as he lay down. Soon, Talking Bear's soft, measured breathing told me that he slept. I lowered my head and drifted into slumber.

Chapter Fourteen

I was drawn from my dream world by the drone of an approaching vehicle. The image of the great tree of life and visions of fire, quickly faded as a truck and trailer ground to a halt near my corral.

The cowboys quickly disembarked and with the help of riders, loaded me into the trailer. For three days, in a place called Rock Springs, I punished each of the cowboys who tried to ride me. The same was true in Oklahoma City, and Durango. Back home now, at the ranch in Santa Fe, I stood quietly in my corral as the sun dipped from the sky.

My owner and Alan studied me carefully in the failing light.

"He's moving pretty slowly, now," said my owner, "But he sure showed those cowboys he could buck, over in Durango! The vote for the top saddle broncs of the year, was held yesterday in Vegas. I just got off the phone with the commissioner's office. Ghost was selected *first horse*, for the national finals up in Cheyenne next month. Have him ready to go, Alan" he said.

"No," said Alan, flatly, "This horse can't buck again this year. He may never buck again. His back was injured in Window Rock when that bull hit him. You chose not to rest him, and it has worsened with each rodeo. Look how he's moving now."

"Ghost is bucking in Cheyenne," said my owner. "He'll take it all, Alan. He will be the number one saddle bronc in the nation."

"You know how wildly he bucks," said Alan. "His anger and determination to throw the riders, blocks any pain that he feels. If you buck him again, he'll likely die in the arena."

"You have a month," said my owner. "Have Ghost ready."

"His name is not Ghost," said Alan. "This horse's name is Son of Banshee. I don't know how you came to own him, but he was taken illegally from federal land near my home in Nevada. His son still runs freely in the desert there. I have gathered samples of his manure and have submitted them to the crime lab in Las Vegas for DNA tests. I am certain the DNA will prove that this horse is his father. By law, Son of Banshee, will be returned to freedom."

My owner's face grew red with anger. "So, that is what you are doing here," yelled my owner. "You are trying to steal my horse. Well, Ghost is not going anywhere. He is going to buck in Cheyenne, and he is going to win me that championship."

Turning toward the men that had gathered around them, he said,

"Mr. Williams will be leaving now. Escort him to the bunkhouse to gather his things. Then, show him to the main gate."

I watched Alan as he walked away, surrounded by the group of men. My owner walked to the edge of my corral and stood for a short while glaring at me from its far side.

"You aren't going anywhere, Ghost," he said angrily, "You are going to Cheyenne." He turned then and stormed away.

I did not know about the place called Cheyenne. Nor did I care. With each rodeo had come a deeper hatred for the two-legged ones who had attempted to ride me. Each time the door of the bucking chute flew open before me, it was simply freedom I sought. Freedom from the kicking and gouging of the rider on my back, and freedom from the two-legged ones that roared in the stands above me. I wanted to walk again without wearing the harness of man, to go wherever I chose. I desperately wanted the freedom in my waking life that the darkness of night brought to me in my dreams.

The last days of summer drew agonizingly by. With the departure of the two-legged one known as Alan Williams, I was again fed large rations of both alfalfa and grain. Alan had cut their portions down, knowing the anxiety and sleeplessness I had endured at their expense.

After Alan's departure, my owner had instructed my new handlers to move me into a pen far away from the other horses. He forbade the other cowboys on the ranch to visit my pen. The solitude, he said, would make me crave freedom even more. I would buck harder when saddled by those who would try to ride me. For weeks, I had paced my corral restlessly. Most nights I stood awake, unable to burn the endless energy given me by my feed.

Early one morning, a truck and trailer ground to a halt beside my corral. I had not been handled by man for a long time, and anger flared within me. With my ears laid back, I screamed with anger at this latest intrusion of man.

The cowboys quickly exited their truck and assisted mounted riders as they entered my corral and threw lariats around my neck. Screaming and kicking, I fought them as they drug me into the trailer.

Peering into my enclosure, one of the men said, "Well, Ghost, I reckon this is it. Ya made it to the big one. Next stop, Cheyenne," he said, as he turned, and trudged forward to the truck.

The cowboys pulled me on the black trail for two days before finally, we reached the land they called Wyoming. When the sun was high overhead we turned from the black trail, and my trailer was drawn into a huge parking lot at the side of a sprawling arena. Kicking and fighting, I was pulled from the trailer and placed alone in a holding pen at the arena's edge. As had always been the case, many other horses milled nervously back and forth in corrals around me.

The trucks and trailers of the two-legged ones still rumbled into the parking lot long after the sun had dropped below the horizon. The darkness was filled with the slamming of truck doors, and the banging of trailers. Horses called anxiously in the night, as they were led past me, and placed in holding pens. Guttural, bellowing outbursts echoed from the arena's edge, as angry bulls kicked, and raked their horns against the thick wooden fences that held them there. Unlike the other rodeos in which I had been, the bulls were held in corrals just opposite the tall, wooden fence that encircled the bucking arena.

The stiffness and pain caused by my confrontation with the bull in Window Rock, had increased with each rodeo. Since then, I had battled the two-legged ones in places the cowboys called, Rock Springs, Oklahoma City, and Durango. Fatigue, a feeling I had never before known, now grew steadily within me. I stood quietly listening through the night, and lowered my head to rest finally, as the skies began to grow light.

Cowboys appeared, and walked slowly around the holding pens when the day became fully light. They carefully studied the horses that they would soon be riding. As the sun climbed higher in the sky, an ever-growing crowd stood before my pen, as cowboys talked and pointed at me.

"This is the one all the bronc riders are talking about," said one of the cowboys to the men beside him. "He's lit 'em up all over the west this season."

"He's rank, that's for sure," said another, as he spat a wad of brown into the dirt at his feet. "I think he'd as soon kill ya as look at ya. He jumps higher than any animal I ever seen, when he bucks. He belly-rolls, bogs, and skip-hops like no other. Ain't nobody figured out his bucking pattern yet, and no one's even come close to ridin' 'im to the buzzer. Don't know if it'd be a lucky thing or not, to draw 'im on the last day, but he'd be the one to ride if ya figured on winnin' it all."

The day was half gone, when cars and trucks began to fill the parking area around the stadium. Men and women poured from the cars, calling excitedly to one another as they walked toward the openings in the arena. There were far more people at this rodeo than I had ever seen at any rodeo I had been to. The noise from the crowded stands was almost staggering.

After the two-legged ones had marched their flags, and sang their songs, cowboys began to move the horses from the holding pens and place them in the bucking chutes. As had become the norm, I was moved into the eliminator's pen at the arena's side. I watched from my enclosure as the rodeo began.

As in all other rodeos, horses exploded from the chutes fighting desperately to throw the riders from their backs. These horses, though, bucked harder than any I had seen. At each thrown rider, or when the buzzer signaled a successful ride, the roar from the stands was so thunderous it made me wince. I was the last horse loaded in the bucking chutes on the first day. When the door of the chute exploded open, I sprang into the arena bucking with such fury that the cowboy on my back was taken by surprise. When suddenly I switched directions with a mighty lurch, the cowboy tumbled from my back and landed in a cloud of dust on the arena's floor.

The two-legged ones did not attempt to ride me on the second day. I stood alone in the eliminator's pen, my anger growing with each horse and bull that I saw buck. Twice, the rodeo was stopped when a rider was thrown to the ground beneath the crushing hooves of the bulls. Both times, the cowboy was taken from the arena on a stretcher and placed into a screaming white truck that carried the injured one quickly away.

The rodeo had long been over at the end of the second day, when a man stood alone in the growing darkness before my pen. A strange feeling settled over me as the two-legged one stood quietly watching. After a long while, the cowboy stepped forward. On the side of his face was a long, jagged scar. The man turned then, and disappeared into the darkness.

My sleep was agonizing. Memories of my mother and Banshee danced in the darkness of my dreams. But finally, as the night drew on, came the smell and peace of the mountains, and I grazed once more on the banks of the Spirit River beside my village.

The season of yellowing grass drew to an end, and the ceremony of the Sundance became a distant memory. The time of ripening berries had come, and our tribe worked diligently in preparation for our yearly journey to the land of the Red Rocks. The clash between Talking Bear and the Crow war chief was nearly forgotten. Talking Bear though, remembered well. He thought often about the angry words spoken between him and Iron Belly.

As the seasons passed, Talking Bear grew increasingly uneasy with our old enemy, the Crow. Now, messengers sent to our village from our old friends, the Cheyenne, brought ominous word of a growing number of Cree that now rode in Crow war parties. The Cree, like the Crow, had long been our enemy. Though Iron Belly had heeded the warning given him by Talking Bear after our great battle with the Crow, Talking Bear knew that the Crow war chief would stop at nothing to defeat the Sioux. Talking Bear cautioned his people to be vigilant at all times when outside the village. The Crow, he told them, could not be trusted.

Our journey to the land of the Red Rocks was uneventful, and the season of renewal was unusually mild. Time passed quickly with the absence of terrible storms and the crippling cold that had threatened our existence in years past.

Soon, it was again the time of ducks returning, and our people anxiously prepared for our return to the Valley of Shining Mountains. Talking Bear sent scouts in all directions of our tribe as we began our journey northward. Without incident, we crossed the great divide, and early in the season of growing grass, our village again stood on the banks of the Spirit River. Talking Bear and I often climbed the west side of our valley and camped in the saddle that overlooked the Valley of Shiny Stones. Often, Talking Bear sat for days carefully scanning the valley's bottom for any sign of the Crow.

When the season of yellowing grass came again, preparation for the ceremony of the Sundance began. Early one morning, long before light, Talking Bear led twenty-one warriors from the village. All had pledged to Sundance and were prepared for the challenges of the vision quest. We crossed the river and climbed the mountain range that lay to the west side of our valley. As we descended into the Valley of Shiny Stones, the men, one by one, left our group. Each traveled onward alone, to the places they had chosen for their vision quest. When at last we entered the valley, all but fourteen warriors had left our ranks.

Crow warriors suddenly appeared at the tops of the hills around us as we moved across the valley. Talking Bear drew our party to a halt and quietly studied the huge war party on the hills around us. Talking Bear immediately recognized his old foe, Iron Belly, on the ridge above. Soon, a rider left the side of the Crow war chief and galloped toward Talking Bear. The brave drew his horse to a halt beside the chief and said breathlessly, "Iron Belly has instructed me to tell you that since there are so few of you in number, a battle would not be worth his while. He will permit you to go. But you must go on foot. The cost of your freedom, he said, will be your horses."

Talking Bear swung from my back, and walked to the side of the mounted warrior. For a long moment he stood glaring into the man's smirking eyes. In a blur of motion, Talking Bear dragged the warrior from his horse. The man screamed in agony as Talking Bear's knife flashed at the side of the man's head, severing his ear completely. Holding the struggling warrior by his hair, he said angrily,

"I told your chief to never again come to our land. I told him should he do so, we would hunt your people down, and finish the battle that you long ago started. Give this to Iron Belly," he growled, as he ripped the man's head backward and jammed the severed ear into the mouth of the choking warrior.

"Tell him that with three ears, perhaps he will at last hear my words. Tell him, it is regrettable that he brought so few warriors with him. The women of my village would defeat the pitiful war party that I see on the hills around me."

Talking Bear then threw the bloodied warrior on his horse's back, and set the horse in motion with a mighty slap on its rump. Talking Bear swung onto my back and with his fourteen warriors, watched as the bloodied messenger returned to his chief.

"Hoka-hey! It is a good day to die!" yelled Talking Bear, turning to his warriors. "Ready yourselves brothers, our vision quest is upon us."

In a terrible din of hideous war cries, the Crow warriors charged at us from all sides. Talking Bear swung from my back and held his lance above his head in defiance, as he faced the charging Crow.

Loosening the red sash wrapped around his waist, Talking Bear drove the lance's point through the shawl's loose end, locking it firmly to the earth. "It is here, we will live or die, White One," he said to me.

There was no hint of light in the sky, when suddenly I awoke. Strangely, my night's journey seemed more than just a dream. Perhaps it was the dark memories awakened by the scar-faced cowboy that had visited my pen, that had brought such turmoil to my dream world. Seized by premonition, I watched apprehensively as the day at last became light.

There was a strange excitement in the air as the two-legged ones filled the stands on this, the final day of the rodeo. The rumble of their voices grew steadily when the procession of flags circled the arena. When their singing was done, the roar of the crowd was so intense that it rattled the stands in which they sat.

Small groups of cowboys walked around the bucking pens. They nervously studied the horses against which they would soon test their skills. Some stood quietly talking, while others sat quietly, visualizing their coming ride.

The voice from the talking boxes could barely be heard above the roar of the crowd when the first of the saddle broncs crashed from the chutes. With each ride, the people in the stands jumped to their feet screaming wildly. With each roar from the crowd, the anger within me grew. I knew that soon it would be my time to battle.

When the last of the horses had crashed from the chutes, cowboys drove me from my pen and placed me in a bucking chute at the arena's edge. I would be the last horse to buck. The roar of the crowd was deafening, as they watched the cowboys strap a saddle on my back.

"Here, use this one, and cinch it tight" said a voice from the past, as a cowboy handed a bucking strap to another at the side of my chute.

Pain ripped through my belly as the bucking strap was tightened. Tossing my head, and screaming with anger, I kicked at the sides of the enclosure.

Unable to hear above the thunderous crowd, I watched with wild anticipation as the one chosen to ride me climbed the side of my chute. I quivered with rage as the rider settled into the saddle on my back.

Leaning forward, he said to me in a raspy voice, "So, we meet again, little man. Like I told you long ago, there ain't never been a horse born that I couldn't ride."

Rage boiled within me as my mind exploded with the memory of the cowboy who had shot my mother. I saw the blood spurt from her chest as the gate before me crashed suddenly open.

The strap around my belly was tighter than it had ever been when I bucked, and a terrible, stabbing pain shot through me with each mighty lunge. The anger that boiled within me though, was greater than any I had ever known. I sprang into the air and twisted with a terrible ferocity, but the crippling pain in my belly robbed me of my strength, and I stumbled to my knees. I saw my mother collapse to the earth shuttering in death, and with new strength I exploded from the ground in rage, dust and sand flying in all directions. The battle with the two-legged one became otherworldly. The deafening roar from the stands was gone. Above the pounding of my hooves on the earth, I heard his labored grunts of exertion and the zing of his spurs as he raked them across my shoulders and ribs. The searing pain from the bucking rig was so excruciating that I could no longer twist and spin. In blinding pain, unable to buck, I crashed across the stadium.

Suddenly, the side wall of the arena was before me. In a storm of rage, I lunged forward with all my might. The sound of breaking timbers filled the air as I crashed through the fence. I spun and kicked with all my might as the scar-faced one flew from my back. I heard the crunch of his skull as my hind feet hit him, and I saw the unseeing look in his eyes as he struck the earth.

Out of nowhere, an enormous bull thundered toward me. I tried to spin from its path, but the unbearable pain in my belly slowed my retreat. The bull hit me full on, in the ribs. My world grew instantly dark.

From in the darkness came the growing sound of war cries. Soon, the frightful screams filled the air around me.

The shrieking battle cries of the Crow were deafening as the screaming warriors descended upon us. Beside me, Talking Bear stood tethered to the ground by his shawl and lance. Man after man fell to the deadly swing of the chief's war club. Blood dripped from the knife he held in his other hand. But the numbers of the Crow warriors were too great, and I soon heard the agonizing cry of our brave warriors as one by one, they were killed. The enemy warriors swarmed all around us now. Talking Bear bled from gashes everywhere in his buckskin shirt, and arrows hung from his back. His breathing was labored, as again, and again, he swung his deadly club.

Suddenly, Crow warriors were at my sides, jerking and yanking my reins as they pulled me from Talking Bear's side. Looking back, I saw Iron Belly and a group of warriors, attack Talking Bear. Tearing against my reins, I pulled free from my captors. I saw Talking Bear grab the Crow war chief and force him to his knees, as I crashed toward them. Talking Bear raised his war club to kill him, but hesitated when their eyes met. In that instant, a Crow warrior behind him, thrust his lance into Talking Bear's back. Its glistening tip appeared through the chest of Talking Bear.

I heard the crunch of bone as my front feet crashed against the head of Talking Bear's assailant, crushing him limply to the ground. Iron Belly jerked the lance from Talking Bear's lifeless body, as I spun toward him and rose again to my hind feet. Iron Belly thrust the lance deeply into my chest as my front feet smashed heavily into his forehead, driving him to the earth. The raging battle grew quiet as I stared into the lifeless eyes of the Crow war chief beneath me. My world began to spin as I slumped to the earth beside Talking Bear.

"Hoka hey, White One," he breathed, as he slowly extended his shaking hand to touch me. Darkness engulfed me as Talking Bear's hand slipped lifelessly from my neck, and fell to the earth.

My eyes fluttered open as I slowly emerged from the darkness. In panic, I fought to rise from the ground when I saw the Crow warriors at my sides, but I could not stand. As my world focused, I realized only white men now crouched on the ground around me. The screaming warriors were gone. The battle was over. Talking Bear no longer lay at my side.

Slowly, I remembered the rodeo, and the torturous battle I had fought with the two-legged one. I suddenly remembered the crashing collision through the fence into the bull's pen, and I raised my head fearfully looking. The storming animal was nowhere to be seen. On the ground near a gaping hole in the arena's wall, lay the quiet form of the scar-faced one.

From somewhere near me, I heard my owner suddenly yell, "Set up the barricades around us, the spectators don't need to see what we're about to do. Ghost is badly injured. We have to put him down."

A man kneeling at my side, pulled a short, white stick from his satchel on the ground near him. As he reached forward to poke the stick into my shoulder, I suddenly heard the screaming voice of Alan Williams as he crashed through the barricade toward where I lay.

I had barely made it in time to save Son of Banshee's life. With a policeman at my side, I sprinted through the gaping hole in the arena's side where Son of Banshee lay dying. I screamed with rage, as I crashed through the barricade they had set up around him.

"Stop," I shouted, as I crashed toward the doctor who knelt beside the stallion.

"You are no longer his trainer, Alan, you have no right to be here," screamed Son of Banshee's owner as he jumped angrily to his feet to confront me.

"Do it," he said sternly, turning to his doctor.

Leaping forward, I kicked the syringe from the doctor's hand as he stuck the needle into Son of Banshee's shoulder.

"I'll have you arrested, Williams," said Son of Banshee's owner, facing me angrily.

"This is no longer your horse, Smith," I said. "I have proven that Son of Banshee was stolen from government land. These papers are from the federal court in Las Vegas," I said, as I thrust the document into his face. "These papers give me full right to the stallion."

Stepping forward, the policeman said, "That's right, Mr. Smith. What this man says is so. These documents give Mr. Williams custody of this horse. For now, you and these others are free to go."

With his mouth agape, Smith stared incredulously at me for a moment, then turned and left.

Kneeling at the side of the dying stallion, I bent and whispered quietly in his ear, "Hang on, White One. I promised you freedom, and soon you'll have it."

Chapter Fifteen

I unfastened the cinch that bound Son of Banshee's saddle, and with the help of cowboys who had gathered, pulled the saddle from his back. When I removed the bucking cinch from around his belly, I quickly understood why he had not bucked. Son of Banshee's belly was gashed, and soaked with blood. Barbed wire had been woven through the sheepskin lining on the underside of the bucking strap.

Carefully, we rolled the stallion onto a sling, and with a small tractor, I carried him into a stable at the edge of the arena. I stayed with Son of Banshee through the night as he hung without moving in the sling.

With my DNA test results, I had proven to the people at the Bureau of Land Management that Son of Banshee had come from their federal land in Nevada. Their land throughout Nevada, they said, had become overgrazed, and they could not permit me to return him to the desert in which he had lived. Their federal range in Montana, they said, could easily support more horses. If I could haul Son of Banshee there, they would allow me to set him free.

The next morning, though his head hung limply downward, Son of Banshee was still alive. With the help of several men, I once again lifted him with the tractor, and carefully loaded him into the back of my horse trailer. Hung securely from the trailer's sides, he showed little evidence of life.

Standing beside the trailer, I said, "I know that the end of your journey is near, White One. Your life has been an endless battle with man. But if you can find the strength to endure one more journey, old warrior, you will soon be free."

I closed the trailer's door, and we were soon traveling northward to Montana.

Late in the afternoon on the second day of our journey, I arrived in a small town in southwest Montana. I ground to a halt in the driveway of a small building complex. A small brown sign at the building's edge indicated that it was the field office for the Bureau of Land Management.

Uneasiness grew within me as I opened the door of my trailer and looked in. I was thankful to see that Son of Banshee was still alive. His eyes were partially open, and he tried to raise his head to look, when he heard my voice.

With a sigh of relief, I said, "You made it old man. We are in the land called Montana."

336

The sun was drawing low in the sky as I followed a BLM range specialist along a narrow highway that wound precariously up a huge mountain. We finally pulled from the highway onto a small dirt road and stopped before a wire gate.

"Go through that gate and over that next hill," instructed the woman. "There's a flat spot there, where you can unload your horse, and there's plenty of room for you to turn your truck and trailer around."

"Good luck," she said, extending her hand.

Shaking her hand, I thanked her, then watched as she got back into her truck and drove away.

In awe, I scanned the amazing view before me. We had climbed halfway up the mountain range on the west side of the valley. At all sides, rocky, tumbling ridges climbed upward still, toward a towering summit far above. The ridge tops were covered with a thick growth of juniper and fir trees that gave way to sagebrush, lower on the ridge's sides. Below us, in the bottom of the sprawling valley, a broad river meandered for as far as I could see. A towering range of mountains loomed on the far side of the valley. A wonderful sense of freedom sprang from deep within me as I beheld the beauty before me.

After opening the gate, I returned to my truck and sat quietly thinking. The reality of the moment began to settle upon me, and doubt began to grow in my mind. I began to question my decision to bring Son of Banshee here. I knew that his life was nearly at its end. I hadn't told the BLM people of his dismal condition, as I feared they would not permit me to set him free on the horse range had they known. I had no idea how I would even unload the stallion without help.

Filled with doubt, I stared at the open gate, and the narrow two-track road beyond. I had made a promise to Son of Banshee, which I wasn't certain I could keep. But then I remembered the relentless determination I had seen again and again in the stallion.

"I will find a way," I said aloud, as I started my truck. "A promise is a promise. We're almost there, old man," I said with a sigh, as we started forward on the dirt road.

On the other side of the hill was a small cabin. From its chimney, smoke rose thinly into the air. At the side of the cabin was a corral, and beside that, stood a tall, white tepee. I pulled into the driveway at the edge of the cabin and shut the truck's engine off.

An old man with long, gray hair appeared in the doorway. His build told of a time when the old man had been strong and powerful, but now, his broad shoulders were stooped, and his steps were difficult as he walked toward me. The old man's powerful grip belied his age as he took my hand in greeting. He told me that he was known as Chief around these parts, and he oversaw the horses on this range. The old man's skin was dark and deeply creased with age. A deep, jagged scar stretched across his cheek to nearly his ear, an indication, I sensed, of the violent life he had once known.

Chief listened quietly as I explained to him why I had come. I recounted the amazing story of Son of Banshee, and I told him about his injury. I explained to him how the stallion now barely clung to life and may have to be dragged from the trailer. With furrowed brow, he nodded his head in understanding as I finished speaking.

"I was told you were coming, Mr. Williams," he said, his dark, unblinking eyes looking deeply into mine. Turning then, he walked to the trailer, and peered through the slats at Son of Banshee. As if to himself, the old man whispered, "Yes, I have been waiting, White One."

For a long while, he quietly studied Son of Banshee. Then, to my disbelief, he opened the rear door of the trailer and entered. I watched curiously as the old man pulled a small bundle of white sage from a leather pouch around his neck. Lighting the sage, he chanted quietly as he stroked the air above and below the stallion. Son of Banshee called out quietly more than once, as the old man sang. In a short time, I heard the creak of ropes as Chief loosened Son of Banshee's sling, and lowered him to the trailer's floor. I heard the thump of hooves, and watched in disbelief as the old man lead him from the trailer. Without speaking, I followed them to the corral beside the cabin. The old man led Son of Banshee into the enclosure and removed the halter from his head. Talking quietly in his native tongue, Chief slowly ran his hands over the stallion's back and shoulders, caressing him gently. Patting him on the neck finally, the old man turned and walked from the corral.

Standing before me, Chief said, "It is a good thing you have done, Alan Williams. Tomorrow, this great horse will be free."

As I drove back to town, the events I had just witnessed played again and again in my mind. How the old man had enabled the stallion to walk from the trailer, I could not explain. And had I not seen it with my own eyes, I would have never believed it possible that he stood calmly beside the Son of Banshee in the corral as he patted his neck.

Darkness was settling when I left the cafe after my evening meal, and the moon was rising over the mountain range to the east when I parked my truck in front of the cabin I had rented at the edge of town.

I sat quietly thinking in the darkness of the cottage as I watched the moon climb into the sky. Tomorrow, I knew, I would say goodbye to Son of Banshee. I quietly remembered those parts of my journey that had brought me to this place. I wondered about the old Indian known as Chief. I puzzled over his strange ability to handle such a wild horse as was Son of Banshee. Chief was the first man I had ever seen touch the stallion. It had been my imagination, I was sure, but after stroking the white stallion's back, it seemed the old man was no longer bent and stooped with age. He had walked from the corral tall and erect, with strong, light steps. I thought it strange that the BLM lady hadn't mentioned him to me.

I climbed into my pickup long before the sun had risen the next morning. Several inches of wet snow lay on the ground, and snow was still falling steadily from the sky. I was leaving the café after a hasty breakfast, when the BLM lady entered.

"How did it go with your horse yesterday?" she asked.

"I am on my way up there right now," I told her. "Chief kept him in his corral last night. We are going to let him go this morning."

"Chief?" she asked.

"Yes, Chief, the old man. Your range keeper," I stammered.

She stared at me in bewilderment for a moment before saying, "We have no range keeper, Mr. Williams, and I've never heard of an old man named Chief."

Totally baffled, a thousand questions raced through my mind, as I left town and drove slowly up the hill. Slush thundered at the bottom of my truck and splashed to the side of the road as I rumbled along. The snow had stopped falling, but the top of the mountain before me was hidden in a wall of clouds. I pulled from the highway when I reached the road that led to the horse range, and quickly opened the wire gate.

I ground to a halt as I topped the hill. The cabin below me, was dark and deserted. The corral and teepee that had stood at its side, were gone.

Sliding to a halt before the cabin, I climbed from my truck and stood in what was now an overgrown driveway choked with weeds. In disbelief, I studied the puzzling scene. The cabin's chimney had long ago crumbled and fallen through the roof. Logs, that one day ago were cleanly painted, now rotted and sagged with age. A shredded curtain moved silently in the wind, drawn from windows whose glass had long been gone. At the side of the cabin where the corral and teepee had been, only tall, yellow grass bent beneath the weight of slushy snow. Lines of rotten wood lay on the ground, marking the place where yesterday, the walls of the corral had stood. A large ring of rocks barely visible beneath the grass and snow, told of the teepee that had stood there one day before. There was no sign of life. Nowhere in the snow around the cabin were there any tracks of man or horse.

As I studied the bazaar scene in bewilderment, a movement far above me on the mountain caught my eye. Obscured at times by boiling, ragged clouds, was the old Indian. Beside him, walked Son of Banshee. Certain that I could go no further in my truck, I started upward toward them on foot.

Strangely, I saw no evidence of their climb as I moved steadily higher. There were no tracks anywhere in the snow. Lost at times, in a dizzying sea of clouds, I climbed breathlessly upward. I could still see Chief and Son of Banshee far ahead. From out of nowhere, I came suddenly upon a set of tracks. A man and horse had walked side-by-side on the ridge ahead of me.

Between parting clouds, I saw Chief and Son of Banshee as they neared the summit. To my astonishment, Chief now sat astride the white stallion. I stood quietly in awe, and watched. Having gained the summit, they turned to face me beneath a twisted old tree at its top. Chief turned Son of Banshee then, and together they disappeared in the clouds.

A blinding wall of fog boiled around me as I reached the summit. What little snow remained on its craggy top was driven in swirling blasts into a great abyss on its far side. My mind struggled to accept what my eyes now told me was so. I stood alone in the raging wind at the cliff's edge. The old man and Son of Banshee were nowhere to be seen.

The gale threatened to blow me from my feet and whistled angrily through the branches of the ancient old tree beside me. Deep gouges coursing the length of its twisted trunk told of its countless encounters with lightning. Though the height of the tree had been stunted by the violent weather on the mountain's top, its immense trunk told of its age. It had clung to this rocky peak for hundreds of years.

At a height just above my head, the old tree had grown into two, reaching trunks. To my amazement, protruding from the crotch where the great tree split, was the partially hidden skull of a bison. The skull had been placed there long ago, and the tree had grown around it. Now, only a horn and one eye protruded from the bark. From a crack in the tree's trunk below the skull, shone a shiny, black lance point. The ageless relics told me that a burial platform had long ago stood beneath the old snag. For reasons that I did not understand, Chief had brought Son of Banshee here. "How did the old man know about this special place?" I wondered.

A sense of timelessness settled on me as I studied the old tree and its ancient contents. Perhaps it was the surreal embrace of the swirling fog, or the strange reality unfolding before me, but I felt very close to the one who had placed those objects in the tree.

The stinging bite of the wind drew me finally, from my thoughts. More baffled than before, I turned and started downward.

Reaching the cabin, I quietly surveyed the bizarre scene once more. As I stood in the ring of rocks where the tepee had been, my eyes were drawn to a glistening, black object barely protruding from the grass at my feet.

A blinding flash of light filled my world as I bent to retrieve the shiny rock, and my eyes were drawn frightfully upward. In the turbulent sky above the peak, sat an Indian chief astride a great, white warhorse. On the chief's head was a long, flowing headdress. He held a lance above his head in a sign of victory. The horse's shoulders and rump were adorned with bright slashes of yellow paint. Feathers hanging from his mane, danced in the wind. I winced, as again, lightning sizzled across the sky. With a deafening boom, the apparition was gone.

Shaking with wonder, my eyes fell to the rock in my hand. It was a long, black, lance point. A translucent band of yellow, ran from its gleaming tip to its tail. It was a gift, I realized, an explanation of sorts.

I had no idea who the old man was, but the bond known between him and Son of Banshee, had been so strong that he had returned for his horse.

Indeed, Chief had been waiting. He had been waiting for Son of Banshee to complete his amazing life's circle. Now finally, their journeys were again, one.

I had been allowed to assist them on their sacred passage.

"Thank you, Chief," I whispered, as I looked back to the sky above the summit.

I knew I had kept my promise.

Son of Banshee was free.

Made in the USA
San Bernardino, CA
20 April 2018